Catamount, A North Country Thriller

Catamount

A North Country Thriller

by
Rick Davidson

Beech River Books
Center Ossipee, New Hampshire

BℝB

Beech River Books
P.O. Box 62, Center Ossipee, N.H. 03814
1-603-539-3537
www.beechriverbooks.com

LIBRARY OF CONGRESS CATALOGING-IN-PUBLICATION DATA

Davidson, Rick.
Catamount : a North Country thriller / by Rick Davidson. --
1st ed.
p. cm.
Summary: "A thriller novel about a rare mountain lion, a catamount, that turns man-killer, perhaps because of a forgotten Indian curse. A pair of young children get lost in the woods and their rescue party battles the rampages of the catamount, forest fire and other dangers in their search"--Provided by publisher.

ISBN 978-0-9793778-3-9 (pbk. : alk. paper)

1. Puma--Fiction. 2. Missing children--Fiction. I. Title.

PS3604.A9497C38 2008
813'.6--dc22
2008028989

Cover design by Ethan Marion.

Printed in the United States of America

This book is dedicated to my wife, Jane,
and my three daughters:
Hanna, Heidi and Gretchen.
Each of them, in her own fashion,
has enriched my life in more ways
than she will ever know.

Acknowledgments

Writing a first novel is not unlike that initial year of teaching that everyone who enters the field of education must endure in order to become competent in the classroom. I would like to express special thanks to my wife, Jane, who always believes in my abilities whatever they may be; to Stephen L. Smith, who simultaneously created the much more ambitious historical novel, *THE BLACK FLAG*, and provided me with the moral support, friendship and commiseration necessary to see this project to the end. I would also like to thank Steve's wife, Joyce, for her on-going encouragement; Andrea Kennett, for reading one of the early manuscripts and taking the time to comment extensively on various aspects of the book. I would also like to express my appreciation to my publisher, Brad Marion, at Beech River Books and his wife, Dawn, for guiding me through the maze of becoming a published author and helping me realize another one of my fantasies before time overtakes me and it is too late to enjoy. Fantasies come from the soul and should come true.

Prologue

Early 1800s, northern New Hampshire.

(In black and white). The old Abenaki comes out the door of the old log cabin. It is cold for November and the long season of snows has come early. The ground is already frozen. Smoke pours from the wide stone chimney. Through the haze of a light snow, the old man watches the smoke rise. A sugary frosting of white barely covers footprints that make their way to an old ladder leaning against the rustic building next to the chimney. Steps on the roof lead to an opening in the chimney where fresh meat is lowered to an open rack and exposed to the billowing smoke from the fireplace below. The smoked deer meat is intended to provide sustenance for the old Abenaki and his aging woman.

Moments before, the man removed some well-smoked meat to create space. Now, he can smell the acrid smoke on his clothing. He goes inside and returns, pulling a heavy bundle wrapped in a handmade patchwork quilt. It thumps onto the snow-covered rock stoop, and then flows more smoothly on the fresh snow as the figure continues to drag the load toward the ladder. He props the bundle against the ladder and climbs halfway up the squared pine rungs, taking the end of the rope that is wound tightly around the outside of the quilt. He works his way up to the low-pitched roof. Once on the roof, he settles his feet securely onto the pine footholds he built many years earlier. Three small steps facilitate the seasonal task of loading large cuts of meat into the smoking chamber.

Skillfully, the old Abenaki pulls his load up to the opening in the chimney. Then he unties the rope and removes the quilt. He lets the quilt slide off the roof. He reattaches the rope to the naked body of a dead woman. He lifts her over the chimney and lowers her into the smoking chamber. In the spring, after the ground has thawed, he will be able to give his beloved wife a proper Christian burial. The smoke will preserve her body until then. The old Abenaki turns away from the chimney. He has reluctantly accepted the inevitable arrival of the white man's ways and has adopted many of them. He worships the Christian God and he has even fought with the local settlers against the Redcoats. Nevertheless, at this moment, he curses aloud the coming of the white man and the diseases they have brought from far-off lands.

Piercing yellow eyes watch from the edge of the clearing. The black apparition blends into dark underbrush as it witnesses the curse and then smoothly moves away. Its eyes, as sharp as they are, cannot recognize color. The black specter lives in a world of black and white.

The *Manchester Daily Sun,* (some 150 years later):

Mountain Lion Sightings in the East
by John Fredrickson

Forest rangers, local police agencies, and scientists at several eastern universities are receiving reports of mountain lion sightings in eastern states. While none have been officially reported as far east as New England, it is clear that the authenticated sightings have been coming closer.

The mountain lion, cougar, panther, or catamount, as it is variously termed, has always been controversial. Many environmental scientists, including Jack Morrison of the University of New Hampshire science department, maintain that the eradication of mountain lions in New England has upset the balance of nature. According to Morrison, deer herd numbers are on the increase and without natural predators, such as wolves and catamounts, deer numbers may increase to the point where they become a nuisance in populated areas. Morrison points to the ever-increasing number of incidents of automobile collisions with deer and moose.

John Harrison, a rancher in Colorado, does not share Morrison's enthusiasm for the balance of nature. According to Harrison and many others in the West, mountain lions in his state and in other western states are a real threat to livestock and pets. Indeed, some human casualties have been attributed to this reclusive predator. Harrison, not generally one to fall for conspiracy theories, is convinced of the existence of an unpublicized, if not secret, organization that is committed to the reintroduction of mountain lions and wolves into the forest areas throughout the United States. Harrison believes that this "radical" organization has gone underground because of the lack of support from government agencies and because of a perceived local fear of predatory animals.

"What sane person would welcome the reintroduction of such a powerful killing machine into his or her back yard?" Harrison asks. He also wonders if anyone would support introducing more sharks to our beach areas.

Wildlife officials throughout New England report that, while they have received numerous reports of catamount sightings, none has ever been verified. The last known mountain lions were hunted into extinction during the early twentieth century. While some officials agree that wildlife management has created an ideal environment for such a predator, they know of no verifiable incidents of mountain lion activity in New England or anywhere near New England. They also know of no official plans to reintroduce the animal into New England. Some others are sympathetic to the concept of realigning the balance of nature in our wildlife areas, but these officials feel that any reintroduction is many years away and that any such action would require the support of local government agencies and the consent of the local population.

Whatever the stand on reintroduction, officials in all of the New England states are unanimous in their conviction that this, in the eyes of some, magnificent beast and, in the eyes of others, dangerous predator, does not exist here or anywhere near here. What is clear is that, in spite of the apparent extinction of this animal in New England, the catamount has taken on the trappings of local legend. Catamount sightings are nothing new. The ghost-like specter has been seen in every New England state, but most frequently in northern New Hampshire and Vermont. In these areas, the locals are more inclined to have their imaginations piqued by a report of a tawny or black panther than by reports of UFO's or ghosts. As one enthusiastic believer in Clifford, NH, pointed out, "It's like we want to believe, on some very basic level, in the supernatural existence of this magnificent animal. It is part of the mystique of the North Country."

Chapter 1

June.

The silence is not normal for the time of year. If Rob Schurman, the local conservation officer, was there, he might notice that suddenly, for no apparent reason, all the forest noises stop. Indeed, after relative silence, he would wonder why every bullfrog, cricket, whippoorwill, and peeper within hearing distance suddenly resumes, creating a cacophony of outback nature sounds. This concert would invariably stop in unison again only moments later. It would not have been unthinkable for someone to be in the woods videotaping the sights and sounds of early summer. Had that person been there, his camera might have caught a glimpse of something black as it slowly emerged from the underbrush. Neither the conservation officer nor a videographer was there. There was only the full moon, a large expanse of field, five deer feeding on the low grass, and a shadowy creature moving slowly just below the tops of the wild grass.

The apparition itself can only see in black and white, but its vision of the unaware deer is sharp and precise. One doe, feeding only twenty feet away, does not appear spooked by the abnormal silence, nor is she cognizant of her impending fate. A muted purring replaces the silence. This sound is unknown to the doe. Frozen for a moment, her head lifted, the doe stares. With no reason to bolt, she resumes feeding. The silence returns and then the wind rustles the grass. It is too late. As the doe turns, a black tail lashes out and the dark apparition springs. Instantly the doe's throat is torn open, her neck is broken, and within seconds, she is dead. The figure hovers over the carcass, then rips open the deer's chest. In the moonlight, the attacker is indistinct as it drags its prize across the field. The deer's legs point straight up as she is pulled through the grass. The indistinct black specter tears into the victim and begins to eat its evening meal. The large black mountain lion lifts its face to let out a mournful, blood-curdling yell. Those who have heard this scream describe it as something like a woman stretched out on a rack, tortured, and in mortal pain. This is as close as the human imagination can come to depicting the magnificence and horror of this sound. The scream ends. Not long after, the sounds of the North Woods return. The peepers, the crickets and the persistent whippoorwill continue their individual performances. What turns them on and off? Can they possibly understand what just took place? Why should they care? Their own lives are short and intertwined with their reproduction and their place on the food chain. Whatever the answer, (if there is an answer we humans would understand), these sounds restore an illusion of peace that will soon attract many city and suburban dwellers to the North Country.

Off-duty Conservation officer Rob Schurman, sits on Ike Roberts' back porch enjoying a beer. The old farmhouse porch looks out over a large tract of open fields surrounded by stone walls. These were built over one hundred and fifty years earlier to enclose and clear fields so crops could be planted. Ike had run an electric fence along the edges of the rugged stone walls. Other than this concession to modern technology, the fields look much as they had when ninety percent of New Hampshire was cleared to provide workable and productive land. The wisdom of the time dictated that unused land was unproductive land. The farmhouse is now rundown. The gray clapboards show through the faded white-lead paint. Who knows when it was last painted? Not in Ike's lifetime. Not in his parents' lifetime, as far as Ike knew. He inherited the old place from them. If he had not, he wouldn't have been able to afford to live there. Folks in his income bracket no longer own such large tracts of land. He certainly could not buy it at today's real estate market prices. More and more people from "away" were paying large sums of money to own "a piece of paradise." It was worse near the lakes.

"Christ, a native cain't afford to live here no more!" Ike would mutter. Then he would get his dander up a bit. "Taxes goin' to put me right out of business."

"Ike, you haven't been in business as long as I have known you," an acquaintance was likely to point out.

Ike would grunt at this observation and light his ever-present corncob pipe. "Sweetest smoke you ever tasted," he would say. What tasted so sweet to Ike smelled like burnt rubber to those unfortunate enough to be nearby when he lit up. Most would allow that it was high time for Ike to buy a new pipe. "Ain't nothin' wrong with this one," Ike would reply as he puffed away.

Since the lumber companies owned most of the surrounding land, the second growth forest crowded in around the perimeters of the Roberts' "working farmland." Back porch philosophers, Ike and Rob Schurman, had already talked the ongoing drought to death. Rural New Englanders generally have to discuss the weather before moving on to other less important subjects. The weather discussion would end with something like, "I guess that's why we live in New Hampshire." Mainers simply insert Maine at the end of their climate observations. Vermonters do the same. In any case, with the weather discussion out of the way, it was time to move on to other topics. This time Rob held his peace and did not comment on Ike's pipe. It was merely coincidental, in spite of what had happened to our previously mentioned deer, that Ike and Rob were discussing panthers and mountain lions. This subject often came up during discussions on back porches and around campfires. Stories passed on from father to son and fishing buddy to fishing buddy.

"Ain't no such thing as catamount as far as I'm concerned," Roberts says as his wife, Marion, brings out a bag of Humpty Dumpty potato chips. "I been here all my life 'n I ain't seen sign of no such thing." He puts down the latest edition of the *Manchester Daily Sun*. "I don't care what the *Daily Scum* says."

"Ike, you've been here all your life and ain't seen much of anything," Marion comments with a grin.

"All I know is that Gregg McDougall claims one ran right out in front of him up on Johnson Pond Road," Rob puts in.

"I don't think state troopers like Gregg tend to hallucinate," Marion says.

"Besides, Walt Simpson claims to have seen tracks up on the river, and Walt ain't no slouch in the woods. Froggy claims to see them all the time."

"Maybe, but it's goin' to take more than that to convince me. I don't believe in nothing till I seen it with my own two eyes. And for Christ's sakes, you ain't going to start quoting that ole drunk Froggy, are you?"

That is Ike's final take on this conversation. Marion, Ike and Rob all look out at the field behind the Roberts' old farmhouse. The warm spring air seeps through rusty screening which partially keeps the relentless black flies at bay. These three locals of Clifford Township sit quietly, contemplating the sounds of emerging insects and wildlife. Winters are long in the North Country and all things living here experience an annual rebirth in May and June. Late spring this year has been exceptionally dry and hot. After months of snow and bitter cold weather, no one complains about the warm evening.

Rob is thinking about how lucky he is to live in his hometown. As a kid, he had loved to play in the woods. He smiles to himself. As a conservation officer, he still gets to do that. He loves his log cabin on Trout Pond. He is very comfortable spending time with Ike and Marion. He enjoys their no-nonsense, down-to-earth ways. Ike and Marion are quite a pair. On the outside, Ike is an old curmudgeon. On the one hand, he would often sit on a stump near his favorite trout stream and make fun of fledgling fly fisherman. On the other hand, he was more than willing to take those same novices aside and share his expertise with anyone who would spend the time with him. He was a helluva teacher and it was amazing how gentle he could be when imparting his knowledge and enthusiasm for the sport.

"One afternoon with Ike was like a week at L. L. Bean's fly-fishing school," Rob thinks to himself. "And afterwards, you had a friend for life."

If anyone disliked Marion, Rob could not imagine who it would be. He is not sure what salt of the earth really means, but the term seems to fit. Everyone knows that, without Marion, the farm, such as it is, would never stay above water. She is there for everyone including old Ike. She runs the local Red Cross. She is the president of the Ladies' Guild at the local All Faith Church. Everyone raves about Mrs. Roberts' casseroles. Like Ike, she is a friend for life. Both are good people.

Rob does enjoy his trips to the outside world. He especially enjoys Montreal, and in his younger years, back from the University of New Hampshire, he had reveled in that city's infamous nightlife. Rob had spent six months hitchhiking around Europe with his college girlfriend, but during his travels, he always knew that Clifford was home and that he would return. The girl was far more seduced by the lure of Europe and stayed in Paris to study at the Sorbonne. He had come home alone, but was at peace in the familiar surroundings that made him feel so content.

Ike puffs on his pipe. Unlike Rob, Ike Roberts never ventures far from home. He makes the occasional trip to the paper mill town of Berlin. That is where he had met Marion forty years ago. Ike feels a sense of warmth when he thinks about the simple but full life they lead together. Living out here is hard. Even with his limited experience with the outside world, Ike knows this life is not for everyone. He is fortunate to have found a companion who enjoys manual labor and the day-to-day endless chores of farm life. When the Roberts' farm stand opens every year in Clifford, the locals and the visitors come not only to enjoy the fresh vegetables, but also to be entertained by the friendly banter between Ike and Marion. Although he never shows it, Ike truly enjoys the fact that his wife tries to trump just about anything he has to say. For the same reasons that Ike is a die-hard Red Sox fan, he is also a Republican. When you grow up in Clifford, you are a Republican. It is as simple as that. Marion, of course, with her flatlander down-country ways is, of all things, a Democrat. When the two of them get "sick of each other", Ike goes on one of his extended hunting or fishing trips. Marion gets together with "the girls" in town. Ike, for all his outward roughness, considers himself a very lucky man.

"I might get a bit riled up on occasion," he realizes, "but I got my rock."

Marion is enjoying the pleasurable aftermath of a good home-cooked meal. She loves to cook. Even the preparation of simple meals is a creative pleasure. Marion's hand-made quilts and blankets help support a number of local charities. Her afghan of local landmarks is a runaway best seller. Her hands are always busy, but she works at her own pace and in her own way.

"How many women can say that in today's world?" she wonders. "I guess I'm a bit old fashioned."

She looks over at her husband and Rob. They are both probably about ready for another beer. Marion does not drink much herself. She never saw much need for it. Ike likes his daily evening dose though. Fortunately, he is not one of those drinkers whose personality changes after a couple of drinks. If anything, the alcohol seems to make Ike mellower, as long as you stay away from politics. It is comfortable sitting here on the porch. She has known both men since what seems like the beginning of time. She is grateful for the space Ike allows her. They have found their own niches on the farm and in the village, and that is that. She could stand for a little more romantic attention, but now and then Ike will surprise her with a bouquet of hand-picked wildflowers or something of the sort.

"Kinda thought you might like these," he would say with a mischievous grin and that meaningful wink. It surprises her that they maintain this interest in each other after all these years. What would the ladies at church think?

She turns her thoughts toward Rob. He is steady and dependable. He can be tough when he needs to be, but he is known for his fairness and is great with the local kids, especially those who show an interest in hunting and fishing. As she leans back and looks at the knotted pine of the porch roof, Marion thinks about all the people in the world who are unhappy with their lot in life while three people sit here on this idyllic evening who have found their place and seem to be doing what they were meant to do. How lucky they are, but she also thinks about the friends and family that are gone. Making the farm pay is hard.

"How fragile life can be," she muses, but there is no need to think about that right now. For this instant, the hard times are forgotten.

Everything seems right with the world. She savors the moment. Then she gets up to fetch a cup of decaf from the kitchen. Ike holds up his can of Bud Light.

"While you're up," he says with a grin. Marion turns to Rob.

"You want another Sam, Rob?

"Nah, I guess one's enough if I am going to hit the road. I don't want to have to arrest myself, you know. Decaf would be good, though."

A moment later, Marion returns to break the silence.

"I was just wondering why you never got married, Rob."

Rob continues to look out into the darkness.

"Just never found the right one," he says.

Chapter 2

Early in the morning, Ed Rollins carries two fly rods out to his family's Ford Explorer. He is a tanned, healthy man of forty-two, sporting a just-graying beard. The sign on the equipment-laden Explorer promotes ED ROLLINS SPORTING GOODS, WINCHESTER, MA. Ed is wearing outdoor, chino-style, synthetic, quick dry pants and a Trout Unlimited catch and release tee shirt; a pair of new and expensive breathable waders is thrown over his shoulder. It is the start of a summer vacation and Ed is in a good mood. Marty, Ed's pretty, thirty-nine-year-old wife is dressed in a Title Nine breathable athletic shirt and running pants. At 5'10", she is one of those women who look better with each passing year. A little gray around her temples only adds to her sensuous, yet classy attractiveness. She is carrying an old rucksack.

"Let's get this show on the road. It doesn't feel like vacation until we hit New Hampshire," yells Ed.

"Come on you guys, let's go. We got a long trip ahead of us," says Marty as she loads her rucksack into the vehicle.

Suddenly the front door of the house blows open and ten-year-old Josey Rollins, and his six-year-old sister, Cindy, bolt down the steps. Cindy is in tears and clutches a love-beaten rag doll.

"Daddy! Mommy! Can't I bring Stina? Josey says I can't."

The boy pushes his sister and pipes in. "We're going to camp. Dolls are for sissies. She wants to bring her pillow, too."

"Do not."

"Do too. Pillows are for sissies. "

Ed and Marty both move quickly toward the kids. Ed grabs Josey around the waist and hoists him up off the ground.

"Hey you guys, we're on vacation. Let's get off to a good start."

Simultaneously, Marty puts her arm around Cindy and says, "Cin, of course you can bring Stina."

Ed puts Josey down. "Let's forget the pillows. There are some at the cabin. We're roughing it, you know."

Cindy turns up her nose. "Yeah, but they stink."

"You stink," Ed jokes as he picks up Cindy, now laughing, and puts her in the back seat of the car. Josey climbs in next to his sister.

Looking at the family vehicle, Marty shakes her head. "I can't believe we got everything into the car. We always bring so much stuff."

"It doesn't much matter whether you are gone for two weeks or two months, you need the same amount of stuff," says Ed.

"We certainly prove that point. Doesn't look like roughing it to me," says Marty as she turns toward the house. "Where's the dog?"

Ed hurries toward the front door. "I'll get him. He's still in the house."

Marty nods. "Just in case, take a look through the house. Make sure we got everything, Ed. I'll wait here with the kids."

"The dog didn't run off this time, Mommy. He's asleep in front of the fire place," says Cindy.

Marty rolls her eyes. "Well, he's not in the car yet, Cin. Last year he took off just when we were ready to go. How about you guys? Are you both all set?"

"Yup," says Josey.

"Are we going to have lunch in North Conway, like always?" asks Cindy as she squeezes Stina. "I got everything, too, Mommy. I want to eat at McDonald's."

"We'll see," says Marty.

Ed comes out of the house. Before he gets out of the door, a large, two-year-old, brown husky/shepherd mutt almost knocks Ed over as he shoots by and begins running in circles around the car.

Ed locks the door of the house and yells. "Come here, Virgil. C'mon. Come here."

Virgil, tail wagging and breathing hard, runs to the Explorer's open door and leaps. Once inside he crawls on top of Cindy, his tail wagging in Josey's face. Cindy lets out a scream as Virgil licks her face.

"C'mon. Over here," urges Ed as he pats the empty place next to Josey in the back seat. "C'mon, good dog."

Virgil steps on Josey as he finally comes over to his place on the seat.

Marty turns toward the back seat. "It's going to be a long day," she says.

Virgil breathes heavily with his tongue hanging out of the side of his mouth. Drool drips onto the floor. Ed climbs into the driver's seat.

"Let's go. We're on vacation!" he announces.

"Can we go to Canada this time?" Cindy asks. "Clifford is boring," she sighs.

"We'll see. We need some peace and quiet," says Marty.

"I want to go fishing," says Josey. "Dad said he'd show me how to do it with a fly this year."

"We have time to do everything we want," says Ed.

"We'll see," says Marty. "We'll see."

Ed looks at Marty as he adjusts the mirrors. Marty, sitting shotgun, buckles her seat belt and, with her head propped up by her right hand, gazes out of the side window. She sighs. Ed glances again at his wife. He starts to say something but decides against it. Avoiding Ed's glance, she continues to look out of the window. Ed starts the ignition, stretches his neck around the high seat and smiles at Cindy and Josey.

"You guys ready?" he asks.

"Ready!" Josey and Cindy yell.

"Okay. Let's go," says Ed.

He slips the SUV into gear, puts his hand on Marty's leg and starts out the driveway. Marty looks over at Ed for a moment and then stares out the side window again. Ed removes his hand.

*　　　*　　　*

Rob Schurman is on the Fish Pond Road. He enjoys his early mornings on the back roads in the North Country. It is one of the great benefits of his chosen profession and one of the reasons why, even as a kid, Rob had always wanted to be a ranger or a fish and game officer. His green government pickup registers every bump in the old dirt road. As he passes the battered town line sign, he smiles. He remembers how his family used to joke that you would know if you went off the road, because the driving would be so much smoother than when you were maneuvering over and around the exposed rocks on the old dirt roads. It is certainly a challenge for the town road agent and his crew to maintain all the dirt roads that web their way through the large, scattered region that forms Clifford Township. Depending on the length of the winters in the North Country, many of the roads are only used five or six months out of the year. Those owned by the paper companies are maintained if they are in use, but tend to deteriorate if they are not. No matter how well maintained, they are a mess every spring during mud season. Even in June, the Fish Pond Road still has deep tire ruts left over from the four-wheelers that have carried the first anglers into the backwoods waters after opening day of fishing season each spring.

The fishing is still good and most of those who are casting lines today are likely to be legal and serious about their sport. The Fourth of July weekend is the beginning of what Rob often refers to as "yahoo season." Then Rob's profession invariably evolves into that of a law enforcement officer. There are the under-age drinking parties, people who fish without a license, the occasional poacher, and the wormers who, although there are miles of open water, insist on fishing areas designated for fly fishing only. As much as he likes summer, Rob cannot help but look forward to the quiet after Labor Day. Leaf peepers and moose gawkers are not much of a problem. Most never make it this far north anyway.

Hunting season is another story. Many locals still depend on hunting for their winter food supply, but more and more flatlanders feel that they can commune with nature by purchasing expensive hunting gear and getting into the woods. Rob is always thankful after an event-free season. Last year only one hunter had been shot. He was hit in the leg when his companion tripped over a root and discharged his cocked rifle. Rob had also prevented a potential fire when he found that a camper had decided to clean out the still-smoldering coals from his campfire and dump them in the woods. "Hopefully, I won't find anything like that today, because it's way too dry this year," he thinks.

Winter brings the snowmobilers. Most of the clubs police themselves well, but last year Rob was called out more than once to rescue a lone sled rider who had not returned after a reasonable or sometimes unreasonable amount of time. Without Rob, in every case, the rider would have died of exposure in the backwoods. One guy ran into a tree after drinking ten beers and started to crawl back to his cabin in the forty-degree-below-zero cold. He did not get far. Fortunately, another group of riders happened on the smashed snowmobile and discovered the badly bruised lump just off the trail. Rob is thinking how modern technology seems to be making his job more complicated, when the radio crackles on his console. "What technological wonder will be next?" he asks himself as he picks up the mic.

"Unit 2, are you still up near Fish Pond? Over."

"Unit 2, affirmative. What's up, Carla? Over."

"We got a strange one, Rob. Eight sheep have been killed, uh…slaughtered, or something like that. Over."

"Huh?"

"At the Roberts' place. Ole Man Roberts is fit to be tied. He's some upset. Says he has never seen anything like it. Over."

Rob looks at his watch.

"It'll take me about fifteen minutes to get over there. I'm on my way. When did this happen? I was over there yesterday evening. Over"

"Rob, I am not sure, but take care. I don't know what this is all about, but Ike's been around for a while. He doesn't scare easily. Cantankerous old bastard! Over."

"Better watch your language, Carla. Ike's one of my best friends. Over."

"I don't care what you say, he's a bit crotchety. Just be careful. Over."

"Can't dispute that. Ike's always complaining about something. Over"

"You can say that again. Just watch out for yourself. If you need back up, let me know. Sounds serious. Over."

"I'm on my way. I'll let you know what I find. Over and Out."

After having lunch at the McDonald's in North Conway and fighting the traffic along the strip of outlets, motels and retail stores, the Rollins family drives beyond Twin Mountain to Route 3. This route will take them around by the Vermont border to Clifford. The village itself is small. There is a fire station, a five-room school, and two general stores. One of the stores features the motto "If We Ain't Got It, You Don't Need It." Outside of the village are a number of well-known hunting and fishing lodges. Various lumber companies own much of the surrounding land. Consequently, most of the land around the lakes, rivers, and bogs is largely undeveloped. On any given evening, the road from Clifford to Canada attracts moose gawkers. The ungainly moose entertain these voyeurs by wallowing in the mud flats next to the road. Those politicians that come to New Hampshire to make a headline by spying a moose would do well to come to this stretch of highway. It is almost impossible not to encounter this noble, lumbering beast here. The moose seem to understand that they are stars. However, few politicians ever come this far north because there are too few voters to make it worth their while.

The Rollins' cabin is on a dirt road that follows Jones Stream up to its source, Jones Pond. Ed inherited the place from his parents—two acres next to lumber company land. Except for the Roberts' farm, a couple other old farmhouses and a few isolated, leased cabins, the family will be alone in the wilderness. The nearest town, as the crow flies, is in Canada. The cabin is a good fifteen miles from Clifford Village. It is late afternoon when the Rollinses finally arrive in the North Country. Although it is a few degrees cooler past Davistown, the New England summer is hot and muggy. Ed drives in silence. The breeze feels good coming in the side window. Marty stares out the passenger's side window. As they have done many times before, the kids are playing a word game to pass the time. The banter in the back seat fades as Ed thinks about the business. His assistant manager is minding the small sporting goods store. Ed has grown to hate the place. He is sick of the day in, day out routine. He is tired of trying to please everybody. He has had enough of dealing with banks and crunching numbers. During the last recession, a big conglomerate bought out his local bank. A "banker" who was more interested in foreclosing than in keeping businesses afloat had replaced his financier.

"We're still in business," he thinks. "But you just can't get ahead. It's just not fun anymore." Marty seems to enjoy working with the customers, but he wishes she would just let him sell out. Ed wants to do something—anything—else. Maybe write a book about fishing. He would not mind moving to Clifford full time, but talking about that or selling the business is not something he should bring up on vacation. Marty just does not understand.

Marty watches the trees fly by. There are now fewer houses. An occasional dirt road leads off the main highway and into the woods. Marty continues to stare out the window. She knows that if she looks at Ed, he might start complaining about the store again. She does not want to hear it all again. She knows she will have to hide her mood for the kids' sake, but she does not particularly look forward to this two-week vacation. It is more work than at home and everything is so isolated.

"Everything you do takes more time and effort," she is thinking.

Then Ed asks, "What letter are you on now?"

"Q, Daddy, we never find Q," answers a frustrated Cindy.

"Or X," Josey pipes in. "What time is it?" he asks.

"Are we almost there?" Cindy wants to know.

Ed looks at his watch. "It's almost four. We'll be there soon. Let's finish the game."

"Can we skip Q?" Cindy asks.

Marty turns away from the window, toward the back seat. "That would be cheating. See if you can find a sign that says "quality." You might see it on the side of a delivery truck."

Leaning forward, Cindy points out, "There are no signs, trucks or anything up here."

"Yeah, there are, I betcha I can find a Q before you do," teases Josey.

In the front seat, Ed says to Marty. "I wish we could live up here full time."

"Let's not get..."

"I saw a sign with a Q," squeals Cindy.

"Did not. Mommy, she's lying."

Now, Ed looks in the rear-view mirror. "Come on Josey, Cindy, we're almost there. Let's not ruin our vacation."

In the front, Marty turns to Ed.

"Let's not ruin ours."

Ed squirms in the driver's seat and speaks in a low voice.

"I hate living down there. I hate the business. I hate everything about..."

"Ed, we've been through this. You're a grown man. You've got responsibilities to me and to the kids."

"I know, I know, but I feel trapped."

Marty snaps, "By us?"

"No, by that damned store. My life isn't what I thought it would be. All I do is put out fires. I hate going in there. I just wish something would change. I just wish..."

"Be careful what you wish for," Marty warns.

"What is that supposed to mean?" asks Ed.

"Mommy, Daddy, Josey doesn't believe me. I did too find a Q word."

"Did not. Cindy is cheating."

Rob pulls his pickup into the driveway leading up to the Roberts' old barn. The clapboards on the side of the house, the shed, and the barn may have once been white and trim, but are now gray and warped from a hundred years of exposure to sun. The shed is serviceable but the roof is concave from the yearly accumulations of snow weighing on its rafters. Rob wonders how many winters the shed has survived. He has helped shovel the heavy snow off the roof more than a few times. He knows the building has been in this condition for quite some time. The barn itself is so weather-beaten that it is

— 19 —

almost black. A couple of ornamental cats grab the side of the house next to the front door. A mushroom lady is stuck into the ground right under the cats. The front lawn grass is long enough for haying, and the Roberts' array of old tractors, trucks and cars are waiting for the time that Ole Man Roberts just might need a spare part. A big iron tripod holds a rusted engine that Ike had thought about repairing two years before. Ike steams through the beat-up screened door. The door slams behind him. He grips a shotgun and hurries across the yard to meet Rob. They both stand in front of the relic of an old pick-up.

"I ain't never seen nothin' like it. The innards is torn right out of eight of my best sheep. 'Nuther one is missing. What'd do somethin' like this?"

The two men start toward the field.

"I don't know, Ike. You okay? Let's go look."

"Christ no, I'm not okay."

"Calm down Ike. Come on, it can't be that bad. Must be a bear."

Marion looks through the screened door as the two men walk quickly to the field. Ike rushes along, leading the way.

"Does that look like it was done by a Christly bear, for Christ's sake, Rob?"

Rob can see sheep carcasses lying scattered about the field. From a distance, in the yellow late afternoon sunlight, the lumps look like mounds of dirty melting snow. As the two men draw closer, the red clumps of blood surrounding the animals belie the winter image and Rob is not prepared for what they find as they approach the first carcass. The sheep's body is ripped open as if something has exploded inside it. The internal organs are in a pile near the dead animal. Splotches of red blood saturate much of the brownish, high grass. Kneeling, Roberts points toward the animal's empty cavity.

"I ain't never seen nothin' like it. The innards is torn right out of them all. There's another one missing. I cain't think of nothin' that could do this, Rob. Can you?"

Rob surveys the carnage. "It doesn't look like a bear. A bear would be sloppier than this."

Rob moves closer to the sheep's neck. "Doesn't look like a coyote either. They always go for the neck, but I've never seen one tear the throat apart like this. Whatever did this was incredibly precise. Are there any tracks?"

Ike appears frustrated. "There ain't nothin'. No tracks. The fence looks fine. I can't find a trace of anything. The electric fence didn't do nothin'!"

"Did you hear anything?"

"Christ no, and I was here all night! I never heard a peep."

Rob sighs. "I guess I better get a hold of Doc Varney. You know, I've spent my whole career hoping to find a mountain lion around here. I think we just might have one."

"Oh for Christ's sake, not that again! And what good's a vet? These animals is beyond help. I can't afford no vet, nohow."

"State'll cover it, Ike. Isn't any animal in these parts that would normally do this. We need an expert."

"I don't need no expert to know this ain't the work of no bear, and I agree I ain't never seen a coyote do nothin' like this. No human coyote neither."

"Well, Ike," says Rob. "I guess that's why we need an expert. You're pretty good at pointing out what didn't do it. I'd kind of like to know what did."

Rob and Ike move around the field. The sheep all seem to have been taken unawares. Rob stares at the bloody mounds.

"Whatever did this must have worked mighty fast."

"I guess probably," is all that Ike can muster. "I'd a noticed it, otherwise."

Rob scratches the palm of his hand. "I'm no expert, but I still think we might have a cat here. This kind of thing happens out in Montana."

"Don't try to sell me on that catamount bullshit again!"

"What else then?" asks Rob.

Ike shoots back. "Damned if I know, but there ain't no one reliable seen no mountain lion 'round here since my Pa was in his heyday! Just drunks. Drink enough of ole Jake's likker, you're likely to see all kinds of shit. Bounty hunters got all those cats long before my time. Just as likely to see a rattler. That ain't goin' to happen neither."

Rob looks at Ike. "Okay, if it isn't a cat, you tell me what you think it was. I wouldn't call Gregg and Walt drunks. Maybe Doc will know."

"Maybe, but I don't put much store in these young vets that been comin' along. I don't know nothing about what Gregg and Walt supposedly seen, but Froggy's always claimin' that he's seein' catamounts everywhere. Don't tell me he ain't no drunk. He ain't breathed a soba breath in over forty years."

"Christ, Ike! Varney's fifty years old and who said anything about Froggy Jones?"

"Fifty is young enough. Froggy's the one always spreadin' rumors about big black cats. All I know is, I'm out nine sheep and I ain't insured or nothing. Besides, catamounts ain't black and if this one is, it ain't normal," says Ike.

"Why aren't you insured?"

"Don't believe in it."

Rob starts back toward the house. "You're a piece of work, Ike! I guess we should keep watch on what you got left. I'll stay with you tonight. Can I take advantage of your hospitality?"

"Sure. I'll get Marion to fix us somethin' to eat. Can you charge that to the state? This whole thing is getting' a might 'spensive. I ain't made of money, you know."

"Yep, that much we do know, Ike."

The road has become narrower and more crooked as the Rollins family drives north. Many of the roads in the North Country follow the original trails used for generations by native tribes. The Abenaki or perhaps other Algonquins who used these trails would find these tarred-over roads wide and straight enough. However, for a family used to the parallel cross streets of suburban Massachusetts, the road is bumpy, curvy and hilly. Inside the SUV, the dog is lying across the kids' laps and whining. He is breathing heavily.

"When are we going to get there? Are we almost there? Virgil is shedding everywhere and he is drooling all over me," says Cindy.

"I gotta go to the bathroom," says Josey, "real bad."

"We still haven't found a sign with the letter Z," says Cindy. "This is getting boring. There aren't any signs at all. Can we play something else?"

"I really have to go." Josey squirms in his seat. "I think Virgil needs to go, too."

"Okay, okay," sighs Ed. "We'll stop over there."

The Ford Explorer eases off the road. Josey and Virgil leap out of the right back door. Ed climbs out of the front seat and walks over to a small clearing with a gated, overgrown road leading to the left. A sign on a large pine tree next to the gate displays the image of a tawny cat. Over the cat is the warning "Catamount Crossing." Underneath is a sign warning anglers that they should only eat two fish per month and that pregnant women and young children should either avoid freshwater fish or limit eating fish to once a month.

Josey walks back toward the road. "Boy, Virgil really had to go!"

"He has been in the car for over three hours," says Ed. "When you gotta go, you gotta go."

Josey looks back at Virgil as he darts back and forth on the road, sniffing first here and then there, lifting his leg and then darting in the opposite direction.

"He's kind of wound up," observes Josey.

Ed walks over toward the sign. "We'll give him a minute to run." Ed yells to Virgil. "You stick around. Come here."

"What's this sign mean?" asks Josey. "Will Virgil be safe in the woods?"

"Of course he will. This is just a joke. People like to pretend that there might still be mountain lions living in the woods. There is no such thing. It's just a myth—you know, a story that people like to tell."

"Is 'catamount' a mountain lion?" asks Josey.

Ed is keeping his eyes on Virgil. "Yes, it is another name for one."

Virgil looks back, but the dog appears ready to bolt. Ed whistles and Virgil pauses, thinks it over, and then starts back.

"I'm not scared of any mountain lion. Are you Dad? I'm not scared in the woods."

"Not around here, son. We don't have any poisonous snakes and spiders. We have black bears, but they don't usually bother anybody."

"Not unless you bother them. Right, Dad?"

"The biggest danger around here is the cold in the winter. That can be very dangerous."

"Could catamounts come back, Dad?"

"No one has seen one for over a hundred years. Come on. Let's get going. I'll tell you about catamounts around the fire tonight. We want to get to camp before it gets dark."

"Can we eat the fish we catch?" asks Josey.

"Not too many, I guess," says Ed. "We need to practice catch and release, like I taught you."

"I know," says Josey. "But it's fun to keep them sometimes."

Ed whistles again and Virgil runs back toward the car. "I know," agrees Ed.

Before Josey and Ed can reach the car, Virgil bounds through the open door and lands on Cindy.

"Ouch! Virgil hurt me, Mommy," shrieks Cindy.

Marty turns to comfort Cindy. "C'mon, Virgil. Over here." She leans over and pats the empty seat next to Cindy.

"Sometimes I wonder why we have this clumsy mutt. It's your father's..." Marty takes Cindy's hand. "You'll be all right, Pumpkin. He didn't mean to hurt you. He loves you."

Cindy sniffles, "I know. I love him, too."

She puts her arms around the dog. He is looking out the window, oblivious to the ruckus he has just caused. Ed and Josey climb back into the car.

"I don't know why you had to get such a big dog," complains Marty.

John Varney's Volvo pulls into Ike's yard. Varney is a tall, balding man in his early fifties. The hair on the side and back of his head is still worn long. It appears his way of suggesting that, even though he's balding now, he still had ties to the 1960s. Doc is always on call and never refuses an emergency, even in the middle of the night. He cannot count the number of times he has dropped whatever he is doing to pull porcupine quills out of the mouths of now-humbled dogs. Many of these dogs are repeat customers. He often wonders how something that painful can fail to make a lasting impression on these great hunters, but some canines just never seem to get it. Delivering newborn calves and ponies make his day. Doc Varney is well liked and respected.

Today's message is unsettling. In his twenty-five years of practice, he has only occasionally been called out because of slaughtered livestock. In most cases the culprit is a coyote or a fisher cat—nothing that would slaughter animals on this scale. He really does not know what to expect. Ike Roberts is not the most easy-going guy around, but he is generally level-headed and reliable. John parks the car and gets out. Ike and Rob come over to the Volvo and the men all shake hands.

"What are we looking at?" asks Varney.

"They're right out back," says Rob. "I've never seen any thing like it."

"I guess that's right. If you've seen anything like it Doc, I'll eat my hat and yours, too, by Jesus!" says Ike.

"Let's go look," says Doc.

The men walk to the field. Marion comes to the door and watches. Doc acknowledges her as he walks by.

"How's it going Marion?" he asks.

"I've been better, Doc. I guess you'll see why. One of those sheep was goin' to win me a prize at the fair down in Lancaster."

Doc Varney appears concerned. "Not the one you showed me last year? She was a beauty. I am really sorry to hear that. I guess I better take a look."

Doc follows the other two. As he approaches the first carcass, he looks around and then kneels down to take a closer look. In spite of years of experience and a hardened response to death, he almost wishes he had not. The carcass is covered with flies. The blood has dried into hardened clumps and the flesh has already started to smell in the hot sun.

"I haven't seen anything like this in a long, long time," he says slowly.

"But you have seen something like this before?" Rob asks.

"Yeah, out West. Well, not really like this. Not on this scale. One or two animals, maybe. Nothing like this."

"What the hell did it?" asks Ike. "You're not going to try and tell me it was a cat too, are you?"

Doc looks at Ike. "To tell the truth, that's what it looks like to me. Are there any tracks? Did you hear anything?"

"Christ no! I didn't hear nothin' and this grass and dirt is so dry, it would hardly show no tracks anyhow," answers Ike.

"Cats sometimes let out a yell. That's why I asked," says Doc.

He gazes around the field and moves to the next carcass.

"Probably wouldn't be any tracks in this grass. I gotta say this is a lot worse than what I saw out in Montana. Look at the precision! Whatever it was knew exactly what it wanted."

Ike glares at Varney. "No shit! We don't need a vet to come all the way out here to tell us that."

"It's okay, Ike," says Doc. "I understand how you feel. One way or another we'll get to the bottom of this. I want to know as much as you do."

"It ain't like you lost any sheep," says Ike.

"You're right Ike, but if this is any indication, I can't help but wonder if anything is safe."

"I don't like the implications of that," says Rob. "Christ, something that can stalk you without making a sound and then create this."

"And then disappear into the woodwork," says Ike. "Fucking A!"

Doc stands up. He stares at the sheep. "Seriously, Ike, I gotta say it looks like a mountain lion attack. Just kind of extreme."

"I guess probably!" says Ike.

"I don't know what else it could be," says Doc. "No coyote or bear would do this."

"What about a fisher cat?" asks Rob.

"Christ, I never saw one do anything like this before. Especially to something this large," says Doc.

Ike picks up a stick and pokes at the fly-covered sheep. "We do have bobcats, but they don't do nothin' like this neither."

"As far as I know, even big cats don't usually kill for the fun of it, but I guess from what I have heard, sometimes they really do. I think it is the only animal that does," says Varney.

He pauses.

"Tell you what. I got an old friend out in Montana. I went to school with him. I know he's had to deal with mountain lion issues out there. I'll give him a call and see what he has to say. I think we better get rid of this mess before we attract just about everything else in the woods. These bugs are awful."

"How we gonna clean this up?" asks Ike.

"Bury them, I guess," says Doc. "Does that backhoe over there work?

"I can probably get it going," says Ike. "What a hell of a mess."

Doc looks around one last time, counting. "You know that missing one? I am almost positive that mountain lions will carry off some of their kill and camouflage it so they can come back for it another time. If we could find it, maybe we could be ready for it when it comes back."

"How does it camouflage the carcass?" asks Rob.

"I think it puts it under brush," says Doc. "Sometimes up a tree. I guess we'd be looking for something that might look like a brush pile."

"A Christly brush pile!" mocks Ike. "How many of those do you think I got around here?"

Chapter 3

Rob, Ike and Marion are sitting on the back porch. The sun is low on the horizon and the yellow rays cast pleasing long shadows onto the grass through the pine trees on the edge of Roberts' field. The three are finishing supper and drinking coffee. The present tranquillity belies the carnage that had been on the field that morning. It is still on the minds of Rob, Ike and Marion as they watch over the open expanse of the back meadow through the screening on the back porch. Ike gets up and goes to the railing to get a better look. Marion picks up her coffee cup.

"Do you reckon it will come back?" she asks. "We cain't afford to lose more livestock."

"That's what I reckon, too," answers Ike. He leans over to the wall, picks up his vintage Winchester 94 lever action 30-30 and cradles it across his lap.

"I don't know what to tell you," says Rob. "I suppose it knows that there are more animals here. I mean, I don't know if we should be out hunting for it, setting a trap, or what. I don't know where to start. It seems like waiting here is our best bet."

Marion is thinking about all the hard work that went into raising livestock.

"We really do depend on the sale of some of those animals to get us through the winter," says Marion. She sighs. "Sure seems peaceful enough right now. The black flies are pretty thick though."

"I ain't got a hankerin' to offer myself up as a meal for those blood suckers. I vote we watch from right here," says Ike.

Rob stares through the screen.

"You'd think with this dry spring, there wouldn't be so many, but they are still pretty heavy this year. I gotta tell you, black fly season is the one time of year when I sometimes wonder why I live around here."

"It does make it hard to work outdoors," agrees Marion, "but chores don't go away."

"That's for sure," says Ike.

Rob gets up and picks up his classic Remington Model 31A slide action 12-gauge shotgun. Both Ike and Rob use older rifles that have been given to them by their fathers. Both men know how to shoot. Hunting, fishing and being comfortable in the woods are still a part of growing up in the North Country. These two men have traversed just about every square foot of the forest around Clifford, but neither man has any idea of how to stalk or trap whatever it was they were waiting up all night hoping to see.

"I guess we can see just as well from in here," says Rob.

"I am also not so sure that I want you men out there in the open," says Marion. "After all we don't know what this is."

Ike pushes lightly on the rusty screen. "I 'magine whatever got them sheep wouldn't have much trouble getting through these screens, if it had a mind to."

Marion starts to pick up the dishes.

"Let's keep the animals penned close by, near like." Roberts points to the right. "We can use that there pen over there. It's a clear view from here to there."

Rob moves to look. "That ought to work, Ike. I guess we should get them moved in there before it gets too dark."

"I even got a spotlight out back we can turn on so's we can see everything. Marion, you wanna turn on the back light?"

Marion turns on the light. Rob turns toward Ike. "Maybe we should warn the Elmers and Peter Schmidt. I don't want to cause a panic, but I hate to see them lose some of their livestock. Maybe we could tell them to keep an eye out for a fox."

"Fox my eye. Ain't no fox done that."

Rob continues to look outside. "I didn't say it was a fox. What else should we tell them? Are we going to tell them there is a catamount loose?"

"Christ if I know," answers Roberts.

He yells into the kitchen. "Marion, you wanna ring up the neighbors? Tell 'em to keep an eye on their animals. Fox might get 'em, iffin they don't."

Marion calls back. "That's really what you want me to tell 'em?

"You got a better idea?" Ike shouts.

Marion comes to the door. "I guess not, and you don't have to yell."

"Christ woman! You're deaf as a bat."

"Bat's ain't deaf. They're blind."

"Christ almighty! Are you goin' to make them calls or ain't ya?"

"I'd a done it a long time ago, if you had asked me civil like. Can you imagine livin' with this old bird, Rob?"

"There isn't anybody in a hundred mile radius that knows what keeps you here," chuckles Rob.

"One of these days I am goin' to be like that Dolly Copp woman and up and leave. What'd she say? 'Fifty years is long enough to live with any man.' We've been at it goin' on forty-five," sighs Marion.

"No doubt about it, you're a saint, Marion," says Rob.

"I ain't disputin' that," responds Ike, "but is anybody goin' to make these Christly calls? I gotta go take care of them sheep. I'll put the pigs in the barn. The cows and the chickens are already in there. It's not as iffin anything would be safe in there neither. The back door is busted off its track."

Marion starts back to the kitchen and picks up the earpiece of an old crank phone mounted next to the more modern dial phone on the back wall. "The wire was okay yesterday. It doesn't always work, doncha know. This old phone is the only way to get through to those summer folk. I couldn't raise them yesterday. Probably ain't up here yet. I wonder if we'll ever get regular phone service out beyond this place. The Schmidts and Elmers are hooked up from over Vermont way."

"Them summer folk ain't got no livestock no how," Ike yells back. "Livestock is all we're worried about, ain't it Rob?"

Rob moves his chair so that he can get a clear view of the sheep pen. "Jesus, I hope so. She said those summer people aren't here yet, right?"

"That's what she said," Ike says as they head out the back porch doors. The door slams. Rob appears relieved.

There is movement on the back of the building. The sound of voices travels across the field and into the night. Human scent on the surface of the ground mixes with the pungent odor of fresh flesh emanating from the new soft mounds of dirt on the edge of the field. Suddenly a bright light illuminates a flat area near the building. Two figures lead a group of animals into a small pen, close a gate and then move back into the building. A door slams.

The apparition watches warily. It starts to move away, looks back and then crouches to the ground. The light from the spotlight on the back of the house reflects in the yellow eyes that stare back toward the movement on the porch and the animals in the pen.

Chapter 4

Outside on the road, the Rollins' Explorer drives past the Roberts' house. Ed starts to slow down.

"Should we stop and tell them we're here? I just saw Ike go into the barn." Marty looks out the window.

"Huh? Rob's truck is here, maybe we shouldn't…"

Ed speeds up a little and continues. "I wonder what he's doing there."

"I don't know. It's far enough out. Maybe he needed a place to stay," says Marty. She stares out the front window.

"You mean like he used to stay with us?" asks Ed.

Marty looks quickly at the back seat and then at Ed. She speaks in a low voice.

"Come on Ed. You know that is all over. Really, I love you."

"I know, I know. I love you too," responds Ed, also in a low voice. "It's just…"

"It was just a bad time for us," says Marty. "This is not the…"

"I know, I know."

Ed calls out to the children. "Fifteen minutes, guys. We're almost there."

Josey and Cindy clap their hands in delight.

"Now we don't have to play any more stupid games," says Josey.

Josey pokes Cindy. "You're just mad because you didn't win."

Cindy pokes back. "I did too win. I found the Q. You just don't believe me."

"You did not."

"Did, too."

Ed raises his voice. "C'mon guys, we are almost there."

Every time Rob's name comes up, Ed feels an uneasy sense of anger. Not jealousy really. He had not been surprised when Marty told him what had happened. He and Marty had been arguing a lot about the store. Ed knows Marty craves attention that is more romantic. Rob is demonstrative and loves to hug. He gives great back rubs. Marty loves both. Ed had not been brought up in a hugging family. He wants to please Marty sexually and otherwise. At least he could offer that, but sometimes it just does not seem to be enough. Marty aches for the attention he finds hard to give. He will have to get better at being romantic. He will work on it. Surprisingly, he finds Marty more attractive because of the affair. Is it because another man finds her attractive? It was always obvious that other men would. She is attractive. It just pisses him off that this had gone on behind his back.

With the commotion in the back seat, Virgil wakes up and spreads out across Josey's lap. Marty turns around. Virgil's tongue hangs out of the side of his mouth, the drool dribbling onto Josey's lap.

"Yuck!" cries Cindy. "That's gross! Are we almost there?"

"Almost," says Marty. "How about if we sing a song? What do you want to sing? How about 'This Land is My Land'"?

"That's my favorite," agrees Cindy.

As has become a family tradition while riding together in the car, the family breaks into a reasonably harmonious rendition of Woody Guthrie's ode to what the United States ought to be like.

Marty always enjoys the family sing-alongs in the car. This time, she sings in a low, uninspired voice. She is hurt because Rob has not tried to contact her and at least talk about what happened. Maybe for him, it is as if nothing has happened. Just sex, maybe that is all it is to him. Well, that would be best if it was that way. Wouldn't it? Nevertheless, she knows it is more than that. What they did had mattered to both of them. It is just that it cannot continue. She knows that, too. "Maybe I'm just a slut," she thinks. "Is that such a bad thing? Sex with Ed is good, too." That part of their marriage does work. Then she thinks about Cindy and Josey. She has to try to love Ed. She does love Ed. It is just so hard. Of course, she has not tried to contact Rob either, but shouldn't he be man enough to…To what?

— 33 —

Then, the song ends and Josey yells. "We're there! I see the house!"

The low yellow moonlight that seeps through the trees and leaves illuminates a small, faded-white, tongue-groove wooden cabin. Ed opens the car window and the sound of flowing water drowns out the sound of the SUV.

"I love that sound. I sleep like a baby when I am up here," says Ed.

"It takes me a day or two to get used to it," counters Marty. "I'm kind of used to fire engines and police sirens."

"I am, too," says Ed, "but I prefer this."

As the car comes to a stop, Josey, Virgil and Cindy all burst out of the side doors of the car. Virgil runs around in circles and the kids run up to the cabin. With the headlights trained on the entry, Ed follows the kids and opens the front door. Inside, he lights a gaslight that is mounted on the wall. Marty turns off the car lights and comes inside. The yellow gaslight reveals a cozy interior. The inside of the tongue-groove board is unpainted natural wood and is yellowed from fifty-some-odd years of cooking, fireplace use and tobacco smoke. Although the stale tobacco smell is long gone, the remnants of the heavy smoking of the '40s, '50s and '60s is ingrained into the knotted wood fibers. Ed gave up the pipe ten years before and Marty had always railed against the evils of tobacco smoke. Marty has never smoked, but Ed still feels an urge for a bowl of Prince Albert when he sits by the fire or casts his fly on a trout stream or pond. Somehow, the sport just does not seem the same without it. Ed yearns for the old days when the health consequences of small pleasures were unknown and a person could truly enjoy a good hamburger, classic french fries and a good smoke. In any case there are now no smokers in the Rollins family and the cabin smells of must and winter mothballs. There is also the damp smell of burnt wood coming from the stone fireplace.

Ed goes to the small kitchen area and checks the hand pump. With a prime from his water bottle, the pump produces gushes of water that flow into the sink.

"We still seem to have plenty of water. I was a little worried. I don't think we have ever been this long without rain," says Ed.

Marty comes over and puts her hand in the flowing water.

"It seems like there is plenty. It's still cold. Like other years. It would be a drag to have to get water from the river and have to boil it. What a pain in the neck that would be."

"I wonder how low the river is," says Ed. "When I was a kid we used to drink right from the rivers and streams. We didn't worry about giardia or anything like that. I wonder where giardia came from all of a sudden."

"I have no idea, but you won't catch me drinking from the river. Not after Pete Johnson's story about getting on an airplane after a fishing trip. I can't imagine what it must have been like to have a giardia attack on a plane to Europe," says Marty.

Ed stops pumping.

"I didn't say I was going to drink the river water. I was just wondering why we suddenly can't anymore. I don't think it has anything to do with pollution up here. What changed? There have always been beavers. I guess there are more now. I heard they were almost extinct. Maybe that's it."

"You're asking the wrong person," says Marty. "It does look like the winter guests had a great time. Look at those nests."

Marty picks up a whisk broom and sweeps piles of chipmunk droppings and multi-material, matted small animal beds onto the floor.

"I love this job every year. Some things haven't changed."

A mouse runs across the floor.

"Looks like some of the winter guests are still here," laughs Ed. "I'll clean the counter. Do you want sprinkles with your supper?"

Josey comes into the kitchen. "You say that every year, Dad."

"I guess I have to find some new jokes. You guys are getting too sophisticated."

"What's *sophisticated?*" asks Cindy?

"It's like you guys already know everything," answers Ed.

"Some of us are getting hungry. We need to get some supper going," says Marty. "I'll do the counter. You guys get the stuff out of the car."

Ed and the two kids head for the door. Ed looks back at Marty.

"God it is good to be here," he says.

Marty continues brushing droppings onto the floor. She does not hide her look of disgust once Ed and the kids have gone out.

"It's still cooking and cleaning whether I do it camping or at home," she thinks to herself.

Ed comes back in loaded with sleeping bags. Marty finishes cleaning the kitchen counter.

"I'll get the rest tomorrow. What do you think? Should I call the Roberts and let them know we are here?" asks Marty. She starts toward the ancient crank phone on the wall.

Ed puts the sleeping bags down. "Maybe we should wait. It is kind of late for them."

Ed goes over to Marty. "I'll help you with the rest of this tomorrow. Maybe we should eat and get the kids in bed."

Marty moves away. "It's been a long day. I'm tired. Is spaghetti okay for supper? It's easy. Are you sure we shouldn't call over to the farm?"

"That's okay, I'll do it first thing in the morning," says Ed. "Where's the dog?"

Chapter 5

From a distance, the Roberts' farmhouse, on the outside, is dimly illuminated by the moonlight. The lights from inside the house glow inside the framework of the windows and the super structure of the porch. The eyes, sharp as they are, can see the lazy black and white movement of the sheep in the pen. They are bathed in a bright light that emanates from the side of the building. The eyes discern the house and the ears recognize the occasional faint sound of human communication. The voices and that bright light had not been there the night before and the prey had been scattered, but there is no cause for alarm. The black and white farmhouse draws slowly closer.

Inside the farmhouse porch, Rob and Ike watch through the screen. They can hear the spring night sounds, the occasional bullfrog down by the small pond outback, and the incessant call of a whippoorwill.

"It's incredible how loud those things are when they are right outside your window," says Rob.

"I guess probably," says Ike.

The field is bathed in faint moonlight and strands of light from the backyard spotlight. There might have been a slight movement at the other end of the field. Rob squints through the screen.

"I think I saw something move."

"What?" asks Ike.

"I don't know. Can you see that black shape over there?"

Rob turns to Ike as he points. He turns back.

"It's gone. I think it was right there. Christ, I don't know."

"Think it might have been a shadow? That cloud just passed over the moon," observes Ike.

Rob looks again.

"Beats me. It was probably nothing. Seeing things I guess."

"They look all right. No panic or nothin'. What do you think? Should we take a look?" asks Ike.

Rob squints through the rusty screens.

"I can't see anything wrong, but maybe we ought to check it out. That's what we're here for, right?"

Standing next to Rob, Ike scans the backyard.

"Well I gotta admit I can't see nothin' stirring, but it's awful quiet all of a sudden. Where's that whippoorwill? The frogs have stopped, too."

Rob turns around and picks up his rifle.

"You got the flashlight, Ike?"

Ike slings his rifle over his shoulder.

"Yup." he says. "Let's go"

The back door slams and momentarily breaks the silence. Two figures come out of the house and start drawing closer as they walk toward the back of the field. As they reach the outer parameters of the floodlight, one of them turns on his flashlight and scans its beam over the tops of the tall grass. Both men wave their arms, periodically, in front of their faces in a futile attempt to discourage the black flies that swarm around them.

"What you saw was right over there, wasn't it?" asks Ike. "Gawd, these damned black flies suck!"

Rob looks over to where the beam of light illuminates the grass.

"I can't see anything now, can you?"

Ike pans the light in an arch over the tall grass.

"Not a God damned thing, but I gotta tell you…"

Rob readies his rifle and follows the light.

"I know. It's like I can feel it, and I don't like it."

"Me neither," says Ike. "For one thing, it's too damned quiet. Whatever it is, it's here somewhere."

"Yeah, I think so," says Rob.

Ike crouches down and aims the light through the grass.

— 38 —

"I can't see a damned thing, but you know what? I'd kinda like to get back to the house."

"Yeah, me too. I'd feel safer on the porch," says Rob. *"To tell you the truth, I've had enough of these damned black flies, too."*

Motionless, the black figure is not disturbed by the insects that swarm around its sleek crouched body. It watches as the beam of light passes overhead and then is gone.

The Rollins' cabin seems a lot cozier now that Ed has started a fire. Ed, Josey and Cindy all pull up chairs next to the fireplace. Virgil is lying on a ratty old rug that is laid out in front of the hearth. Marty still rummages around in the kitchen.

"What are you doing in there? We did the dishes," calls Josey.

"Dad is going to tell us about catamounts."

"You go ahead without me. I'm not too worried about catamounts."

Ed pokes the fire.

"In the old days, there were a number of animals that lived in New Hampshire that don't now."

"What animals, Daddy? Were they dangerous?" asks Cindy.

"Actually some of them were, Sweetie. These woods once had rattlesnakes, wolves and mountain lions."

"What happened to them, Dad?" asks Josey.

"Well, because they were considered dangerous to people and farm animals, most were killed off. Local governments even offered a bounty for each dead animal."

"Were they really dangerous?" asks Josey.

"What's a bounty?" asks Cindy.

Ed pokes at the fire again and puts another log on the fire.

"I don't think there is any proof that wild cats or wolves normally bother humans, but they were certainly interested in farm animals. I suppose it was scary to hear the wolves howling at night. I guess I wouldn't want to run into a wolf pack in the middle of the night. Killing a mountain lion must have been quite a trophy. I guess the bounty, receiving money for each animal that was shot, also made killing all these animals attractive. Some guys even made their money by collecting the bounties."

Josey leans closer to the fire.

"They were called bounty hunters. Right, Dad? Why didn't they get all the foxes? They go after farm animals, too."

"That's a good question, Josey. I'm sure they did kill many foxes. Maybe they just weren't considered as threatening as wolves. One thing is sure. I've never seen a rattlesnake, but I have heard of people who have. Once when I climbed Green Mountain in Effingham with Camp Wakuta, the ranger said one had been seen near the top. I don't know if he was just trying to scare us, or what. There are no more wolves around here, and the last mountain lion bounty was paid, I think I read somewhere, around 1881."

"That's okay with me. I'd be scared of rattlesnakes and lions," says Cindy.

"Not me," adds Josey. "I'll bet the catamount is still around. I'd like to see him."

Ed leans forward in his chair. He puts his arms on his legs.

"The chances that you will are pretty slim. Supposedly, there have been some sightings. Around 1941 a bunch of cattle was killed not far from here. Someone claimed to have found mountain lion tracks. They never found another trace of a catamount though. Now and then, someone claims to have seen something. It's kind of like UFOs."

"What do they see?" asks Cindy.

"There are stories. One of the old time game wardens claimed that one jumped right out in front of his truck. Old Bill Thompson, the guy with the fly-fishing shop down in the village claimed the same thing. He said it looked like a streak of black lightning. Another guy said he saw fresh tracks along the edge of our river not too far from here. He hurried home to get a camera, but by the time he got back the rain had washed the prints away."

"Do you believe him?" asks Josey.

"Well neither Bill nor Walt is the type to make things up. So I guess I do believe it's possible."

"I believe there are still catamounts around," states Josey.

"You are not alone," says Ed. "The legend has it that, strangely enough, a catamount prowls silently and without leaving prints. Most of the sightings are of a ghost-like animal. It is even said that everything goes quiet when a catamount is around. There are no sounds in the forest."

"Is a catamount a ghost?" asks Cindy somewhat disturbed. "I'm scared of ghosts."

"No, I don't think so. It's just a story, Cindy," continues Ed. "I don't think we have anything to worry about."

Holding a dishtowel, Marty comes into the room. "Hey you guys. It's time for bed."

Josey turns around. "Do we have to? I want to hear more about catamounts. I want to see one."

Marty puts her hands on Josey's shoulders. "I don't think you do. Not up close anyway, unless it's in a zoo. Besides they don't exist around here."

"Daddy, are there any real catamounts?" asks Cindy.

"Well yes, sure enough out West, but I think that it's the last thing we have to worry about here. Our biggest worry is poison ivy," says Ed.

"Daddy, do you promise? I don't want to get eaten."

Ed puts his arm around Cindy. "There is nothing to worry about. I promise."

Cindy turns around and opens her arms wide. "I believe you Daddy. Now I know I am safe cause you said so. I love you this much."

Ed opens his arms even wider. "I love you this much."

Josey comes over and gives Ed a hug. "I love you, Dad."

Cindy hugs Marty. "I love you, Mom."

Then Marty hugs Josey and Cindy hugs Ed. "I love both of you. Now off to bed," urges Marty.

The kids go into the back room. Ed goes to the cooler.

"You want a beer? I'll get the ice for the ice chest tomorrow."

Marty sits down in front of the fireplace.

"I'd love a beer. Roberts said he was still going to cut some ice from the pond last winter."

Ed approaches Marty with two opened bottles of Sam Adams.

— 41 —

"Not many people cutting ice like that anymore," says Ed. "I guess there aren't many like old Ike left." Ed sits down and plays with the fire.

"Isn't that the truth?" Marty appears pensive. "I know you love it up here Ed. For me, though, vacation up here is just like being at home. There is so much to do. It's still cooking and cleaning. It's just like there, only here we have to worry about ice, gas, wood and all that stuff. And the bugs are awful."

"I help with all that."

"I know you do Ed. It's just that you complain about your life, but…"

"Come on. Let's not argue. Come sit closer to me and enjoy the fire. We'll all help tomorrow, okay?"

"Okay, but some year I'd like to go to a hotel and be pampered."

Ed puts his arm around Marty. From the back of the room, the husband and wife are silhouetted against the fire.

"That can probably be arranged," says Ed.

"Ed?"

"Yeah?"

"You know there is nothing to be worried about. I chose you, not him."

"I know."

Chapter 6

Early the next morning, the sun is about to come up. It appears across the horizon and its first rays seep weakly through the screening onto the Roberts' porch. Both Rob and Ike are dozing. Ike suddenly awakens, jumps up and looks out to the sheep pen.

"Shit!" cries Ike! "Shit! Oh, shit! Oh, shit!"

Rob wakes up with a start.

"What's the matter?"

Ike throws his hands up in frustration.

"For Christ's sake! I knew that thing was out there," he says. "I could feel it. I can't believe I fuckin' fell asleep! Jesus Christ!"

"Christ, so did I," says Rob.

"Shit! Shit! Shit!" says Ike again. That is all he can muster.

Both men stare out at the pen. Of the eight sheep that were in the pen the evening before only six remain standing. One is missing and one is gutted on the ground. The surviving six seem undisturbed by what has happened to their pen mates.

"How the hell did that happen?" asks Rob. "I didn't hear a thing. I know I didn't doze that long."

"Me neither. I didn't hear nothin'. Even when I sleep normal, I usually wake up at the drop of a hat. Shit! Them sheep cost me a fortune. I cain't afford this bullshit. I'm sittin' out there with them, tonight. I'll blow the begeezus out of whatever is doin' this!"

Rob gets up and goes to the door. "I guess we better take a look."

"I don't know what the Christ for. I know what it looks like. God damned lamb chops. That's what." Ike sighs and looks at Rob. "What the hell? Let's go look."

As Ike and Rob approach the pen, the six remaining sheep are grazing contentedly. The dead carcass is lying on the ground. The legs are pointing straight up. The chest cavity is ripped open. Most of the blood has been lapped out of the interior cavity. The liver, heart and lungs are all missing. A number of ribs have been snapped off and picked clean. Apparently, the predator has enjoyed a substantial nocturnal meal. Off to the right is a shallow but noticeable trough in the grass. A trail of blood leads to the forest at the edge of the clearing. The missing sheep has been dragged across the field and out of sight. The two men follow the bloody path into the woods. About one hundred yards into the trees Rob spies what looks like a pile of brush. They come closer. Ike picks up a long branch and uses it to push the sticks and leaves off the top of the mound. Once the loose vegetation has been removed, the missing sheep lays gutted and apparently put away to be a future meal.

"The Christly thing took my best one again. I suppose he left the other ones over there just for spite. I'm gonna get the sonna bitch."

Rob picks up a stick and pokes at the carcass.

"This wasn't dragged here very long ago. The blood is hardly dry. I guess we should be happy that it only took two this time."

Roberts looks up angrily. "That's easy for you to say. They ain't yours. Christ, I'm pissed!"

"Do you smell that?" asks Rob. "It can't be from here. This one's fresh."

"It smells like rotten meat," says Ike. "I think it's from over that way."

Further into the woods is another pile of brush.

"That's got to be the missing one from yesterday," says Rob. "I don't particularly want to, but I guess we better look."

"I reckon so," says Ike. "I don't know that it makes much difference, but I guess we gotta know." The two men walk deliberately, but slowly toward the next mound. They don't pay much attention to the ever-present black flies.

Ike starts to pull the top branches off the mound of loose brush. Then he stands back.

— 44 —

"Man, that's ripe," he says. "I guess the heat yesterday didn't help much."

Rob picks up a long stick and pries the next layer off the already decomposing sheep.

"Looks like that is it, all right. Not much blood though." Ike hunkers down, put his hands on his knees, and peers at the carcass.

"It must've had more time to clean up the first time. There wasn't no blood trail like today."

A shiver goes up Rob's spine. He looks around.

"I think it's here, Ike. I have that same feeling I had last night."

Ike looks around. "Me, too. I don't like it none."

Rob shudders. "I wonder if it was in a hurry today because we came along. I think we might have interrupted it."

"You think it is watchin' us right now?" asks Ike.

"I think so," says Rob. "It is kind of eerie. I feel its eyes on me, but I can't see it."

"I know what you mean," says Ike. "Do you think it would go after us?"

Rob looks back toward the house. "I don't know, but I would kind of like to get back to the house. I am sorry Ike. I guess we were both asleep at the switch."

"I just don't get it. Neither one of us heard a thing. We got this trail but still no tracks," says Ike. "Unbelievable. Me and my 30-30 will be sittin' right outside tonight. Bugs or no bugs."

"I think I would want my back against the house," Rob says. "There is no telling where that thing might come at you from."

Ike gets up from his crouching position. "We should've brought our guns."

"I guess we better get back," says Rob. "I'll call in. Maybe Varney has come up with something."

"Varney can't fix 'em now," says Ike.

"Nope he can't, but if we can figure out what we're dealing with maybe we can do something about it."

"I know what I'm gonna do. I'm gettin' my gun and I'm goin' to take a look around."

"Let me call this in. I'll join you." Rob starts back toward the house. *A loud screech permeates the woods and the fields. Rob stops. He shivers.*

"What the hell was that?"

"Christ," says Ike. *The just-rising sun shines on Marion as she comes out the back porch door.*

"What was…?" The door slams shut behind her. *Something slides away into the trees.*

"I think I saw it," cries Marion, shaken.

Rob turns around. "What did you see?"

"I don't know. It was black. It was very black." Marion shudders. "It looked right at me and then it was gone."

Ike goes to his wife. He puts his arms around her. She buries her head in his shoulder.

"Oh Ike, it was like she looked right into me!"

"Why do you say she?" asks Rob.

Still being held, Marion turns her head around. "I don't know. I just know I don't want to see it again." She puts her head back on Ike's shoulder. Ike and Rob look out over the field. Nothing.

"I thought mountain lions were brown," says Rob. Then the phone rings inside the house.

"I better get it," says Marion. "This one is black."

Marion turns and walks back into the house. Ike and Rob follow. The dial phone is still ringing as they come in the porch door. Marion picks up the earpiece, speaks into the mouthpiece, and hangs up as the two men enter the kitchen.

"Rob, we got another one. Mary Schmidt's fit to be tied. She just called. Hear her tell it, most of her cows are ripped apart." Rob sits down heavily in one of the kitchen chairs.

"Man! How many?" asks Rob.

"About twenty-five," says Marion.

"How many?" asks Rob again. "Is that possible?"

"I don't rightly know, but one way or another I guess you better get over there," says Marion. "You want a cup of coffee to take with you?"

"Thanks Marion. I could use it." He takes the coffee and heads for the door. "Marion, could you call around? I'll call in and get Doc Varney. He'll want to come over there, too. I think we might want to get some help. I'll call Troop F."

Marion picks up the phone. "There's about five of us on the line. I'll try everybody." Marion looks at Rob. "Could only one do all of this?"

Rob opens the door and looks back. "I don't know Marion. I really don't know. Are you all right?"

"Yes," she says. "I'll be fine, but it was like it looked right through me." She shivers.

Rob nods. He smiles and goes out the door, gets into his truck and pulls out his microphone.

Ike stands at the door with his rifle in his hand. "I'm gonna get the sonna bitch."

Inside, Marion starts calling.

Chapter 7

Cindy Rollins is playing with a Raggedy Ann doll on the front steps of the cabin. Virgil is lying in the sun. Suddenly the dog looks toward Cindy's right. A slight rustling in the thick scrub oak next to Cindy holds his attention. He watches. Cindy has not noticed the activity in the underbrush and continues to play. Suddenly the scrub brush moves violently. Cindy looks up, startled. A low growl emanates from behind a large pitch pine tree and then stops. Virgil's ears twitch and his nostrils open and close rapidly. The growl starts again. Cindy does not move.

Then the scrub oak shakes again. Something leaps from behind the brush.

Cindy screams.

The figure lands in front of her and yells, "Catamount's gotcha!"

Cindy continues to scream and runs into the house.

"Mommy! Daddy! Josey scared me!"

Ed and Marty are sitting at the table. Cindy runs to Marty.

"What are you two fighting about, now?" asks Ed. "Josey get in here, now!"

Cindy is still sobbing. "He jumped out at me like a catamount. He scared me."

Josey shuffles in. "I was just kidding. I didn't do anything. She's such a sissy. I wish I had a boy to play with."

"Josey doesn't like me," wails Cindy.

"Of course he does," soothes Marty. "Josey, your sister is only six years old. She's only a little girl." Cindy's cries turn to sniffles.

"Can you say you're sorry?" asks Marty.

"Come on guys. You two need to get along," says Ed. "It will be a long vacation if you can't stop fighting."

Ed looks at Josey and puts his hand on the boy's shoulder. "Do you think it was a good idea trying to scare your sister?" he asks.

Josey looks down and shrugs. "I guess not," he says, "but you guys fight, too."

Marty glances quickly at Ed. "Will it be okay if Josey says he's sorry?" she asks again.

Cindy nods, sniffling.

"I'm sorry," says Josey. "But you and Dad don't always say you're…"

Ed looks quickly over to Marty and then down to the floor.

"I'm still afraid of catamounts," interrupts Cindy.

"Maybe we need to do a better job of settling our differences," says Ed.

Josey looks away. "You and Mom fight more than we do," he says.

Marty goes over to Josey, puts her arms around his waist and pulls him close.

"We're just having some difficult times," she says. "Just because we have disagreements doesn't mean we don't love each other."

Marty tries to hold back her tears. "We are a family," she sobs. "We both love you two so much."

Cindy comes over and puts her arms around Josey and Marty. Ed opens his arms around his wife and his two children.

"I love you, too," says Cindy.

"Let's all try to get along better," says Ed. He squeezes tighter.

"Let's," says Marty.

Cindy is the first to pull away. "I'm still afraid of catamounts!" she says.

Ed takes Cindy's hand. "There's no such thing, Cindy. You don't need to be afraid," he says.

"There is too!" says Josey, animated. "I saw tracks down by the river. Down by the fishing pool."

"You saw no such thing!" says Marty. "If you guys are going with Dad to get ice, you need to get ready. Why don't you get going?"

"Are you staying here?" asks Cindy. "Mr. Roberts scares me."

"Everything scares you," says Josey. "I really like Mr. Roberts."

Cindy sniffles. "He says naughty words," she says, "and you did not either see catamount tracks."

"I did too see tracks!" says Josey. "There are tracks down by the river."

Ed stands up and heads for the door. "They're probably deer or moose tracks."

"Dad, they aren't! I know what deer and moose tracks look like. You showed me."

"Josey, we'll look at them when I get back. Are you all coming or not?"

The kids run out the front door. Marty stays in her seat.

"You know what? I think I will stay here. Boy, I wish you had never brought up this catamount thing and you know we need..."

"I know, I know," says Ed. "I didn't realize how much the kids have picked up on all of this."

"Ed, can't we find a way to be happy, if only for the kids?"

"I don't know. I hope so," says Ed. "The catamount thing will pass. I'll try to play it down. It's the least of our worries. Maybe if the kids stay here, it won't come up again."

"All right, I'll fiddle around here. Say hello to Ike and Marion. It's probably best if I don't see..."

Ed looks back at Marty.

"I guess I'm not aching to see Rob either. We'll have to sometime, though."

"I know. I know this is hard for you. I do appreciate that you're trying to understand. It really is over. I promise," says Marty.

Ed starts on his way out. He looks back for a quick moment. "I love you," he says.

"Me, too," says Marty. "If the kids want to stay, they can. It's up to them."

The kids are running around the Explorer. Ed gets into the vehicle.

"Do you guys want to come or stay with Mom?"

Josey runs around to the driver's side. "Let's stay. We can hunt for a catamount."

"I don't like catamounts. I'll stay inside with Mommy," cries Cindy.

"Guys, could we just forget about catamounts?" pleads Ed.

"Okay, we won't play Catamount," says Josey.

Cindy runs toward the house. "Let's go help Mommy."

Josey turns back toward his father. "Dad, I really did see big cat tracks out back. I even looked them up in the wildlife book."

"Okay son, we'll take a look when I get back, okay? Please don't scare your sister."

Josey nods and heads for the cabin. Ed drives away and disappears in the dust of the dry dirt road.

Out behind the house, the river is low. The fishing pool still holds enough water to shelter a population of native brook trout. These trout hover under the cover of three blown down overhanging trees and are calmly waiting for whatever mayfly nymphs, stoneflies, caddis flies, ants or midges that may drift into the range of their waiting mouths. This section of the river is not heavily fished, but it generally takes a well-laid fly and a practiced drag-free river mend to fool these trout into falling for even the most artistic of tied flies. The trout, while they might react to the heavy step of an approaching angler, are not at all aware of the two mountain lion tracks that are imbedded in the narrow wet stretch of bank on the far side of the river.

The Old Abenaki.

The old Abenaki steps outside. The snow has started to melt. Soon it will be time. The sun is bright. It is comfortable and fine to be outside. Soon he will be able to take his beloved wife and give her a proper burial, a proper Christian burial. He has accepted the white man's God, but it has not always been that way. He is the son of a chief. His father was a warrior. It was his duty to protect his people from the invading white men. The old Abenaki remembers killing his first white man, but after attending the white man's school for Indians, he became convinced that his people would perish if they did not befriend the English settlers. The great

Pennacook Chief Passaconaway influenced many chiefs, including his father, to this way of thinking. At first, he had fought with the French. The French were more open to the Indian ways. Their priests preached of a great God, the God of all men, good and bad.

Later he would side with the colonists against the English and would disown his living sons for siding with the British during the War of 1812. One son is killed. It is with more sadness that he thinks of his infant son who was killed by a pack of wolves. The wolves have paid. The old Abenaki killed every wolf in the pack. He has spent most of his adult life helping the white man. He believes in the one God, the one God of his French friends. He has chosen the way of acceptance. He has not chosen the way of many others, who prefer to stand and fight, but he is still an Abenaki. He believes in the spirituality of the great White Mountain. He believes in the still waters of what will later be known as Chocorua Lake. Any human voice heard on those waters offends the Great Spirit. The humans who will break this silence will immediately sink in their canoes to the bottom of the lake. Only a white man would commit such a sacrilege.

He believes in the great healing power of the six sacred springs where he himself has witnessed the power of the magic water that flows out of the ground near the great river. Once again, the white man has come and tries to make money from the springs. He knows of the Curse. No one shall profit from this healing gift of the Great Spirit. Many whites have sought the springs, but up to now, none has tried to make money on the springs themselves. He is sure that will change, but he also knows in his heart that any attempt to profit from the springs will fail dramatically.*

Yes, he has helped the white men to learn to live off his people's land. He has guided them through the dense forests and he has helped secure food. Many would not have survived without his help. He knows the local tribes cannot stand up to the numbers of settlers coming to his people's land.

In spite of the death, in spite of the disease, in spite of the loss of land, and in spite of the ripples of political change among the whites, he has made the right decision. He has followed the way of his adopted God. He accepts the changes that have come, but still he resents their coming.

Had he truly meant the curse that he cried out in anger at the loss of his wife? Can a curse be undone? Is he powerful enough to evoke the Great Spirit to carry out his repressed revenge? He has been taught that the spirits could never actually injure anyone. Harm can only be brought on by oneself, but fear alone can be very dangerous. Can his curse create such a fear? He does not know. Soon, he will bury his wife.

He does not see the quick movement or the yellow eyes that watch him intently while he contemplates his life. The old man is beginning to lose his eyesight. He does not realize it yet, but soon he will depend totally on those who for many years depended on him.

---

* Indeed, attempts to profit directly from the springs result in the destruction by fire of three different grand hotels. To this day, the area around Brunswick Springs has been the sight of a number of tragedies and is considered by many to be haunted. Of course, the old Abenaki knows none of this.

Chapter 8

Rob is driving down the road to the Schmidt place. He needs to get over to the Schmidt's place. He has not eaten. The coffee he had at Ike and Marion's burns in his stomach. He is trying to piece together what happened back at Ike's farm. He is not looking forward to poking around again in mutilated flesh. In his twenty years as a conservation officer, he has never seen or heard of anything like this. Up ahead at the crossroads, Rob briefly sees a car come from the right and continue toward him. He recognizes the Ford Explorer right away. Rob pulls over to let Ed approach him on the left. Ed rolls down his window. Rob speaks first. He is hesitant.

"How's it going Ed? I didn't know you were up here yet."

"Got here last night. I was just going down to Ike's place to get some ice and eggs. How are things up here?" Ed asks, trying not to show his discomfort. The fact that Rob and Ed had once been good friends as well as hunting and fishing buddies is not evident from the stilted exchange they are now having.

"Actually, I can't say that everything is great right at the moment, Ed," says Rob. "Roberts just lost a number of sheep to some animal. Peter and Mary Schmidt had twenty-five cows killed last night. I'm heading to their place now."

"What in hell would do that?"

"That's what we're trying to figure out. If you see Doc Varney, tell him to get over to the Schmidt place."

"Is there anything else I can do?"

Rob starts to inch forward.

"We might need you later. We may have to go after this thing. I am not sure I'd go wandering in the woods right now. At least until we figure this out. Have you got your hunting stuff?"

"Not all, but I've got my Winchester Magnum back at the cabin. I'm not sure why I brought it. I thought I might check the sights, I guess."

"We might just need that kind of power. Do you want me to swing by and tell Marty about what's going on?" asks Rob. "You know while you get the ice and…"

Ed hesitates. "Well, I…"

"Don't worry Ed. I'll just tell her what happened. You know I'm…"

"I know Rob. I guess you had better do that. Tell her I'll be back in about an hour. I'll see you…"

"Okay we'll talk later," says Rob. "We don't want to create a panic, but we have been trying to notify everyone who lives out this way to be careful. I'm glad I ran into you. We didn't know you were here."

Ed puts the Explorer in gear. "All right, Rob. I'll probably see you later. Let me know what you find out."

Rob continues toward the crossroads. How long has he known Ed and Marty Rollins? Almost as long as he has been working in the North Country. He was attracted to Marty right from the start. In the early days, he was still going with Megan. That was before she tired of the slow life around Clifford. She moved to St. Johnsbury, and it hadn't taken a young, pretty girl like her long to find someone else. Thank God, they had not married. At least they were spared the grief and expense of a divorce. Megan wanted out of Clifford and Rob could not imagine living anywhere else.

It was still hard after a seven-year relationship to walk away. Rob has dated a few women over the past years but nothing has lasted long. There just are not that many women who are interested in staying full-time around Clifford. One or two thought they might be, but on returning to livelier places, they were once again caught up with their previous lives and drifted from Rob. There are, of course, woman who relish the rural lifestyle, but they seem to be either taken or so set in their ways that they do not need a man hanging around. So what happened with Marty? Christ, she does not even like coming up here on vacation all that much. Moreover, she is taken.

"By one of my best friends, for Christ's sake," he almost says aloud. "What kind of guy…?"

When it happens, it certainly does. When the two of them unexpectedly find themselves alone at her cabin, an awkward silence turns passionate when their bodies accidentally brush together in the doorway. The initial discomfort they both feel freezes both of them in the front doorway. Marty is not expecting Rob, nor does he expect to find Marty there that fall afternoon. She is there to spend some time away from Ed. She does love autumn in the cabin. Rob is simply doing one of his courtesy drive-bys to make sure the cabin has not been broken into.

When they both move simultaneously to let the other pass, they instead walk into each other. Their eyes meet and Rob can feel the warmth of Marty's breast. He cannot really remember exactly what happens next but the two lean backward into the cabin kissing. Without conscious thought, their tongues explore each other's mouths. Rob has never known that lovemaking can be like this. Marty seems to be in the same state of arousal. For Rob it may be nineteen years of suppressed desire for a forbidden woman. What was it for Marty? Maybe it is just the vulnerability after another major confrontation with Ed. He has known for a long time that their outwardly good marriage is not what it seems to be. Maybe, he hopes, she has always nurtured a hidden desire for him, too. Whatever it is, Rob finds it hard to regret the entire weekend he and Marty spent exploring their mutual attraction.

Of course, it has all ended. Reality arrives when Ed shows up late Sunday evening. Rob leaves hastily after saying that he has only dropped by for a few moments. He has not seen Marty since that mid-October weekend, last year. Indeed, he was not sure whether Ed ever found out what happened. After their meeting in the road, Rob now knows that Ed has. What can he do now but respect Ed and Marty's twenty-year marriage? Why can't they all do this in the open? Why do we make it necessary to do it behind someone's back? He loves Ed as a friend, too. Why do relationships have to be exclusive? However, he realizes he has to respect that, for good or bad, the Rollinses are a family. They have a life together and there are also, of course, Cindy and Josey to consider.

He, Marty and Ed are not swingers after all. Could the outcome of openly exchanging partners be any worse than this? He doubts it. The guilt is terrible. Christ, Ed is probably his best friend. Yet he cannot wait to see Marty. He starts to get excited just thinking about her. Is this a good idea? He'll have to face it sometime. He will just stop by to warn Marty and the kids. He has to get on down to the Schmidt's in any case.

Then, the radio crackles on Rob's dashboard.

"Unit 2, Come in."

Rob picked up his mic. "This is unit 2. Do you read me, Carla? Over."

"Load and Clear. Concord wants to know what's going on up there. Over."

"I wish I knew. Has Varney called in? Over."

"From what he saw over at Ike Roberts' place, he's convinced it's gotta be a cat. Over."

"Man, I guess it's got to be. I don't have any other theories that make any sense. I guess you can tell that to Concord. I'll call in after I see what's up over at the Schmidt's place. Over."

"Varney wants to bring in a cat expert from out West. Over."

"Can he get him? We really could use some help on this one. Tell them, as far as I am concerned, to go for it. You know, Marion Roberts is sure she saw a cat. I was there but I didn't see it. Over."

"Okay. Anything else we can do from here? How'd she see it, if you didn't? Over."

"I don't know. It was almost like she—it—wanted Marion to see it, not Ike or me. Marion's convinced it is a female. Over."

"That's weird. How does she know? Over."

"I don't know. I really don't…Ah, just tell Concord that we'll need some back up. We'll need some good hunters. I want to go after this thing before it does any more damage. Over."

"You got it. Over."

"Carla, you know what? Tell them to do whatever they have to and fly that cat expert up here ASAP, whatever it takes. Over."

"No problem. We'll get him up there by helicopter. Where do you want to meet? Over."

"Let's do it at Roberts' place. We know whatever it…the cat has been there. It's as good a place as any to start. Send the backup there, too. I'll get back there as soon as I have checked out the Schmidt's cows. Over."

"Okay. Varney should be heading to Ike's place. Over."

"Okay. Carla. Get some troopers up here, as well. I'll talk to you later. Over."

"Okay to that. Hey Rob, be careful and keep your radio on. Concord wants it on all the time. Over and out."

"You got it. Over and out."

After making the right turn at the intersection, it takes Rob only a few minutes to reach the Rollins' cabin. "Maybe it would be best if I just drove by," he thinks to himself. "I can't screw up again. Christ, she may not even speak to me!"

The cabin comes into sight. It is too late, now. Cindy and Josey are playing in the yard. They look up and immediately recognize Rob's vehicle. Josey stands up and waits for the approaching vehicle. Cindy runs into the house. A moment later, Marty appears at the front door.

Josey calls out, "It's Uncle Rob."

Rob pulls into the driveway and gets out of his pickup. Virgil rushes over wagging his tail. Josey and Cindy run toward Rob. They both hug him warmly and Rob captures both kids in his arms.

"We haven't seen you in a long time, Uncle Rob," cries Josey. "I really missed you."

"Me, too," pipes in Cindy.

Virgil tries to edge his nose in. Rob lets the two kids go and gives Virgil a vigorous pat on his head.

"I've missed you guys, too. And you too, Virgil."

Marty cautiously walks toward Rob. The two hug quickly and formally.

"It's good to see you, Marty," says Rob. Marty pulls back.

— 58 —

"It's good to see you too, Rob."

"I just ran into Ed. He's heading over to Ike's."

Josey runs up to Rob. "Can I show you something, Uncle Rob? I found some…"

Marty interrupts. "Josey, can you guys play out back for a couple of minutes? I need to talk to Uncle Rob for a second."

"But I have…" Josey starts to say.

"Please just go out back," says Marty. "You can tell Uncle Rob in just a minute."

"But…"

"Josey!" snaps Marty.

"Okay. We'll go out back." The kids start toward the back door of the cabin. "Will you come to see us afterward Uncle Rob?"

Rob leans against his truck. "I sure will, Josey. Just give me a few minutes. Okay?"

"Okay, Uncle Rob." The kids run around to the back, Virgil leading the way. Marty tentatively approaches Rob. She cautiously takes his hand.

"Rob, I'm sorry I didn't…"

Rob puts his hand on hers. "It's okay. It was hard not to see you, but I understand."

"I couldn't. I just couldn't." Marty starts to cry. "I have a family. What about Josey and Cindy? I have Ed. I didn't know what…"

"It's okay. I just don't know what to say." Rob plays nervously with Marty's right hand. "I really missed you. I have never been with anyone like you. I didn't know that it could be so…"

"I know," sniffles Marty. "But I can't…the children. I want to, but I can't."

"I guess Ed knows."

"We've been together a long time. I just couldn't hide it."

"How does he feel about it?"

"He seems okay, but I don't know. It keeps coming up."

Rob continues to clasp Marty's hand in both of his. The breeze lets up and the black flies continue to get heavier. Marty swipes her face with her left hand.

"God these things are awful," complains Marty.

Rob lets go of Marty's hand and swipes around his own head. He feels a loving concern as he sees the flies attached to Marty's leg. He wants to lean over and wipe them off her leg. The thought of touching her leg.... He understands clearly, now, how some men cross the line between fantasy and propriety and force themselves on the object of their desire. He would not do that, but God, he wants to have this woman again. Instead of allowing his desire to take control, he swipes the tiny annoying black vampires away from his own face again.

"They're all over your leg," he says. Marty leans over and brushes the feeding insects off of her leg.

"I don't dare invite you in."

"That's probably not a good idea. You're right. We don't need to have Ed think…"

Rob leans back against his truck. Marty looks at Rob's eyes.

"It's not easy right now. Ed still is unhappy with—it seems like everything. He wants to live up here. I'm so sick of it. I'm sick of talking about it. Sometimes I just feel like telling him to shut up. Every night I have to hear about the damned store."

"Maybe it is time for a change, Marty. It's not impossible, you know. You could live up here. I like it up here."

"I don't want to. Besides, you make a living. What would Ed do up here? All he wants to do is write that damned book. You cannot support a family by writing books. I am tired of hearing about it."

"It's not that bad. You'd have some money, if you sold the store. You said you might be willing to live with me."

"Rob, you're different. You are not unhappy. I'm just so frustrated with Ed's disappointment."

"All I am saying is that maybe Ed and you could be happy if…"

"Rob, let's forget it. I don't need you taking Ed's side. This is just a difficult issue for me right now. It is probably why…"

"Okay, okay. It's just that I care about both of you."

"I know that is why we can't continue to….If only Ed could be happy. I could be happy if he were happy. Why do we have to change?"

"I don't know, Marty, sometimes we just do. I guess that's what came between Megan and me."

This time Marty takes Rob's hand. "I'm sorry. I shouldn't bring this all up. In some ways, I wish it could be different between you and me. I guess right now it looks like I wish that everything was different. Well sort of. I want things to be the same. I want Ed to, you know, change."

Rob smiles. "I guess it is hard to get what you want. What I want, I can't have."

Marty looks at Rob. "Rob, I would do anything to repeat that week-end, but it will never be the same."

Rob looks down. "You're probably right, but we have to stay friends Marty."

"I'll try, Rob, but that will never ever be the same again. In some ways we forfeited that by what we did."

"Don't I know!" Rob puts his arms around Marty and she returns a long lingering hug. Neither wants to break away and both avoid lip contact until Marty finally gives Rob a quick peck on the cheek.

"I guess we better just let things be."

Rob stares at the ground. "Well, actually Marty, I'm here for another reason, to tell the truth. Something killed a bunch of sheep over at the Roberts' place. I was just heading over to the Schmidt farm when I ran into Ed."

"Why are you going way over there?"

"Something slaughtered something like twenty-five of their cows."

"Twenty-five? What would do that?"

"We don't know, but Doc Varney seems to think it might be a mountain lion or something like that."

"A mountain lion? I thought they were extinct around here. Could it be a bear?"

"I suppose, but I never heard of a black bear killing anything like twenty-five cows."

"I haven't either, but…"

"I guess it is fairly rare, but a mountain lion will sometimes kill for the hell of it."

"But there is no such thing around here. For God's sake, Ed has got the kids all wound up with this business about a catamount."

"What do you mean?"

"You know he's been telling them outlandish stories about seeing a black panther cross the road and stuff like that. Josey thinks he has found catamount tracks out by the fishing hole."

"Huh? I wonder if that is what Josey wanted to show me. Have you looked? Ed's stories might not be as off the wall as you think."

"Do you think that there really could be a…?"

Rob moves toward the house. "I don't know but, given what's happened, maybe I should take a look."

"Do you think Josey found catamount tracks? My God! Do you think this could be…?"

"Marty, let's not jump to conclusions. We're only talking about farm animals."

"Yeah, but anything that would kill twenty-five cows might do anything."

"Marty we don't know that. Let's go find the kids." Rob and Marty go quickly around to the back of the house. There is no sign of Josey, Cindy or the dog.

The back of the cabin opens into a small field surrounded by pine trees. The grass underneath the brown covering of pine needles can hardly be seen. The drought has turned even the healthiest patches of crab grass to a pale tan. The grass and the pine needles crackle under foot as Marty and Rob work their way to the river down back. The sandbox that Ed has built shows signs of small-scale villages and construction projects, but there are no young city builders in sight.

An old wooden Thompson motorboat stands empty towards the back of the clearing. It belonged to Ed's father who towed the boat all over New England and Eastern Canada on fishing excursions. After inheriting the boat in the mid-1980s, Ed managed to keep it running for a number of years. When the 35-horsepower engine finally ripped the motor mount off and the engine fell to the bottom of Aziscoos Lake, Ed towed the boat back to the cabin where it has served as a realistic toy ever since. Today, Josey and Cindy are not searching for buried treasure or chasing pirates off the coast of Cape Cod. The boat stands empty.

Both Marty and Rob yell, but there is no response. They follow the path down the banking created by the annual spring run-off to the river. This year, due to the long period without rain and due to the abnormally low snow season, the river has not come up to the annual flood plain. The river itself, though, seems to flow in its normal path. The source is a spring-fed pond about thirty miles north of Clifford. The path cuts through a large patch of poison ivy. Ed has cleaned out enough of a pathway that it is possible to pass without coming in contact with this annoying weed. The poison ivy, unlike just about every other form of growth in the area, does not seem in the least bit affected by the lack of water from the drought and is as prolific as ever.

The path opens up to a small sand bar. To the right, a large bend in the river has carved out a deep pool. A number of substantial trees have already fallen into the river. A number of others are leaning precariously over the water waiting for a strong high water current to continue to erode the high bank into which the trees planted their roots. Soon it will be their turn to careen into the water. Across the river, a sandy bank projects into the bend. The water immediately in front of the sandbar is shallow and allows for easy access to the edge of the beach on the other side.

Marty sees dog tracks in the wet sand near the edge of the river. They lead off in various directions but ultimately head toward the river. Four small sandal prints betray the fact that Josey and Cindy have also waded the river to the other side.

"They know they are not supposed to go over there alone," says Marty.

Rob unlaces his boots, takes off his socks and starts across the river.

"They can't be far."

Marty takes off her sneakers and starts across. On the other side, the tracks lead to the dry sandy bank. In this area, any definable tracks disappear into a continuous series of small mounds. Rob goes over to the furthest point of the beach. Here again there is a small wet area.

There is evidence of Virgil searching in a variety of directions. There is no evidence of sandal prints, but in the midst of Virgil's chaotic pattern of prints are two less distinct prints that do not fit the configuration. The four forward pads do not have the familiar sharp nail protrusion typical of a dog print. The rear pad is softer and features a clear indentation at the top. The bottom of the pad has two indentations that are unlike the rounded back part of the dog's rear pad. Each print appears to be at least three to four inches long. The dog's prints are about half of that.

Rob kneels down to look. "I'll be. This surely does look like cat prints, and these weren't made by any house cat."

Marty runs over. "That must be what Josey saw. Where are they?"

Both Rob and Marty continue to call out for the two children and their dog.

No response.

Marty's calls begin to border on hysteria.

"Oh my God! Where are my kids?" she wails. "Josey! Cindy! Where are you?"

Chapter 9

At the Roberts' farm, Marion passes out cups of coffee to her husband, Doc Varney, Ed, Ralph Hudson and John Barnes. Ralph and John are both state troopers. Everyone is sitting around the kitchen table. A map of northern New Hampshire lies on the table.

"This is a pretty large area," says John. "I think we might have to get some cooperation from Vermont and Canada. Maine, too. What do you think?"

Ralph looks closer at the map.

"I guess we could call them in. Why don't we see how far we get first?"

Doc Varney stands up and traces a circle with his finger.

"According to my friend from Montana, a normal mountain lion might cover up to twenty miles a day. That is all pretty much within our boundaries."

"Sort of. It does get us into Vermont and Canada. Let's, at least, let them know what is going on. This twenty mile radius is certainly the place to start," says John.

"How far is the Schmidt Farm from here?" asks Ralph.

John draws his finger across the map.

"We know it was here this morning and over there at some point last night. As the crow flies the Schmidt place is only about five miles from here. Have we heard from Rob?"

"Not yet," says Ralph.

Ed looks anxious. "I saw him over by my place just a little while ago. I told him to tell Marty and the kids to stay close to home."

"That's probably a good idea," says Varney.

Ike stands up. "You can bet your sweet ass that I'm stayin' close to home. Me and my Winchester. Whatever this thing is, it's sure as hell developed a taste for my animals," says Ike.

"Actually, you know, it probably is a good idea for you to stay here," says Ralph. "It has come here two nights in a row. When Rob gets back, the rest of us can see if we can get a jump on hunting this thing down."

"They're supposed to be bringing in my friend from out West," says Doc. "The state police is also bringing some trained dogs up here."

"Maybe one of us should stay here with Ike," suggests John. "The other two could go to the Schmidts. I don't see how we can trail this thing till we get those dogs."

Ralph looks up at Ed. "Ed do you want to have a crack at this? Both Rob and Ike claim you know your way around these woods."

"Yeah, I would. I got a .338 Winchester Magnum I bought to hunt grizzlies in Alaska. I never managed to get up there. That'll bring just about anything down."

John gets up from the table. "Can you go get it? What else have we got for rifles?"

Ed goes to the kitchen sink with his coffee cup. He rinses it out and puts it in the strainer.

"You didn't have to do that," says Marion. "I can take care of the dishes."

"That's okay," Ed smiles. "I wouldn't want Ike to overexert himself."

"You don't have to worry none about that," says Marion. "One thing Ike hasn't got is dishpan hands."

"Ralph and I brought our deer rifles. So I guess we're all set that way," says John.

"Ike, could I get some of that ice?" asks Ed. "I should get back. It's getting late and I want to check in on Marty and the kids. I'll get my rifle."

Ralph puts his cup in the sink. "After that, why don't you come back here? John and I will head over to the Schmidts. Doc, when your friend gets here, have Rob let us know by radio. Do you want to stay here with Ike, for now? Or do you want to come?"

Doc looks at Ralph. "Why don't you two check it out? It's getting late. I'll wait for George. It'll be awhile but he's on his way. When he gets here, we'll head over to take a look at the Schmidt's. George will know what we need to do to hunt this thing."

Ike heads for the door. "The ice is out back. Why don't you drive round back?"

"I'm on my way," Ed says.

Suddenly the old crank phone rings—one long, one short and one long. Marion picks up the phone.

"Yeah. Hi Marty. What's the matter? Yeah, he's right here. Hold on."

She goes to the door and yells, "Ed! Come back. Marty is on the phone. She sounds upset. You better get in here."

Ed rushes through the door and picks up the phone. "Marty, what's the mat—…?" He listens. "They're what? How did that happen?" He listens again. "I'm on my way. Just wait for me. I'm coming."

Ed hangs the phone back in the C-shaped cradle and heads for the door.

"What happened?" asks John.

"My kids are missing. I'm not sure what happened."

"Do you need help?" asks Ralph.

"I don't know. Rob is still there. I have to get over there. Marty wants to go after them." As he rushes out he adds, "I'll have Rob radio you when I get there."

He looks at his watch.

"God, they will be out there in the dark if we don't get going."

Chapter 10

"Damn it," says Ed, slamming his fist against the steering wheel as he drives away from the Roberts' farm. "Here we go again. How can they let this happen? What really pisses me off is that they screwed around behind my back. Now they are at it again. Well, maybe not that. I can imagine that Rob finds Marty attractive and she him. Were they so glad to see each other that they lost track of the kids? I know I am not always what Marty wants me to be. What is it that makes me so damn angry? The idea of the two of them having sex doesn't piss me off as much as being cheated on. What's more, I am the one who is supposed to change to make everybody happy. I am who I am. I don't want to change. I want my life to change. This bullshit about the business is hard for her to live with. Some of it is my fault. I know it is. It was my idea to have the business in the first place, but it isn't what I thought it would be. Nothing ever is. Does wanting to change make me such a bad person? I'm trapped and now Marty doesn't feel that I'm giving her what she needs. What is really weird is that I find her more attractive than ever. The sex is actually better for both of us. How do you figure that? Damn, are they so wrapped up with each other that they can't even watch the kids?"

Sometimes he can not suppress the anger that hits him like a wave. It is a little like the grief that welled up in him, unexpectedly, after his Dad had died.

"For Christ's sake, how could they lose track of the kids? Why is everything so messed up? We're all good people. We just want to be happy. Marty and I do love each other. I know we do. We love our kids. We both, in our own way, love Rob. We're all trying so hard to fill our own voids that we can't seem to accept each other as we are."

"The rest doesn't matter," he says again aloud. "It's the God damned cheating that pisses me off. Behind my back, that's what sucks."

Ed pulls into his yard. When he sees Rob's truck, anger, frustration and grief swell up in his throat. "Let it go," Ed whispers to himself again. "The kids are what matters."

Then he sees Marty burst through the front door. Rob follows behind. He was carrying his 12-gauge.

"Ed! Ed!" cries Marty. "I don't know where they are! Rob and I were talking and they…"

Ed jumps out of the Explorer. "Where did they go?"

Marty runs up to Ed. "They went out back."

"We found some of their prints by the river," says Rob. "They headed into the woods."

"Christ!" Ed says. "They know not to go into the woods alone." He looks at Marty. "What were you and Rob…?"

"Nothing we were just…"

"Christ, I can't even trust you for a couple of hours."

"Ed, we thought they were out back."

"Calm down! We have to find…" interrupts Rob.

Ed advances toward Rob. "Screw you! Screw you Rob! Why don't you just get out of here?"

"Ed!" Marty screams. "We need Rob. We have to find the kids."

"I can do that without his help," screams Ed.

"Ed, calm down," says Rob. "We also found some large cat prints. This is serious."

"Oh Christ!" says Ed, more subdued. Stunned, he sits on the front step.

"You mean this cat everyone was talking about? Here? In our back yard?"

Marty sits next to Ed and takes his hand. "We have to go after Cindy and Josey. Now! Virgil is with them. We have to find them."

Rob stands in front of man and wife. "It looks like they went to look for the cat. A catamount or whatever you want to call it."

"Josey tried to show it to us," says Marty, "but we didn't pay attention."

"I'll bet you didn't," says Ed, his anger building again.

"Ed!" says Marty. "We have to go after our kids."

"Come on, it's going to be a full moon. With that and the headlamps, it should be easy to find them," says Rob. "Let's take advantage of the rest of the daylight."

Ed leaps to his feet. "Rob, we don't need your help. This is all your fault. If you and Marty had not…"

"Ed, for God's sake!" cries Marty. "This is not the time. We need Rob and we need you. Our children need us! Just go get your stuff."

Ed looks at Rob and Marty. He knows they are right, but his heart is pounding. He stomps past them into the cabin and slams around inside. A few minutes later he returns with his backpack and his Winchester Magnum. He glares at Marty. She and Rob pick up their gear.

"If you paid attention to the kids instead of…"

"Ed, not now! Please let it go! Maybe if you paid attention to me…"

Rob steps between Marty and Ed. "Come on! Let's go find your kids." He heads toward the back of the house. "I'm going!"

Marty puts her arms on Ed's shoulders. Then she melts into him. "I know all this is hard for…"

Ed begins to regain control as he embraces his wife. "It's that…Never mind! I'm all right."

Ed and Marty follow behind Rob.

"We're coming," says Marty.

Chapter 11

The Schmidt farm, unlike the Roberts' place, is well kept, clean and modern. Peter and Mary Schmidt bought the old 1812 farmhouse, then gutted and remodeled it. The interior, while still colonial in style, is crisp and new. The freshly painted gray exterior clapboards are the original color recorded in the early records at the Clifford Town Hall. The Schmidt's even paid an exorbitant amount of money to have power and phone lines run to the farm. A small satellite dish provides TV and Internet access. Peter Schmidt, a successful litigation lawyer, is able to afford the time and money to spend most of the summer on his gentleman's farm. Mary, his Radcliffe-educated wife, much to the surprise of her New York society lady friends, also seems to enjoy her summers horseback riding and sipping late afternoon martinis on the big screened-in porch that had been added to the side of the original kitchen.

The Schmidts are thought of as either "them city folks" or "flatlanders." The terms are not derogatory as the Schmidts are amiable and friendly. They also employ a number of locals to keep the farm running. The expensive Scottish Highland cows are an exotic curiosity in a part of the world that is known for its frugal, unassuming practicality. Some of the Schmidts' city slicker friends raise a few eyebrows. On occasion, after only one night, someone will cut short their trip and be driven back down to Lancaster to catch a plane to the comfort of the city. In spite of its modern conveniences, the Schmidt farm is still too quiet and isolated, especially in the late fall and winter.

"How can you sleep?" one fellow asked. "It was so quiet I couldn't sleep. There was no noise at all."

The locals know that the Schmidts pay on-time and are easy to work for, so they accept them as a part of the local wallpaper, even if one of their cows costs more than the average Clifford citizen can earn in three months.

The two troopers, John and Ralph walk up to the front door of the screened-in porch. Before they can knock, Mary Schmidt opens the door. In spite of the beginnings of a cultured summer tan, Mary looks pale.

"I've never seen any thing like it," she says as she gestures out over the manicured lawn to the clean white-slated fence that is across the yard.

"There. Over there. All twenty-five of them! All dead!"

"Do you know what did it?" asks Ralph.

"None of us heard anything. My husband is in New York. Jake woke me up this morning and took me out to…" gasps Mary as she takes a sip of her Martini. "Oh, I forgot my manners. Can I offer you anything?"

"No thanks," says John. "I guess we better go take a look."

Mary hesitates. "Do you mind if I stay? I mean those cows were like pets to us. It is so gross and they've been lying out there all day."

John and Ralph head out the door. "No, that's fine," says Ralph. "We can take a look ourselves. Where is Jake? We apologize for taking so long. It's been a long day."

"It hardly matters now. Jake is probably in the barn," Mary replies.

Ralph and John enter the huge restored barn. The original weathered barn boards are still in place, but the interior is immaculately rebuilt to house the thoroughbred horses and high-class cattle that are Peter Schmidt's passion, pride and joy. Jake, the Schmidts' stable manager comes out of one of the gleaming, highly polished stalls to meet the two troopers.

"Mr. Schmidt is probably going to have my ass for this."

"It isn't like you could have done anything about it," says John.

"Well it ain't like I could of. Schmidt is a nice guy, but he isn't going to like this. I am paid to look after his animals, you know."

"Most likely he's insured," says Ralph.

"Oh yeah, no doubt about that. But he was mighty partial to those animals. They were shipped all the way from Scotland," says Jake.

"You suppose whatever got them could tell the difference between prime beef and Ole Man Roberts' mangy sheep?" asks John.

"I don't know," says Jake "but whatever got them seemed to enjoy the meal."

"Did it eat the cows?" asks Ralph.

"Not all of them. It looks like it ate one or two. One was dragged off. The others looked like it was done for the fun of it," says Jake.

"Did you see where the one was dragged off to?" asks John.

"Nope. I just went in, told Mary and she called Marion and you guys. It took you a while to get here. I thought Rob was coming."

"This isn't exactly right around the corner," says John. "Rob is looking for some lost kids and we had to go to the Roberts' place first."

"I don't suppose it matters much," says Jake. "We can't bring them back."

"No, we can't, but hopefully we can get whatever did this. I guess we better go look," says Ralph.

Jake starts toward the wide-open door at the back of the building.

"We can go through the back way. Follow me."

A long ramp is built into the back door and the three men walk down the small dirt hill that holds the ramp in place. The lawn on both sides of the ramp is healthy and green in spite of the drought. Further into the field, the men can see the bloody lumps in the browning pasture. They approach the disemboweled animals. The area is thick with black flies and large houseflies. The blood has congealed and is thickly matted on the grass and on what is left of the carcasses. Most of what made up the various body parts of these once magnificent beasts is now strewn helter-skelter all over the dry ground.

"Christ! There is hardly enough left to butcher a good steak," says John.

"Not much mercy shown here," says Ralph. "Can any of this meat be salvaged?"

"I don't see how," says Jake. "Even if we could, I'm not sure I'd have any appetite for it. I know that Mr. and Mrs. Schmidt won't."

John moves back to follow the carpet of blood that leads to the woods at the end of the field. His foot squishes into what were once the functioning innards of a nearby animal. "Shit! Damn! I just stepped into a…I don't know. What the hell is that? A liver? A kidney? Man this will never come off."

To avoid making the same mistake, Jake and Ralph step over similar piles of organic gore.

"Jesus! It's in my shoe," complains John. "Man!"

"I got an extra pair in the trunk of the cruiser," says Ralph.

"Or I can hose you down when we get back to the barn," says Jake.

"What do we do now?" asks Ralph.

John squishes toward the trail of blood. "I guess we wait for Doc Varney and the vet from Montana. Let's go see where this goes."

Ralph looks at John, "You going like that?"

"What difference does it make?"

"Hey, I don't care. It's not my foot," says Ralph.

At the end of the field, the blood leads the three men into a small clearing. The blood disappears into a pile of brush.

"What the heck is this?" asks John.

Ralph picks up a stick and pokes at the pile. He lifts up the top layer of scrub and pushes it aside. Looking pale under his sunburnt face, Jake simply watches. John picks up another long stick and helps Ralph remove the loose, interwoven mesh of cut branches.

"I just cut some of this brush a few days ago," says Jake "If we don't keep at this stuff, it just keeps growing in on us."

"I know, it's like a jungle," says John. "My property is surrounded by scrub oak. You can't get rid of it."

"We got another one," says Ralph, as he pushes off the last of the top layer of sticks.

"Nicely hidden," says John.

"What in God's name would do that?" asks Jake.

"I don't know exactly," says Ralph. "The rumor is that it might be some kind of mountain lion."

Jake comes closer. "What a mess. Looks like whatever it is, it's planning to come back."

"What do you think?" asks Ralph. He turns to look at John.

"I don't know. Why else would it hide its kill like this?" asks John. "Maybe we should cover it back up."

"I'm thinking we might be able to get it when it comes back," says Ralph.

"You sure it will come back now that we have messed around with the pile?" asks Jake.

"I don't know," says Ralph. "But it's worth a try. Let's cover this back up and go back and get our rifles."

"It'll be a while before the vets get here," says John. "Maybe we can settle this thing right here."

The three men place the branches on the pile. The eyes watch as the men make their way back to the distant farm. The gray clapboards of the farmhouse are lit by last strong rays of light as the sun approaches the horizon. She can hear the footsteps in the ultra-dry hay field. One of the figures looks back nervously. It does not understand the language, but it does sense the fear that Ralph shows when he asks if the others feel as if they are being watched.

Chapter 12

Ed, Marty and Rob each carry small backpacks. Both Rob and Ed have their hunting rifles slung over their shoulders. They stop to look at the river's edge.

"The prints are over here," says Rob.

Ed looks. There are dog prints everywhere. "Where's the cat...?"

"Right there." Rob points toward where a small path leads into the woods. Ed crouches down.

"They are big."

"They do look just like a house cat only bigger," says Rob.

"Come on," screams Marty. "Are you two just going to stand around talking about those tracks? I want to find Cindy and Josey. Please, let's get going."

Ed stands up. "Okay, it looks like they went in over here. Let's go. How far can they be?"

Rob heads toward the path. Marty moves toward Rob.

"They are all alone. They don't know what to do."

"I'm sure they just got disoriented," says Ed. "I taught them to stay put if they get lost. Josey knows how to use his compass. I told them to never go in the woods without matches."

Marty stumbles on some rocks. "Ed, he's only ten years old."

Rob takes Marty's hand to keep her from falling.

"We'll find them," says Rob. "If he lights a fire, we'll see the smoke."

"It's awful dry. What if...?"

"Marty, we'll find them," says Rob.

Marty leans against him to keep from falling. With his right arm, Rob pulls up to keep Marty from falling. His left arm steadies her at the waist. Ed looks away and hurries into the woods.

Josey and Cindy are sitting next to each other near a small fire. Virgil is lying nearby.

Cindy is crying. "I wanna go home. I'm scared and I am tired. I'm hungry and I want Mommy."

Josey puts a piece of wood on the fire.

"It's your fault that we are lost," cries Cindy. "I told you we shouldn't go."

Josey pokes at the fire with a long stick. "Please, stop crying. We are not lost."

"Yes we are. You lost the compass thing. We are lost and we are going to get eaten."

"We are not going to get eaten. Dad told us to stay by the fire. He'll find us." Josey puts his arms around his sister.

"We'll be okay. I promise."

Cindy waves her hands frantically in front of her face. "These bugs are horrible."

"I know, but we will be okay," says Josey. "Dad will find us."

"Daddy said that there was no such thing as a catamount. Why are there tracks? I don't want to get eaten."

Josey gets up from the fire. "We won't get eaten."

He walks toward the edge of the clearing. "They're some small raspberries over there. Want some?"

"I don't know. Are you sure they are safe?"

"Dad showed us about them."

Cindy turns around. "Don't go away."

Josey looks back but keeps on walking away. "Virgil will protect you."

Josey starts to pick the sparse, not yet fully ripe berries. Cindy sits by the fire. The crickets and the peepers discordantly create a wall of sound around the tiny campfire. Suddenly Virgil growls. The sound stops. Cindy looks around and Josey stops picking. Virgil starts to run towards Josey.

Cindy turns around and screams. Virgil speeds by Josey, knocking him onto the ground.

From behind the raspberry bushes, a black apparition springs into the clearing past the campfire. Frozen, Cindy watches as the dog spins around and, growling, pursues the streamlined black figure into the surrounding trees. On the ground, Josey rolls over to see his sister clutching her doll. Josey jumps up and runs to her. As the night creatures resume their clamorous performance, Josey throws his arms around his sister and holds her head to his chest. He can still hear the dog in pursuit. He pats and smoothes her hair.

Cindy begins to cry. "Josey, I want Mommy. I want Mommy."

Virgil barks in the distance.

"I don't want Virgil to get eaten."

"He won't," says Josey. He whistles for the dog. "Come here, Virgil. Come here."

The dog's bark grows more distant.

"What are we going to do, now?" wails the little girl.

Josey holds Cindy. "We have to wait here so Mom and Dad can find us. Let's build a bigger fire."

"Josey?"

"Yeah?"

"I think Virgil just saved us from a catamount."

Josey and Cindy still sit motionless by the fire.

"I know," says Josey.

"Do you think Virgil will come back?" asks Cindy.

Chapter 13

Ralph and John return to the grotesque brush pile at the edge of Schmidt's field. It is starting to get dark, but the full moon lights their way. They find a small open area behind a large white pine. It is enough to offer a clear site of the brush pile and cover from whatever might come to claim its hidden treasure. Both men lay low on the ground.

"We'll have to keep very quiet," whispers John. "Have you got the radio on?"

"Yeah I do," says Ralph, "but I think it's nuts. If that squawk box comes on, it'll scare the damned thing off."

John settles into a better position. "I know it but I guess we've got to follow the Colonel's directives."

"Sometimes it's like these guys never worked in the field," says John. "We haven't got a choice if we want to stay out of trouble. Leave the blasted thing on."

"All right! It's on, but I turned the volume down," says Ralph. "Let's see if the damn cat or whatever it is comes back."

(Later). The pile is where she had left it. As she draws closer, she can smell the fragrant odor of ripened flesh. She also catches a whiff of that two-legged animal she generally tries to avoid. The crickets fill the night with sound. The flesh will make a nice evening meal. "Might not have to kill tonight," she muses as she comes closer to the clearing. The white moonlight shines through the shadows of the black trees and brush. Then it is very quiet.

Ralph looks at John. Quietly he points to the edge of the field. He aims his rifle. John nods and looks through the sites on his rifle. The sleek black animal approaches the pile. Both men draw a bead on the dark figure and tensely hold their fingers on their triggers, ready to fire. They know they cannot afford to miss. The first shots must count. The night is silent. Suddenly the radio on John's belt comes to life.

"Unit 20, come in. Over." The crackle, though muted, invades the stillness.

The black apparition springs into the darkness of the forest. Both men fire. Too late. It is gone.

"Unit 20, come in. Over." John grabs his radio.

"Unit 20, what do you want? We had him! By God we had him!"

"Had who? Over." responds the voice. John looks at the radio.

"We had the cat. This damned radio scared him away. Over."

"Where are you? Over." asks the voice.

"At the Schmidt place. Over." replies John.

"We need you to check out the Allard place. Over."

"Why? Over."

"Couple of guys out fishing didn't call home when they were supposed to. The wives are worried. Can you check it out? Over."

"Okay to that. I guess we have blown it here anyway. Over."

"Call in when you get there. Over."

"Okay we are on our way. Over and out."

"Damn it!" is all that Ralph has to say as the two troopers head back to their cruiser in the black and white moonlight. John looks at Ralph. He does not say anything.

Chapter 14

The old cabin stands on the edge of Boulder pond. The once-white tongue and groove clapboards are now a weather-beaten, dull gray. A gas light inside shines through two cloudy glass windows that face into a small clearing at the dead end of a five-mile dirt road, one that runs almost exclusively through lumber company land. The cabin is rented by an agent of Great Northern to hunters and fishermen and has stood, and will stand undisturbed, until a whim of the great logging conglomerate decides that the timber in and around Boulder Pond is ready to be harvested. At the moment, there is no logging taking place anywhere near the old one-room hut.

The sound of the crickets is carried to the cabin by a warm breeze that barely stirs the dry evening air. Outside, a Chevy blazer is parked in the clearing. A blue Trout Unlimited sticker is displayed right above a bumper sticker that reads: "A bad day of fishing beats a good day at work." Inside, two fishermen, Eric and Dave, sit at an old cribbage table made out of a solid pine slab. In one corner, four fly fishing rods are safely packed in protective tubes. In front of them are two fishing vests, thrown haphazardly on the floor on top of small bags containing reels, leaders and boxes of flies. Two wrinkled crushable-felt fishing hats lay to the side.

Eric leans back and stretches. "I'm tired, but that was a pretty good day of fishing. Those two you caught by the falls were good size fish."

Dave heads for the cooler and pulls out a Sam Adams. "You were really into them with the sinking line down in the pool below the snowmobile bridge. Do you want some wine?"

Eric nods and David pours out a glass of Merlot and opens his beer. He places the beverages on the table and goes over to the piles of fishing gear. He hangs the vests on some pegs placed judiciously near an old Vermont Castings wood stove. In the winter, the pegs are close enough to dry out articles of wet snowmobiling clothing without burning them. He picks up his bag of gear and tosses both of the hats on the bed to his left.

Eric jumps up. "What are you doing?" he cries.

Dave watches as Eric goes over to the bed and quickly takes the hats off the covers and hangs them on the pegs.

"Didn't you know that putting a hat on a bed means someone is going to die?" asks Eric.

Dave shrugs and comes back to the table, takes out his reel and starts replacing part of his leader. The idea of death makes him shiver momentarily, but he does not intend to show it.

"I can't say that I had heard of that one, but I'll take your word for it."

Eric comes back to the table, sits down, sips his wine, and takes out a book called FISHING THE NORTH COUNTRY.

"Where do you want to go tomorrow? According to this, we should hit Long Pond. That's the one we couldn't do a couple of years ago, because we were there in the middle of that thunderstorm."

"We've been doing this for so many years, we have fished just about everywhere around here," says Dave. He smiles.

"Since when have you been so superstitious? You're the one who goes to church every Sunday. I wouldn't have thought a hat on the bed would have bothered you."

Eric laughs. "I don't believe stuff like that, but why tempt fate?"

Dave continues to work on his leader. "You know I still remember what you said about God back when we were at Bowdoin. You said that we should figure out whether we believed in God or not and then either decide to worship him or to stop worrying about it. It's funny, I think you are right, but I haven't given up questioning."

"It's who you are, Dave. You were a philosophy major. What more can I say? I believe in heaven and hell and that I am responsible to God for my actions."

"I believe that, too, but I don't find it in church. I feel God more out here when we are in the woods. Know what I mean?"

"I do," says Eric. "If we are going to get philosophical, do you want some of the Chivas Regal that I brought?"

"It wouldn't be tradition without it and this is a wonderful tradition. Eric, I look forward to these trips every year." Dave finishes his beer.

Eric pours the Scotch into two tin cups. He brings the cups over to the table and hands Dave one of the cups.

"This is one of the high points of the year for me. Here's to good times to come," he says and takes a sip. "It's true what Robert Traver says in TROUT MADNESS: 'This does taste better out here.' We even have the tin cups."

"Yup," says Dave. "We're lucky to have had so many good times over all these years. I have to say that I'm glad that not every year has been like this one."

Eric leans back in his chair. "The older we get, the more we lose. I had two colleagues die this year who were younger than I am."

Dave takes a sip of his scotch. "I guess if there are things we want to do, we better get to it. Losing both of Mary's parents and my Dad going into the nursing home makes you stop and think. We're not far behind."

Eric picks up his cup. "I don't think we're quite ready to be put out to pasture yet. At least I'm not. Here's to few more years."

The two men clink their tin cups together.

"I'll drink to that," says Dave. "We may be losing our parents, but we also got our first grandson. Sometimes it feels like heaven and hell are right here together on this planet."

"We have to grab times like these while we can. Even with all the medicines they have us on, we can't live forever. Don't let me forget to take my Lipitor before I go to bed and my blood pressure pills in the morning," says Eric.

Dave gets up from the table. "I guess we have to do our part to support the pharmaceutical industry, but right now I need to relieve this fifty-eight-year-old bladder of mine. Another one of the bad habits you got me started in during college—beer just goes right through me."

"I'm not taking responsibility for your bad habits. The way I remember it, you were the one who corrupted me."

"Truth be told, we both contributed quite a bit," laughs Dave. "I suppose we should clean up our act before we start bringing grandkids up here. What do you think?"

"Yeah, right. Go take your leak. I'm going to try to figure out the best way to get to Long Pond. Supper is almost ready and it is getting past my bedtime. Five o'clock comes around pretty fast."

Dave opens the door and goes outside.

"All right, all right," he mumbles on the way out. "I don't want to be responsible for your not getting your beauty sleep."

Eric grins and takes another sip of whiskey. He opens the DeLorme map of New Hampshire that is lying on the table. Suddenly he feels a chill. He turns his head and looks out the window. Did something move? Must be Dave, he figures. No, probably not. All he can see is the darkness of the night. Even though Dave is right outside, he suddenly feels very alone. It seems almost too quiet.

Outside, the calm, yet alert, eyes gaze at the sharp black-and-white image of the cabin and the pond. The side door opens and a dark figure descends a series of stairs down to the ground. Dave comes closer and closer. He stumbles a little in the darkness. Finally he stops. He unzips his fly.

This trained move is his last. It happens so quickly that he hardly reacts as something very large and very black springs out of the night and tears into this father of four, this husband, ardent flyfisher and high school history teacher. The cat looks up when the screen door opens a second time.

"Dave? Dave, where are you? What the hell are you doing out there?" (No answer as a flashlight scans back and forth over the clearing). "What was that noise?"

Chapter 15

John and Ralph pull the cruiser into the Allard place. It is quiet. The gas light in the cabin shines through the side window. A Chevy Blazer is parked in its usual place. Everything seems normal except for the screen door that is opening and closing quietly in the evening breeze.

"Not a good idea when the black flies are out in full force," thinks John as he gets out of the cruiser.

"These guys have probably been hitting the bottle. What do you think?"

Ralph nods. "It wouldn't be the first time a couple of fisherman lost track of time."

"Yeah, I suppose," says John.

Ralph leans into the cruiser. "We better check in or they'll think we have lost track of time, too."

He picks up the mic. "Unit 20 to base. Over."

"Loud and clear, unit 20."

"We'll be out of the vehicle. We're at the Allard place. Their truck is here but no one has come out. We're checking it out. Over."

"Okay to that. Have you heard from Rob? Over."

"He's still out looking for the two Rollins' kids. We'll check on that after we check this out. Over."

"Keep an eye out for that cat. Over."

"We had the darn thing in our sites. It is big. Over."

"Be careful. Over."

"It hasn't bothered any people, has it? Over."

"No, but be careful. By the way, John's kid called. He wanted to know when you would be coming back. Over."

"I'm not sure. It looks like it could be a while. I guess we will be needed to help getting that cat. Should be interesting. We don't get much excitement up here. Over."

"Sounds exciting all right. Just an excuse to go hunting out of season. I know you guys. Over."

"We'll bring the pelt back to you. But I gotta tell you. It is scary what this animal did to that livestock. Over."

"I'll be waiting. I'll tell your families that the great white hunters will be back after they bag their prey. Over."

"You do that. In the meantime, we'll check out these two guys. Over and out."

John and Ralph head toward the cabin.

"Seems like they should have heard us by now," says Ralph.

John looks around. "Probably dead to the world by now. You know, after a day of fishing and a couple of beers."

"Not to change the subject," says Ralph, "did you see the game last night?"

"You call that a game?"

Ralph approaches the steps to the cabin. "Yeah I know. Typical Red Sox."

"What they need is pitching," says John.

Ralph arrives at the door. "They always start out strong and then they blow it."

"Well they're not even doing that this year," says Ralph.

John grabs the partly open door, closes it and knocks.

No answer.

Ralph knocks again. "Man, that cabin must be full of bugs."

Ralph knocks one more time. "Police," he calls out.

Still no answer.

He looks at John. "What do you think? Do we look inside?"

John starts to open the door. "I guess we got no choice. Police," he calls one more time. "Anyone here?"

John opens the door. Ralph knocks one more time. "Police," he says again. There is still no answer.

"Anyone here?" he asks.

Nothing.

The two troopers enter the cabin. The door swings sharply and slaps against the frame. Ralph goes ahead while John waits by the door. Ralph looks around.

"Holy shit!"

He runs out of the cabin. The screen door slaps the wooden doorframe. He leans over and is sick. He looks up as he spits out the sour saliva in his mouth. He sees something move through the zebra like slits of moonlight and shadow. He tries to focus but the motion is gone. He feels lethargic as he turns his head to look back toward the door. John stands still, his image frozen in the rusty screen and silhouetted by the lone gas lamp hanging from the cabin's rafters. John starts to speak. This image is Ralph's last as he straightens and takes a step toward the cabin. He hears his name and feels the pain. Then nothing.

The cat springs from out of the moonlit darkness. She grabs Ralph by the neck and spins around. Ralph's body flops in the cat's mouth like a rag doll. She runs into the clearing in front of the cabin. John bolts out of the front door. It slams. The cat stops and drops the inert form from its mouth. John pulls out his service revolver. He fires twice as the cat leaps in his direction.

Chapter 16

Ed, Marty and Rob continue to search. In the hopes that Josey and Cindy have done the same, they follow what appears to be the line of least resistance through the thick scrub oak—a deer path. Rob leads the way. He holds back an overhanging branch and passes it to Ed before the thin limb can snap into Ed's face. Ed turns to do the same for Marty and then freezes. He holds the low hanging appendage in place. Two shots interrupt the silence of the night. Then they hear a painful piercing screech.

"What the hell was that?" asks Ed.

"Sounded like something straight from hell," says Rob. "Do you think that was the cat?"

Ed looks around. "Those shots weren't that far away. The Allard place is just across the bog."

"Do you think somebody shot it?" asks Rob.

"It couldn't have been the kids. They don't have a gun," says Marty. The group stops in a clearing.

"It could be John and Ralph," says Rob. "Let me try to raise them on the radio."

"Unit 20, do you read me? Over."

No response.

"Unit 20, do you read me?"

No response.

"I don't like it. Those guys are never supposed to be away from their radio."

"What should we do?" asks Marty. "We have to find the kids. They wouldn't be over there, would they?"

Rob tries one more time. Then he calls dispatch.

"John and Ralph called in from the Allard place," he reports. "I've got to check this out. What do you two want to do?"

Ed puts his pack on the ground.

"We could split. Marty and I will keep looking for the kids and you can go over to the Allard place."

"What if they are over there?" asks Marty.

"Christ, I don't know! What if they aren't?" asks Ed.

"I'm just not sure we should split up," says Marty.

Ed looks at Marty. "You just want to stay with Rob."

Marty responds sharply, "For God's sake, Ed! I just want to find my kids."

Ed looks back. "They're my kids, too."

"This is getting us nowhere," says Rob. "The Allard place is over that way, beyond the bog. We'll all go. Maybe if we meet up with Ralph and John, they can help us out."

Marty starts toward the bog. "Let's do it then. Let's go."

Ed picks up his pack. Rob pulls Marty back.

"Careful, we'll have to skirt the edge of the bog."

Ed moves toward the edge of the bog. "The water level should be lower in this drought."

Rob is still holding Marty back. "The muck around this place is slippery as hell. You can still sink in over your head. A place like this never dries up."

"Well, at least this breeze is helping to keep the bugs down," says Ed.

"For the moment anyway," agrees Rob. "Let's go."

The three work their way gingerly around the edge of the bog. They try to avoid the slimy black goo that makes up the bottom and the side of the swampy quagmire, but the underbrush grows densely right down to the edge of the black water. More than once the dark ooze tries to take possession of one of their wet boots. Sometimes it seems to wish to suck their entire bodies into the murky blackness.

"This place is eerie this time of night. I hope the kids didn't get too near here," says Ed. "It's funny how I normally think of these woods as peaceful and safe, a place for a vacation."

"Not much of a vacation so far," says Marty. "These woods don't seem safe or peaceful at all. I used to like the sounds of peepers. Now they sound threatening and ominous. I just want to find Cindy and Josey and get out of here."

"Nature can turn mean," says Rob, "but Josey has been in the woods before. He knows to stay clear of the bog."

Marty takes a step. "It's really slippery here." Her feet fly out from underneath her.

"Ed!" she cries.

She splashes hard into a black pool of water. Thrashing, Marty tries to find something to grab. There is nothing. She slaps her hands on the water.

"I can't get out of here. It's all muck. This is gross. I'm sinking. I can't get out."

Frantic, Marty tries to reverse the suction of the unyielding swampy mire.

"Help me! I am stuck! I'm sinking fast!"

She sinks down to her waist.

Ed throws his pack and his rifle onto the ground. He dives for the ground. Crawling forward, he reaches for Marty's hand. He slides closer to the edge of the pool. The black ground under him is slick and slimy and he cannot quite reach Marty's hand. Marty continues to sink.

"Keep your hands above the water," yells Rob.

Ed slides forward and extends his hand. Marty stretches forward and connects. Just as Ed's hand reaches Marty's, he slips into the pool.

"Christ! I'm going in, too!" yells Ed.

Marty lets go of Ed's hand. She is now up to her rib cage.

"I'm still sinking!" she screams. "Ed, are you all right?"

Thrashing, Ed tries to reach the edge of the shoreline.

"Shit! I'm sinking, too!"

Rob, on the edge, pulls a rope from his pack. He makes a loop. He throws the loop to Marty, but the rope falls undershot. Marty tries to move toward it.

Rob retrieves the rope. "I'll try again. If I throw it out further, can you grab it?"

Marty is now up to her neck. She raises her hands above the slimy water. Ed is up to his waist. Rob throws hard. The rope sails just beyond Marty's head. The water is close to her mouth.

"Can you grab the rope if I pull it in?" Rob yells.

Blowing dirty water out of her mouth, Marty yells back. "I'll try."

Rob pulls carefully and Marty grabs the rope.

"Hold on."

Marty grabs with both hands. Rob loops the rope around a large tree and starts to pull. Ed is continuing to sink. He is now up to his chest. Rob keeps pulling. With a sucking sound Marty starts to emerge from the black, thick liquid.

"My hands are killing me!" she yells. Rob holds up.

"Can you get the loop around your waist? I'll stop pulling."

Marty lets her hands slip on the rope until they slid down to the loop. She tries to flip the loop over her head but fails.

"Let me give it some slack," yells Rob. "Try again!"

Marty moves her hand further away from the loop. She flips the rope again. This time the loop sails over her head and down to her chest. She pulls it down to her waist. Rob, using the leverage of the tree, begins to pull again. Marty holds on and with the extra lift from the loop around her waist, she slowly comes out of the pool. With Rob's help, she crawls up to safety. Gasping for breath, she turns back toward the pool.

"I'm okay. Get Ed! For God's sake!"

Ed is up to his neck. His hands are extended into the air.

"I can't move!" yells Ed. " I'm sinking!"

"This is it," he thinks. "This is what it all comes down to. No way to help myself. Just buried in the muck."

Rob pulls the slimy rope off Marty. He tosses it to Ed. Ed thrashes in the murky water. The muck below continues to pull downward like a giant vacuum. Ed grabs the rope and works it up his arm and over his left shoulder. Rob loops the rope around the tree, then starts to pull, but Ed does not budge.

"The muck is sucking me in!" Ed yells. "Hold on! I need to get this around my body. Give me a little slack."

"If I can do this," he thinks, "they might get me out."

Ed continues to sink. He grasps the rope with his right hand, tugs and stretches it over his right shoulder. The rope hangs loose in the water around his torso.

"Now!" Ed yells.

Marty, tired and weak, drags herself to her feet and joins Rob. Rob and Marty strain and pull. The rope tightens around Ed's chest. Suddenly the suction lets go and water sloshes in a near perfect circle around the drowning figure. Then, Ed starts to move upward. He is able to move the loop down to his waist. The rope grips against the tree. Marty and Rob continue to haul. The rope stretches and inches forward around the tree. Slowly, Ed emerges from the water. With one final pull, Marty and Rob help Ed struggle onto safe ground. Panting, Marty collapses as if melting to the ground. Rob sits next to the slackened rope, winded. He rubs his raw, wet hands. Ed lies flat, hugging the ground. Marty forces herself to her feet and staggers toward Ed. Ed pushes himself up as Marty throws her arms around him.

"Thank God, Ed!" she cries. "I love you. I thought I was going to lose you, too."

Ed hugs Marty tightly. "I love you, too."

Rob is still sitting. "Come on, both of you. Get back over here. You don't want to go in again."

Rob stands up slowly. Both Ed and Marty look at each other and then back to Rob. Ed extends his hand. Rob takes his hand and helps him onto his feet.

"Thank you," says Ed. Rob lets go of Ed's hand and helps Marty regain her footing.

As Marty gets up, she looks down at her legs.

"Oh my God! I'm covered with leeches.

Ed pulls up his pant leg. "I am, too. Get out of these clothes."

Both Marty and Ed frantically pull off their clothing. Both are soon completely naked. Ed starts to pull leeches off Marty's breasts.

"Once they start sucking, they're a bitch get off."

Marty jumps up and down. "I hate leeches."

In spite of her discomfort, she pulls leech after leech off Ed's welt-covered body. Rob works on both victims' backs. They throw the squirming black bodies into the woods and back into the pool. Leeches are writhing all over the ground. Although it is not cold, Marty shivers with disgust.

"I got them all, I think," says Rob. "I have some dry clothes in my pack. I'm always prepared. I used to be a boy scout."

He pulls out two small towels and hands them to Ed and Marty. Both are covered with red welts that sting as they dry off the slimy bog water.

Rob and Marty are putting on Rob's clothing.

"I hate those things," Marty says as she ties up her wet boots. Marty bends to pick up her wet clothing, then straightens up.

"Should we leave these here? I don't want to carry this stuff. It's heavy and wet."

Rob is kneeling next to his pack.

"Leave them in a pile. We can always get them later."

He closes his pack.

"Come on. Let's get out of here before something else happens. I'm not easily spooked, but this place is giving me the willies. Where are the peepers?"

The bog is silent. Then…

"What's that?" cries Marty.

The underbrush on the right sways quickly, as if in the wind. Then it bursts open. A black mass flies out of the darkness into the moonlight. It speeds by and into the darkness on the other side of the clearing. Marty does not move. Rob looks toward the woods where the apparition has fled.

"What was that?" he asks.

Ed has been leaning over to pick up his pack.

"What?" he asks. "I didn't see anything."

Marty moves toward Ed. "I don't know. It was something big. It was black."

She looks at the two men. "I don't think they shot the cat. I think I just saw it."

Ed puts his arm around Marty. "What did you see?"

Marty shivers. "I saw the cat! I saw the damned catamount, that is what I saw!"

Rob is still unable to move. "I think she is right. Something just…we need to get out of here!"

Marty clings to Ed tightly. "We can't stop looking for the kids."

"I know," Ed agrees.

"Maybe we can get some help over at the Allard place," says Rob. "We can go this way."

"You know this used to be one of my favorite places," says Ed, as the group carefully makes their way around the bog again.

"I'm sorry this all had to happen," he says, looking at Marty.

"Yeah, I know," she manages, starting to cry. "It's nobody's fault. I just want our kids back and I want all this to end!"

Chapter 17

Ed, Marty and Rob approach the clearing at Allard's cabin. Soft ribbons of moonlight filter through the trees. They all stop and survey the scene. The cruiser sits at the top of the hill. The Blazer is parked in its usual place. Light from the gas lamp radiates out from the windows. In the warmth of the early summer, it is the quintessence of tranquillity. Yet it feels oddly cold. Marty shivers and folds her arms over her breasts.

"Where are they?" asks Marty.

"I don't see anyone," replies Rob. "I can't hear anything."

Ed shudders. "It is incredibly quiet. Almost like in the middle of winter."

"What do you think we should do?" asks Marty.

Rob pulls out his radio. "Let me see if I can raise John or Ralph." Rob brings the radio to his mouth.

"Unit 20, can you read me? John? Ralph? Are you there?"

The silence is broken as a tinny version of Rob's voice echoes throughout the clearing from the open window of the cruiser. Then silence covers the scene again like a thick feather-down blanket. Rob returns his radio to his belt.

"Anyone here?" he yells. "Hello! Is there anyone here?"

Silence.

He calls out again and again.

Nothing.

"What do you think? Should we check the cabin?" Ed suggests.

Without speaking, the three figures move slowly toward the dim yellow light emanating from the open door of the cabin.

"What's that on the ground in front of the stairs?" gasps Marty.

Rob hurries over to the stairs. "It looks like…oh my God, it's…it's Ralph!"

Rob kneels down to make sure he is right. Ralph's deadened eyes stare back. The weak light from the open door reflects faintly on both retinas, but that will not bring them back to life. Ralph's face is pale from the loss of blood that had once flowed but now drips from the missing right side of his throat. In contrast to the blackness of the night, the lifeless face appears almost white. The blood…

"My God!" The thought flashes into Rob's head.

The blood, in black and white, looks like shadows. What a time for that old John Prine song to pop into his head. Momentarily, the words dominate his mind. His head throbs as the rhythms of "Shadows, Shadows," and Lake Marie scream out in his skull. Before him lays a friend, a father, a husband, a trooper, a baseball fan….All that he was is lost. "Shadows, Shadows," he whispers as he spits out the last of the bitter vomit from his mouth. Rob does not remember leaning over to the side, but as he slowly recovers himself, he looks back at his companions.

"Don't come over here!" he warns.

Both Ed and Marty turn away but they have come up close enough to glimpse the gore. It is enough. Marty doubles over and throws up. Ed's skin turns gray. Rob closes Ralph's eyes. Rob suddenly feels very distant. His emotions are gone. He is now an observer. This is just another TV story on the news. He turns to Ed and the sound of his own voice surprises him.

"I've never seen anything like this," he says woodenly.

Ed puts his arm around Marty's shoulder and tries to help her up.

"If I stand up, I'll faint," she says. Marty feels darkness starting to take over her consciousness. Her eyes began to lose focus as a spinning haze creeps over them. Then it stops. Her entire body has broken out in sweat. She stares, unblinking, at Ed as her clothing absorbs the stale perspiration.

"Are you okay?" asks Ed as he finally pulls his wife up. Momentarily, she sways unsteadily and leans against him as Ed's arms slip down Marty's arms. He pulls her close to him and hugs. She hugs tightly back.

She sobs, "I can't stand it. This can't happen! Not to them! Not to us, not here! Not to our kids! This isn't happening!"

Ed strokes her forehead. He is numb. He is comforting his wife. He feels her anguish, but none of this is real. Just an illusion. He blinks his eyes as if that will end it, as if that will take all this away.

They are back in their cabin. Ed is telling Cindy and Josey about….Everything is as it should be. Marty brings in hot chocolate.

He opens his eyes. He is still embracing Marty. Allard's cabin is still there. Peaceful, mellow light fills the windows. The cruiser is still there. The Blazer hasn't moved. The pile is on the stoop. The pile of…Ed pulls his wife even closer. Nothing is all right! Nothing!

"I am so scared. I can't take anymore." Marty slowly pushes herself away. She puts her hands on her knees. Head down, she glances around. "Oh my God! What is that over there?"

Ed's eyes move toward the truck. He sees Rob get up to go over. Another lump lies between the SUV and the cruiser.

"Is that John?" wails Marty.

Rob wipes his mouth on his sleeve. He trudges over and looks. It is another body. He turns it over.

"Don't come over here. There is nothing to be gained by looking."

Ed and Marty have moved away from what remained of Ralph. Rob approaches the couple who are still huddled together. Ed looks shocked but is quietly comforting his sobbing wife.

"Both of those men have families….young children," says Marty, as she thinks about her own lost kids in the woods. "This isn't fair," she sobs. "What did any of us do to deserve this? What did those two troopers do?"

Rob tries to gain his composure.

"I have to do my job. I'll have to go inside and see if I can find out what happened to those guys who were staying here."

"We have to find Josey and Cindy," sobs Marty. "We have to…I can't take…"

"I need to go in," repeats Rob.

"I know," says Ed.

"We'll get more help. I just need to look," says Rob.

He takes out his gun and approaches the cabin. He steps over Ralph. He looks back.

"I don't know if..." But he continues toward the cabin. He opens the door and goes in. Ed holds Marty and gently strokes her hair.

She looks wild-eyed at Ed. "I can't find them that way...not like this."

Ed keeps stroking. "We won't," he says. "If it was here, it wasn't around the kids."

Suddenly, the door slaps. Rob steps carefully over Ralph and comes back from the cabin.

"There's nobody in there," he reports, "but there is a lot of blood on the floor. I wonder where they are."

"What do we do now?" asks Ed.

Rob lets the air out of his lungs. "I don't know. I've never. I wasn't trained..."

"Rob, we still have to find the kids!" says Marty. "We can't let them down. As much as I'd like to, we can't do anything for Ralph or John or whomever was in that cabin."

Rob holsters his pistol.

"No, I guess we can't," says Rob. "I'll radio for a search party and get a helicopter. With their help, we'll find the kids."

Rob looks down at the ground and says, "I'm sorry. I didn't know how..."

"None of us did," says Ed. "I'll help you."

"Marty, why don't you sit in the cruiser?" suggests Rob. Avoiding the remains of John's body, Marty gets into the cruiser.

Rob and Ed shuffle over to John's body. Carefully Rob picks up John's service revolver. He smells the barrel.

"It looks like John got off a shot."

"The cat must have gone toward the bog," says Ed. "That's where you and Marty saw it."

The sun is about to rise and the clearing becomes lighter as the two men check around.

"Look over there, it might be blood," says Rob. "John may have hit it."

"Or that could be from one of those fishermen," suggests Ed.

Rob goes over to the edge of the clearing, then hesitates.

"Whatever it is, it leads into there. All we need is an angry, wounded animal. This thing does enough damage when it isn't mad."

The day is getting brighter. Rob glances around. "Do you feel like we're being watched?"

"Yeah, I do. This whole place feels like death, like being watched by ghosts." Ed shudders. "Worse than that," he thinks.

The cat creeps backwards and then away.

"We'll get some dogs and a crew. I bet they can track this thing," says Rob. "We definitely need help. We're in over our heads."

"I'm scared," admits Ed. "I'm really worried about the kids."

"Me, too," agrees Rob. "Let's go back and radio in. And don't tell Marty about the blood."

The two men survey the scene one more time.

"Funny," says Ed. "I don't feel like we're being watched anymore."

They hurry back to the cruiser. Rob picks up his radio.

"Do you think we should head back and meet up with the search dogs?"

"I think we have to go back into the woods. Marty won't want to stop looking."

Rob puts the mic to his mouth. "All right, we'll keep looking. I had better warn everyone that the cat might be wounded. I don't know what else to do."

"I don't either," replies Ed. "I'll get Marty."

Chapter 18

The sun appears over the low hill behind the clearing where Cindy sleeps in Josey's lap. She is clutching her rag doll. Josey is still sitting upright. He has dozed off in spite of his attempts to stay awake and watch for the catamount. The fire has burned out. The black flies compete for their attention as both Josey and Cindy awaken. Their first reflex is to wave their hands around their heads to discourage the attacking black kamikazes. Virgil lays next to the two kids, sound asleep and oblivious to the flies swarming around him. He is breathing hard and in a dream. Panting and moaning, his body and haunches move in a rhythmic chase. Virgil is dirty and wet.

Cindy leaps up. "Look! Virgil is back!"

Josey leans over toward the dog and pats him on the head. Virgil wakes up and lets out a loud yip. He licks Cindy's face. She throws her arms around him. Josey continues to pat him. The dog jumps up and races in circles around the clearing. Josey whistles and the excited dog stops and then comes over to him. Josey strokes him to calm him down.

"You're a good dog," he says.

Cindy pats him, too. "Oh Virgil, I love you. That catamount didn't get you."

Josey hugs Virgil's head next to his. "He saved us," he says, "from a catamount."

Cindy breaks into tears. "Please, I don't want that thing to come back. I'm still scared. I'm very hungry and I want to go home."

Josey holds his sister.

"Please can't we just go home?" she begs.

"Now that it's light, Mom and Dad will find us," Josey promises.

"I want Mommy and Daddy," she cries. Virgil licks her face.

"Me, too," says Josey, hugging his sister. "Come on, let's build another fire. They'll find us."

Cindy pouts. "I am hungry."

"Come on, we'll eat some berries. Maybe I can figure out a way to catch some fish. That catamount is gone."

"How do you know?" asks Cindy. Virgil lies quietly next to the burned-out fire.

"Look at Virgil. He's not afraid. He'd know if a catamount was around."

Josey leads his sister over to the small berries.

"I don't want to stay here. It knows we're here," complains Cindy.

Josey starts to pick the barely ripe raspberries. "These berries aren't very big, but we've got to eat something."

"What is Virgil going to eat? Are you sure these are safe to eat?" asks Cindy.

"These are the kind Dad said were safe. I'm sure they are okay. Virgil will be fine. Besides Mom and Dad will…"

"Where are they? How come…?"

"They are coming," says Josey. "I don't know. Maybe we should go down the river. Maybe the catamount won't smell our tracks, if we walk in the water."

"But, Daddy said to always stay in one place."

"You're the one that said the catamount knows where we are," says Josey.

Cindy starts to whimper again. "I don't know what to do."

"But you're right. That catamount does know we are here," says Josey. "I saw on TV that if you walk in the water…"

"But Daddy said…" begins Cindy.

"I think we need to move," insists Josey.

"Where? Are we really lost?" asks Cindy.

Josey looks down the river. "If we walk up the river, it must come to our house."

"Is this the same river?" asks Cindy.

The boy looks up and down. "I'm not sure. There are a couple of rivers out here. We shouldn't have gone into the woods."

"I told you we're lost," cries Cindy.

"I bet this comes out by the bog, down by that fishing cabin," says Josey. "I think we should follow the river. It has to come out somewhere."

Josey eats some of the small berries. "Here eat some of these." He hands her some berries.

"I just want to go home," she insists. "I just want to go home. Why did Daddy lie about the catamount?"

"What do you mean?" asks Josey.

Tears well up in Cindy's eyes. "He told us catamounts don't exist. He promised. Why did he lie?"

"He didn't know," replies Josey.

"Why not?" she asks.

Moving toward the river's edge, he says, "I don't know. He just didn't. I don't think anyone did. Come on. Let's go."

"I don't want…"

"Cindy, do you want to get eaten by a catamount?"

"No, but…"

Josey takes Cindy's hand. He whistles to Virgil. "I'll make a mark in the sand to show which way we have gone."

Josey draws an arrow in the sand. "Come on, I'm pretty sure this goes near the Allard cabin. Maybe we can find help."

Virgil runs ahead of the girl and boy. He doubles back along the other side of the river. He sniffs the large cat prints that are heading down stream. One of the prints is bloody, but the two kids don't see this as they continue. They are busy swatting the swarming flies, sloshing and slipping as they make their way along the rocky-bottomed river. Above them, the sky is growing darker and they hear the distant rumble of thunder.

"Josey?" Cindy asks.

"What?"

"I thought Dad knew everything."

Josey keeps moving. "Nobody knows everything."

"Josey?"

"What?"

"We can't stand in the river if it lightnings. Mommy said so."

*   *   *

The front yard at the Roberts' place resembles the parking lot of one of the outlets in North Conway. Police cruisers, Fish and Game pick up trucks, press vehicles and several private vehicles trample the uncut grass in front of the house and barn. Cars are parked in a row along the winding dirt road. People are approaching the Roberts' place and comparing stories. Some carry hunting rifles and holstered pistols. Three troopers are positioned in front of the yard. It is their duty to keep the press and the ever-increasing number of curious bystanders and would-be great white hunters at bay.

Channel 8, Channel 13, Channel 6, and Channel 9 all have their satellite vans set to broadcast the latest on "The Mountain Lion Crisis, Day 2 in the North Woods." None of these TV stations is local, but the loss of a boy and girl in the woods, the death of the still-unnamed fishermen and two New Hampshire troopers is the biggest news from Bangor, Maine to Burlington, Vermont. Even the nationwide feeds are carrying the story. Radio and newspaper reporters mingle among the crowd hoping to out scoop their competitors. Four more troopers guard all the possible entrances to the farmhouse. Occasionally, someone decides that the rules do not apply to him or her and attempts to get closer to the action. No one succeeds.

Inside, the Roberts' kitchen has been converted into a crisis command post. Radios flick off and on. Marion Roberts pours endless cups of coffee, while trooper Ben Southard carries on a conversation on his two-way. Conservation officer Roger Wright is looking at a map. Ike Roberts comes in the front door.

"I hear a 'copter coming."

Southard is holding the radio to his mouth.

"The helicopter is here. Can we send the bodies back? I heard Charlie couldn't get his hearse out here because of all the cars in the road. We can't find one of the fishermen either. Over."

"Yeah, Charlie couldn't get through. That's why we sent the 'copter. The pilot is also looking out for the kids. The vet from Montana should be at the Fryeburg Airport soon. Harry is coming with a couple of dogs. What about the kids? Over."

"We haven't found them yet. It's a big woods. The dogs should help. Over."

"What about the cat? Is that what it is? Over."

"It looks like it. That guy from out West should be able to help us figure that out for sure. Over."

"The TV is calling this 'The Catamount Tragedy.' Over."

"Well, I guess they always are way ahead of us. How are John and Ralph's families taking it? Over."

"We haven't been able to contact everyone yet. Dave is coming up from Conway. Over."

Ben's voice breaks. "Good, they will need a chaplain. He's the best there is. I met him when Henry was killed. Over."

"That was an awful time. Over."

"This could be even worse before it is over. I guess it already is," says Ben and then looks at Ike. "Mary, I've got to go. Make arrangements for the bodies and don't let the families near them until Charlie has had a chance to work on them. It's that bad. Over."

"I'll make sure Charlie gets them to the funeral home. We still have to get in contact with the other families, too. The wives and kids are away somewhere else. We're working on it. Over."

"Man they don't even know. Over."

"No they don't. It's a nightmare. If they see the TV… they're bound to figure it out, even if the names haven't been released." Over."

"Mary, the 'copter should be returning to you before long. See if you can get the Montana guy on it when it comes back. It looks like we are going to get a serious thunderstorm on top of everything else. Over."

"Yeah, no rain for two months and now this. They're predicting hail and high winds. Over."

Ben looks outside. "Damn!" he says. "It's getting darker. I am going to try to get that bird loaded and out of here. Over."

"Okay to that. Over and out."

Roberts is sitting at the table. Everyone is drinking coffee.

"Leastwise, it left my Christly sheep alone, last night."

Roger looks up from his map. "Is that all you can think about? You want to tell Ralph's and John's wives what happened? What about the two kids in the woods?"

Ike looks at his coffee. "I didn't mean nothin'. Just makin' an observation. I got my own reasons for wantin' this son a' bitch. That's all."

Roger looks at Ben. "I just don't get it. John and Ralph were armed and trained in the use of deadly force."

Ben drinks some of his coffee. "It must have happened awful fast."

"How fast are mountain lions supposed to be?" asks Roger.

"I don't know. If it is a cat, they don't normally attack humans," says Ben.

"I heard of 'em eatin' babies out West," says Ike.

"John and Ralph weren't babies," says Ben. He heads for the door. "It sounds like the helicopter has landed. We need to get those bodies back to town. Thank the two officers who went and brought the remains here."

"Do you need help?" asks Roger.

"I don't think so. There are enough of us out there. We'll move the bags from the barn to the helicopter and get them out of here before it starts to rain. You decide where we should start to search. The kids are top priority. Get in touch with Rob." Roger puts down his coffee cup.

"Maybe we should wait on the bodies. We could use the helicopter to start searching."

Ben looks out at the landing helicopter. "A storm is coming up and we need to get that other veterinarian. I think we should get the bodies to Charlie and get the 'copter out of here ahead of the storm." Ben hurries out the front door.

Roger takes out his radio. "Thanks for the coffee, Marion."

Marion picks up the cup. "It's the least I can do, Roger."

Roger studies the map. "I think we should start east of the Rollins' place. That cat can't be everywhere, can it Ike?"

"It sure as hell seems to be," says Roberts.

"We can take Harry with us and get some of the kid's clothing from the house," says Roger. "The dogs should be able to track them."

"Even after the storm?" asks Ike.

"I guess the storm won't help much, but it's worth a try," says Roger. "I'm not a canine trainer, but I believe these dogs are trained to find the proverbial needle in a haystack. I don't think these cats hunt much during the day, do they? Of course, they don't normally do what this one is doing."

"Darned if I know when they hunt," says Ike. "Normally they don't exist—least not around here. We ain't dealin' with nothin' normal."

Wright looks up from the map. "I wonder how a wounded cat might act."

Ike scratches his head.

"Ain't none of us know, but I ain't sure I like the idea of that."

"I'm not sure I want to think about that, either," says Roger.

Roger radios Rob as he watches Ben and two other men carry three black body bags into the back of the helicopter. The bags flutter in the ever-increasing wind. When he is done, Ben comes back to the kitchen door. The helicopter takes off and the chop, chop fades into the distance.

Chapter 19

Marissa Hudson is sitting on the beach at Wallace Sands. Seth, age four, and Lisa, age five, are building sand castles. It is a bright sunny day, but beyond the row of weather-beaten, wooden beach houses, the northern horizon has started to look more threatening. She plans to meet with Joyce Barnes and spend the afternoon with Joyce and her kids, Bobby and Willie, over at Odiorne Point. John Hudson and Ralph Barnes have been partners and friends for over ten years. They went to the Academy in Concord together. Their wives also became close friends and the kids are about the same age and often play together. The two families often get together during their time off.

Marissa and Joyce often enjoy time at Wallace Sands while their husbands are on-duty. Marissa's family purchased the beach house on the water in the early 1950's for $6,000. Ralph and Marissa would not be able to afford to buy the house today, but they both enjoy the place enough to pay high taxes in order to hold onto it. On a summer day like this one, the beach will become very crowded, but their favorite time is a beautiful fall day when everyone has left after the main season is over. Ralph and Marissa sometimes rent out the cabin during part of the summer to help with expenses, but this summer they decided to use it themselves. The cleaning between rentals is tiresome, and outside of a few of those treasured fall days, they seldom get to use the place themselves.

Marissa looks at the sky. "Lisa, Seth, I am going inside to check the news and see what the weather is going to be."

She gets up and heads toward the house. Inside, she turns on an old TV. She flips to Channel 9. The news is already on, which surprises her. The news usually comes on at noon, but it is only ten-of. The announcer is talking about a mountain lion crisis in Clifford.

"That's where John and Ralph…"

The announcer then starts to talk about two state troopers: "The names have been withheld. The next of kin have not yet been notified."

Marissa's knees feel weak. She collapses into the old worn gray sofa and picks up Lisa's beat-up, ratty old doll. She holds it close.

"I've got to go to the phone down at the clam shack. I've got to…"

Then through the back window, she sees the cruiser pull in.

"No! No!" she cries aloud.

Moments later, there is a knock at the door.

Chapter 20

It is suddenly very dark. Without the passage of time, day has turned to night. The once-distant thunder now crashes violently overhead. Bright chains of lightning repeatedly flash in the sky.

Rob, Marty and Ed enter the clearing where the kids recently spent the night. Marty races to the remnants of the small fire.

"They were here!" she cries. "It has to have been them."

Ed kneels down and inspects the ashes. "This is definitely a recent fire. I wonder why we didn't see the smoke."

Rob looks up. "The trees are pretty high here. This is going to be a hell of a storm."

Now, the deep warlike crashes of opposing weather patterns tear the sky into crescendos of cannon-like roars. The sharp, jagged swords of lightning rip the sky with an ear-shattering crack as they seek ground. The rain pours out of celestial buckets. Within seconds, all three are drenched. They crouch to the ground, heads down and wrap their arms around their knees. There is nothing else they can do. The rain hits their faces like nails sprayed from a stud gun. Each climax of rolling thunder brings a brilliant chain of light that seems to hit the small clearing as if aimed at an archery target. Behind the clearing, there is a larger crack. A large tree is shredded at its core and screeches to the ground. An earthquake-like tremor passes quickly through the earth. Then, as suddenly as it had arrived, the storm stops. The violent wind turns into a mild, whispering breeze. Otherwise, it is almost silent. The only other sound is the gurgle of the brook as the new water runs off downstream.

Suddenly, on the other side of the river, a vagrant flash of lightning reveals the yellows slits of light reflected in two large eyes. White whiskers are momentarily set off by a large black face.

No one notices. The thunderous sounds are now distant snare drum rolls and occasional flashes are more like a bare light bulb being switched off and on.

Rob gets up. "I haven't seen anything like that in years."

Ed stands and looks around. "I thought it was the end of the world."

Marty gets to her feet and brushes her soaked hair away from her face. "I've had enough," she says. "Josey and Cindy were out in this, too."

Ed puts his arm around Marty. The sun starts to filter through the drenched trees. The silence is punctuated by dripping residue from the leaves, enough to give the impression that it is still raining. The air is thick with moisture and the muggy heat becomes oppressive. Marty walks over to the small, makeshift campfire. Sweat and rain drip off her skin. Rob picks up the bottom of his wet shirt and wipes his forehead.

"Any sign of where they might have gone?" he asks.

"No," says Ed. "Damn it! I told them to stay put, but…"

Marty takes his hand. "Ed, we don't know what…"

"I know." He kneels down where Josey has made his mark in the sand. A washed out line is barely visible. The pointer has disappeared.

"They may be trying to show us where they're going," says Ed.

Rob looks closely at the line. "It doesn't show us which way they went."

Ed paces back and forth. "It looks like they are following the river. We have two choices."

"Thank God, they were okay when they were here," says Marty.

"It seems so," agrees Rob. "God, this rain really came down."

Ed looks across the river. "I can see blue sky over there."

He turns around toward his back. "I feel like we are being watched."

Marty moves closer to Ed. "I do, too. I've felt it ever since we got here."

Ed spots a small box on the ground. He kneels down and picks up a box of waterproof matches.

"What's this…? These are Josey's. I gave them to him. The kids were definitely here."

"Now they can't light a fire," says Marty.

The black figure moves closer.

Rob, Marty and Ed are all kneeling by the river.
"Look!" says Rob. He points out the washed out, fading dog tracks going into the river. "It looks like Virgil is still with them," he says.
"What good is Virgil?" asks Marty.
"I believe even large cats are intimidated by dogs. They use them to hunt and corner them out West," says Ed.
"I can't imagine Virgil cornering anything," says Marty.
"What's that?" yells Marty.

The brightening sunlight through the trees reveals the glare of two yellow eyes peering coldly through the underbrush on the other side of the river. The next moment there is nothing. The sunlight intensifies the colors in the post-storm dew.

"I saw it again!" Marty cries. "It was right there."

"You saw the cat again?" asks Ed.

"The eyes! It! A catamount! It was watching us from over there."

"Where? Exactly where?" asks Rob.

"Over there across the river," replies Marty, pointing to the spot. Rob grabs his rifle.

"Are you sure?" he asks.

"Yes," she says.

Ed grabs his rifle. The river has risen in the storm and is hard to wade, but the three slosh through the water to where Marty has seen the cat.

"Right there behind those bushes," says Marty. She points to the spot. Rob pulls back the scrub branches. The outlines of the cat's prints are fading in the mud.

"It was here. It was watching us," says Marty.

Ed kneels down for a closer look.

"Look at the size of those paws. This thing is big."

"And it was this close," says Marty. "Is it still watching us?"

Ed starts back across the river. "Let's go back to the other side." The sun is now beating down in full force.

"It's going to get hot today," says Rob as he starts across. "I'll radio for a crew. We'll go down the river and have the others go upriver. We have two choices."

"Maybe we should continue upstream because there have to be troopers over by the Allard place," suggests Ed. "What do you think?"

"Let me radio and see if we can find out what is going on over there."

Rob goes over to his pack. He radios in.

"I can't help but think about John and Ralph," says Ed. "I knew those guys. I fished with John a few times. None of this makes any sense. This is the twentieth century. Things like this don't happen."

The day is getting sweltering. The black flies are swarming around all of them. The more the sweat rolls off their bodies, the more inviting they become to the insidious blood-sucking insects.

"It is hotter than hell, but I felt really cold when I saw those eyes watching us," says Marty, swatting around her face. "I don't know if I can stand it. Even 100% Deet doesn't work."

Ed hugs his wife. "I know what you mean," he says as he wipes the sweat from his brow. "I wonder why the cat didn't bother us."

"I don't know," says Rob. He puts his radio back in its holster.

"Let's go down the river. That's the way I would go, if I were in their shoes. Let's get out of here. These bugs are awful."

"We're heading back toward the bog," says Ed.

"Help is coming from your place. They are bringing dogs," says Rob. "They'll see if they can pick up the trail, so they'll be coming from the upstream direction."

"We didn't see any sign of them by the bog," says Marty.

"They were probably here while we were in there," says Rob. He takes out his GPS. "I'll radio in the coordinates so they can start the search from here."

Marty flings her hands around her head. "God I am miserable. It must be even worse for the kids."

The sun continues to beat down, indifferent to their trouble, and the black flies are persistent in their attraction to human sweat and carbon dioxide.

The Old Abenaki.

The winter melt is over. There has been very little rain. It is very dry. The bundled corpse of the old Abenaki's wife is strapped to a flat boat the old man has often used to carry furs and pelts down the river to the white man's village. The forest between the wide bend in the river and the great lake is dense, but the quiet water that flows into Mackapaque provides an ideal conveyance to transport a heavy load. He will paddle the bundled body of his beloved down the mild current to Mackapaque. He is thinking about his wife's name. It is a variation on Mary, the name the white man uses whenever a female native is baptized. Not unique. There are hundreds of Mollies in the North Woods, but he will bury his wife on the island she loved so well, an island that will be the only one of its kind, as it will forever bear the name of Moll's Rock. It will be their island. He will show no other living being the way to this private and sacred place. He pushes the float into the river and starts out. He looks to his left across the pond-like bend in the river. He can see the smoke from the great fires burning to the north, a raging inferno. This is the curse he will put on anyone who desecrates his Molly's resting ground.

The black creature lies quietly next to a large blown-down tree. The cold yellow eyes watch as the lonely figure moves away steadily into the distance.

Chapter 21

The helicopter takes off from the Roberts' farm. The storm appears to be in the distance. Josh Jenkins, under normal circumstances, would avoid flying with a severe storm on the way. These are not normal circumstances, however, and Josh wants to prove to his superiors that he can come through in a pinch. Josh completed his flight training a year before and doesn't have a lot of experience flying under adverse conditions. He is young, but well thought of in the State Police. He has a great family consisting of two boys, ages five and eight, and a wife who is very supportive of his career. He has made his reputation not by being hard, but by being fair, and everyone likes him. It is not that Josh does not have an air of authority. All troopers are trained to have that. He is confident and can take charge, but right now, he is growing nervous as the winds from the northwest rapidly increase and attack his helicopter. Suddenly, the rain opens up and visibility in front of the helicopter is reduced to zero. The instruments tell him where he is going but he can see nothing except sheets of water flowing like the incoming tide off his bubble. Lightning flashes around him and the aircraft shakes in the winds. Josh wrestles with the controls. The stick shakes but he holds on. He is heading out of the storm.

"If I can only get ahead of..." he thinks.

Then, there is loud crack. Josh does not feel a thing as one of his blades breaks into splinters and the helicopter immediately goes into a spin. Before Josh can try to regain control, call mayday, or before he can even think to unbuckle and bail, the 'copter hits the top of a tree and flips over. The second blade clips off the top of another tree as it snaps and hurtles into the forest. The bubble spins to the ground and breaks into flames on impact. Although the rain has been heavy, the dry forest all around the helicopter bursts into flames. The dead bodies inside are incinerated, as is the still-living body of Josh Jenkins, a man with a promising career and a wonderful family.

Rebecca Harrison starts her car and turns on the air conditioner. "That's it," she thinks. "We have everything for the trip. When Eric gets back from up North we'll be ready to go."

Even when the kids were growing up, Eric and Rebecca always took time together. Sometimes it is a weekend at a condo in Wells Beach. Sometimes it is just a hotel in Portsmouth. Sometimes Portland. Now that the three boys are all grown, Eric and Rebecca still look forward to their trips away. This time they have rented a cottage on the Cape. Rebecca cannot wait to get away from her job as a legal assistant in a Laconia law firm.

Eric is a history teacher and, even though he works part-time doing carpentry, has more free time in the summer. One of his yearly traditions is his annual fishing trip with Dave Johnson. Eric and Dave have taken three days together during the beginning of the summer for as long as Rebecca can remember. Eric and Rebecca met in college and have been married for thirty-two years. She knows how much the two friends enjoy this annual outing. She wonders how the fishing is going. She also appreciates having some time to herself. The couple has weathered hard times, but now, in their mid-fifties, they relish their work, their time together, the fact that their three boys have each found their own niches in society and are off on their own. All in all, it is a good marriage. Both will be able to retire within the next few years. The mortgage will be paid off and it looks like their long-term plan to travel across country might just happen. The sex is still good, if not as frequent. In fact, it's probably better.

"I could use a little," she thinks to herself as she pulls into her neighborhood street. All in all, with vacation just around the corner, the world seems good. Then she slows down.

"What is that trooper doing in our driveway?" she almost says aloud.

* * *

Josey and Cindy are sitting on a small sand bar. They are drenched after the heavy rain. Virgil is sniffing, moving quickly around in a circle. The thunder and lightning are now distant and blue sky has returned, bringing with it hot, muggy air.

"I'm not afraid of lightning anymore. I wish I could tell Mommy," says Cindy. "It was scary, but it didn't hurt us."

Josey rummages for something in his pocket. "It's a good thing we got out the water. Dad says that you shouldn't stand in the water during a thunderstorm."

"What do we do now?" asks Cindy.

"Keep following the river," says Josey.

He searches his pockets again. "I lost the matches. I can't find them anywhere."

"You're stupid!" says Cindy. "Now they'll never find us." Cindy starts to cry.

"Be quiet Cindy. I am not either stupid."

"You be quiet. This is all your fault. I just wanna go home. I'm sorry I followed you."

"I want to go home, too," says Josey quietly. "We'll find a way. I'm sorry, too."

"How?"

"I think the Allard cabin is down the river. I think I can see the bog."

"But Mommy said to never go near the bog." Cindy is still crying. "I don't want to go to the bog. I don't want to stay here. I don't want to be in these woods. I want to go home. I hate catamounts. This is all your fault."

Josey grabs Cindy by the shoulders. "Cindy we have to keep going. Please! We have to go to the bog. Please!"

He pulls his sister to him and slowly massages her forehead and dripping hair.

"Josey, it's so hot and I'm so tired and I'm so scared."

"I know you are, but we'll get out of here. Mom and Dad will find us. I know they will."

Josey starts to lead his sister down the river. She takes his hand.

"Josey?"

"What?"

"Do you smell smoke? Where's Virgil?"

Chapter 22

George Mason drives his car up to the tollbooth, hands the attendant a dollar bill and heads north. He cannot help but think of all the states he has driven through in his life where you can drive toll free. "As soon as you hit 'tax-free' New Hampshire," he thought, "you better start digging for change." George studied Biology at Dartmouth so he knows the routine. It will cost him two bucks before he leaves the Spaulding Turnpike. Then he plans to travel up Route 16 to North Conway and over to Fryeburg, Maine, where he is to meet his helicopter. It must be serendipitous that he was already planning to head to the Conway area when his cell phone rang yesterday.

He turns on his car radio and listens to the news coming out of northern New Hampshire. George has never heard of anything like this, but he can at least identify mountain lion signs when he sees them. He is well qualified to determine one way or another whether this is the work of a mountain lion. On the phone, he promises to help, but he hopes another vacation won't be completely shot. Mary and the kids left Montana a few days earlier and are already at the condo in Jackson. His veterinary practice has been financially rewarding, and it is definitely George's calling, but being the expert has more than once interrupted his other plans. He wants to spend this vacation with his kids. This may be the last chance for everyone to be together. Next fall the third daughter is off to college in Florida.

"It goes by so fast," he thinks, "and I have been so busy. All in all, the kids have turned out all right. We still like to be together. It will be good to see Varney again."

It has been a while, although they do keep in touch after graduating Dartmouth. In fact, they have managed to get together a number of times over the years. The tradition, while not yearly, is the sort that, when they go off alone on a fishing trip, hiking excursion, or camping, the two men always start wherever they left off after the last trip and carry on as if no time has passed at all.

"Christ, probably like those two guys up at Allard's cabin," he thinks. "Doc and I have stayed there more than once."

George knows that Doc Varney is not one to panic, and that he is more than capable of handling any veterinary emergency. George is glad that he happens to be close by and that Doc has traced him down. The situation does not sound good. George has dealt with an occasional renegade mountain lion at home out West, but nothing like this. Going down Wakefield Hill, George wonders how many times over the years he has covered this stretch of road. He remembers skiing at Mount Cranmore as a kid. His parents owned a small ski chalet in Intervale. He met his wife at a barn dance at Stafford's in the Fields in Tamworth. He wonders if the inn and barn are still there. He hasn't been there in more than thirty years. In those days, there were live bands everywhere.

"I'll have to take Mary and the kids back there when I get done. It'll be fun to see what is still there."

Should he call the kids? He was able to talk to Mary quickly. She knows he will be up in Clifford.

"I'll call the kids later," he decides. "I don't like driving and talking on the cell phone at the same time. I better get going." Fryeburg is not far, but today it seems like a long drive. The sky is starting to darken and George hopes that his helicopter will not be delayed.

Except for the rushing water, it is as if the storm never happened. The hot sun is high in the sky. Ed and Marty walk slowly along the riverbank. Rob is talking on his radio. He turns to his companions.

"They've been able to get the veterinarian from out West. It turns out he is a friend of Doc's who was heading this way on vacation anyway. He should be getting on the helicopter any time now."

"How does that help us?" asks Marty.

"Well, if nothing else, he may have some ideas on how to hunt a catamount," answers Rob.

"They are putting together some search parties back at Ike and Marion's place. They have ordered more search helicopters and they'll be able to use the one that left before the storm."

Ed stops and looks around. "Do you smell smoke?"

Both Marty and Rob stop.

"It smells like it's coming from over there," says Rob.

"That's no campfire," says Ed. Suddenly, Rob's radio comes on. He answers.

"Shit!"

"What?" asks Marty.

"What now?" asks Ed.

Rob signs off the radio.

"There is a fire. They think the helicopter evacuating the bodies went down."

Ed looks at Rob. "What do you mean?"

"It went down in the storm and crashed in the woods."

"You mean that's the fire?" asks Marty.

"That's it, and it is already out of control," says Rob.

Marty sits down on the ground. She puts her hands over her face.

"What is happening? There is something wrong with this place. What about Cindy and Josey? Are they over there?"

"I don't know. No one knows. Wright and Southard are headed for the crash site," says Rob. "They all know to keep looking. It is the number one priority."

"God!" says Ed. "What are the odds of all this happening at once? It's as if this placed is cursed."

"I'm sure it's not a curse," says Rob. "Everything has just come together in a horrible way."

"I guess!" says Ed.

Ed goes over to Marty and extends his hand to help her up. "We will find them. I know we will."

"We have to. I can't live if we don't. I can't..." says Marty.

"I know," says Ed. "I know."

"They're sending in more helicopters. Harry should be here any time now with some dogs," says Rob. "I think they are our best bet."

Ed pulls Marty to her feet. He kisses her on the forehead.

"Let's go meet them. We have a better chance of finding the kids with their help."

Hearts pounding, Cara Johnson and Paul Horton roll over on their sides. Their breathing slowly returns to normal as they lay back on the motel bed. Their arms are criss-crossed under their heads.

"You know I look forward to these times," says Paul. "How long is Dave away?"

"He should be back the day after tomorrow," says Cara.

"How about tonight?" asks Paul. He pulls back the hair falling on Cara's ear, leans over and kisses her. "I'll be here, but I better get back to work, now."

Paul gets up. "I got to…We really shouldn't…"

"Don't ruin this," Cara interrupts.

Paul continues to dress. "I know. I am sorry. Just sex."

"Paul this is special. No guilt—okay?"

Fully dressed, Paul bends over to kiss Cara goodbye.

"I'm not the one who should be guilty. I'm not the one who is married."

Cara pushes herself up and kisses Paul back. "Now get out of here before I decide to see if we can do it again."

"All right, all right, I'll see you tonight."

"It'll be worth your while," Cara giggles.

"I am sure it will be. You're going to wear me out," Paul says as he goes out the door.

Cara leans back on her pillow.

"Guilt?" she thinks. "I don't feel guilty. What would my husband think? What would Paul think? What about her two daughters? Did they inherit this deep sexuality? Can you have a lover and still love your family? Can you have a good sex life with your husband and still want more, still need more? Is this normal? I love it. I want it. More than thirty years of marriage, a good marriage…Pamela and Amy are doing well. My family is my world. Here I am in a hotel room. A lover has come and gone. No commitment. Just sex. Do I feel guilty?

"No. No, I don't," she sighs and sits up in the bed. She reaches for the TV remote.

She wonders, "Do I really want to be with another man?" She clicks on the TV. "I do!" she decides quickly. "I really do!"

"What's the news doing on now?" she wonders.

"Oh my God!" she gasps.

"Two unidentified fisherman in the township of Clifford have been killed by what authorities believe may be a mountain lion," drones the newswoman. "Names are being withheld pending notification of next of kin."

Cara turns down the sound. She picks up the phone and dials her eldest daughter.

"Oh Mom, where have you been?" her daughter asks. She is crying, crying hard. "It's Dad!"

Chapter 23

Josey and Cindy are moving slowly along the edge of the bog. After the recent downpour, the top layer of leaves is slick and wet. Underneath, though, the decaying debris is dry and crackles as they walk. Heavy black smoke is blowing overhead. Light pieces of black soot fall to the ground as if part of a black snow shower.

"Come on, Cindy!" Josey urges and starts to move a little faster. "I think we better get out of here. Everything is burning and it's getting closer. Let's go!"

Josey starts to run. He turns a corner near the water's edge and almost slips in, but is able to keep his footing and continues to run.

"Wait up!" calls Cindy, trying to keep up.

"Hurry!" cries Josey. "We have to get out of here."

The smoke is getting thicker and is now billowing through the trees. Josey stops to wait. He looks back, frustrated.

"I could do this much better by myself," he thinks. "She is slowing us down."

"Come on, Cindy!" he yells.

Cindy comes around the corner. Breathless, running, she trips on an exposed root. Josey sees Cindy's doll fly into the air. He hears a flopping sound hit the water, but he cannot see Cindy. He rushes back.

"Cindy! Where are you?"

Then he sees her. She is lying face down in the bog. Her bare legs, not covered by her shorts, are peppered with black splotches of muck and red bug bites. Her hair is matted against her head as if glued in place. She is not moving. The inky black bog water is slowly coming up around to engulf her. Suddenly, he feels regret for even momentarily thinking life might be better without his sister. Josey races to the edge of the bog. Leaning out, he is just able to grab her foot. He starts to pull her back and manages to flip her over.

"Cindy, come on! Are you okay?" He pulls again.

"Come on, move! Cindy, come on. Please!"

This time Josey jerks Cindy's motionless body and hauls as hard as he can. He gets her up against the side of the bank. He needs to maneuver her up over the rough overhang. The exposed, washed-out roots catch on the short sleeve of Cindy's muck-covered T-shirt. Josey tries to muscle her up over the dirt ledge to more level ground. The sleeve rips as the root refuses to let go of the young girl in its grip. Then Cindy begins to move her arms. Her eyes pop open, confused.

"Josey!" she cries. Josey lowers his sister a few inches.

"Grab the root up at the top," he yells. "Help me pull you up." Josey chokes on a sob. He has never been so thankful in his life. Cindy is alive!

Josey's frantic struggle catches her attention. The human girl clutches something on the side of the bank. The human boy yanks hard. The girl slides roughly onto the narrow slice of flat ground. The two children become larger as the cat draws closer. The boy leans over the girl. The cat can hear human sounds.

"Cindy! Are you okay?"

Cindy starts to get up. She spits out some water. She looks at Josey but things are so blurry. He seems far away. Her body aches. It hurts to open her eyes. She closes them and tries to sit up. It is hard to move, but she knows she must. She hears Josey's question.

"I think so," she tries to say. She opens her eyes again.

The cat is ready to spring.

Cindy feels as if she is in the middle of the Ball Crawl at Story Land. She wants to move faster but everything is happening very slowly. She is sure that she is awake but her movements are thick and methodical. This is no dream.

"Jo…Josey! It's…!"
Josey turns. "What?"

Suddenly, Virgil rushes out of the woods, barking angrily, and charges the cat. The catamount pulls back and lets out an enraged screech. The dog keeps coming toward the cat. With one swipe of its paw, the cat sends Virgil flying into the bog. Virgil yelps and then, as if in slow motion, the cat springs over Josey and Cindy and flees into the woods.

For a brief moment, both Cindy and Josey remain frozen. Once back to her senses, Cindy starts to wail. The smoke is thicker than before. Josey checks his own sniffles. He cannot let himself cry. The need for action is too urgent. A loud roar can be heard rushing toward them from the forest. A red glow engulfs the treetops above the ever-increasing smoke. Josey tugs Cindy's arm.

"Cindy, come on! We have to get out of here!" he screams. "The fire's coming this way! It's everywhere!"

Cindy starts to run, and then she stops.

"What about Virgil? What about Stina?" Virgil is lying motionless far out in the bog. The muddy doll lays closer to shore, but still too far to reach. Josey approaches the edge of the water. The smoke grows thicker.

"I can't reach them." He looks back at Cindy. "It's too far. We have to get out of here!"

Panicked, Cindy begins to shake. "I want Stina! I want Virgil!"

Josey grabs Cindy. "We haven't got time!"

Josey drags the resisting girl along the edge of the bog, away from the oncoming fire.

When Southard, Wright and Roberts reach the helicopter wreckage, black smoke is still rising from the remains of the burned-out aircraft. The smell of burning oil and fuel saturates a clearing created by the ball of fire that had been a state police helicopter. The fire had leapt immediately into the treetops and then jumped from the top of one tall pitch pine to another. On the ground, the fire is spreading through the fallen pine needles and dry scrub oak just as fast as if gasoline has been poured on the forest floor. The three men carry heavy Indian pumps, but these are of no use as the fire has already escaped the point-of-origin and is now taking control of the forest.

"Damn! Using these pumps is like pissing into the friggin' ocean! I ain't never seen so much go wrong at one Christly time, and I've been here almost sixty years!" says Roberts.

"What are you belly-aching about now, Ike?" asks Wright. "Why don't you just start pumping that thing?"

"Ain't no use. This pump is just about as potent as my sex drive. I vote we get the hell out of here."

Southard backs away from the fire. "I think he's right for once. We're going to need some serious help to deal with this."

The three men are forced back by the heat.

"We are going to experience the real thing, a wild fire," declares Wright. "It's so damned dry!"

Roberts turns around to look. "Least we know what hell is going to be like."

"You got that right!" says Southard as he grabs the radio.

Southard waves them back into the woods. "Let's get out of here before the wind shifts and the fire heads this way too."

"This is going to be out of control by the time the crews get here," says Wright.

Southard holds his hand over his hot forehead. "I think this is already out of control!" he says. "Let's go, that truck is a ways back."

"All I can think about is that flash fire that killed all those jumpers," says Wright, as they look back one last time.

"Yeah, the Man Gulch Fire," agrees Southard. "I read that book, too. Do you suppose the fire will force that thing—that cat or whatever it is—to come this way?"

"Wouldn't surprise me none," says Roberts. "It's about the only thing left that can go wrong."

In the woods near the bog, Josey and Cindy are forcing their way through the heavy underbrush and ever-increasing muck. At the moment, there is no fire, but the smoke is thick and acrid. Both of the children are covered with dirt and sweat and scratched by the sharp branches of the scrub oak that form an almost impenetrable web growing out of the forest floor. In their haste to flee the fire, neither child has noticed the leeches that have attached themselves to Cindy's skin. Cindy and Josey are panting and the drops of sweat sting their eyes as they stop to catch their breaths. The second they stop, the black flies swarm around them. They both wave their hands wildly as they attempt to fend off the blood-sucking insects.

Cindy screeches, "What are those big black things? What are they? Josey, get them off me. Please help me."

Josey jumps to help his sister. "They are blood suckers." Still waving his arms to swat flies, Josey pulls on one of the leeches. It sticks to the girl's skin.

Cindy screams, "I hate blood suckers! Get them off of me."

Josey pulls again. He digs his fingers under the black form and rips it off. One after the other, Josey pulls and rips. Cindy cries out after each leech is separated from her exposed skin. The black flies have no sympathy and the leeches hold on to their prey with amazing tenacity. Finally, Josey pulls off the last of the red-bellied creatures and throws his arms around his whimpering sister. They both sit on the ground. The leeches squirm all around them and the black flies relentlessly swarm around the two sweating bodies. The two children are almost too weary to care. They both shake in each other's arms. They hold each other as tightly as they can as the smoke starts to thicken through the tangled underbrush.

Suddenly, flames leap over the treetops. A burning clump of pine sails to the ground and lands next to the quivering children. The fire overhead intensifies and flaming fireballs of branches, pitch and cones begin to pelt the ground below. Josey and Cindy start to run. One ball of flame lands on Cindy's back. Her drenched, sweaty shirt retards the flames, but she feels the heat as the fireball slides off her back onto the ground. It scorches her ankles as it hits and she jumps. Josey is waving his hands trying to fend off the missiles that are coming down on him.

Josey grabs his sister and yells, "This way, into the bog! We have no choice!"

Cindy acquiesces and moves with her brother.

"I'm scared," she cries. "I don't want to go in that water." Josey pulls her again.

"We have to. We have no choice."

Cindy balks. "No!" she cries. Flames burst through the bushes behind her. Scrub branches snap in the heat, and flaring tongues spring out after the two children. The fire seems to hunger for the human flesh that stands inert in front of it.

"Come on!" Josey cries. "We've got to jump over the muck into the water."

At last, Cindy starts to move. She trips. The flames reach out for her. Josey springs back and jerks her to her feet, pulling her forward.

"Come on!" he urges. They run to the edge of the bog where there is one small opening of shallow clear water that leads out onto the more expansive black water in the middle of the bog. The flames are reflected in the inky surface, but neither Josey nor Cindy notices as they leap into the water. The flames make one last attempt and flare out over the water. Falling grenades of pine branches spring out of the trees and sizzle as they hit the water.

"Keep swimming!" warns Josey. "If you try to stand, you'll get caught in the muck."

Chapter 24

Black ash is falling from the sky even twenty miles away as George Mason and Harry Ames drive toward the township of Clifford. George has been flown into the small airport down by Lancaster. Even there, a vague smell of smoke is in the air. Soon firefighters, jumpers and firefighting planes will be taxiing the limits of this small landing strip. Harry has driven his K-9 cruiser to the grass landing strip and has picked up George. The dogs are riding quietly in the back.

"The smoke is getting thicker up there," says Harry. George looks out of the window to the north.

"God, you can see it already. How did it start?"

"A helicopter crashed. It is so dry that the woods just broke out into flames. We need a lot more rain than that thunderstorm to change that." George continues to watch the smoke through the front windshield.

"I have to tell you, Harry, I have never seen nature piling up so many disasters and misfortunes at one time. Is this place cursed?"

"Well, I doubt that," says Harry. "Pure chance, I guess. I could have predicted the fire. It was just waiting to happen."

"Yeah, it gets this way out West, too. All it takes is one cigarette," says George. "It's nice and cool in here. We won't have the luxury of this air conditioner when we get there."

"If we get there," says Harry. "The fire engines are trying to get through all of the press and other gawkers up there. It's a real mess."

"Won't the fire drive them all out?" asks George.

"Maybe, but right now the road in is completely jammed up with cars and fire engines," says Harry. "Those dirt roads are so narrow, no one can turn around. It's got the makings of a real disaster, if the fire does blow that way."

"How are we going to get in?" asks George. "We have to find those kids. What are the odds of them being okay?"

Harry gave the cruiser more gas. "I don't know. It depends on where they are. The dogs should be able to find them."

George looks out of the window. "It's getting worse. Can we get to that family's house?"

"I think so," says Harry. "There is an old logging road that comes in from the other side. It's gated but we can get the key in Clifford. I've also arranged for a four-wheel-drive vehicle to take us and the dogs out there."

Harry hits the siren as the cruiser heads into Clifford.

"We need to make some time. It's going to take a while to maneuver those back roads."

Streaks of afternoon sun pierce through the small paned windows in the Rollins' living room. The windows are closed to keep the increasing clouds of smoke on the outside. The wooden crosses that hold the panes in place cast a shadow on the fireplace. Ed, Marty and Rob, though exhausted, sit anxiously waiting. A two-way radio sits on the pine slab cribbage board / coffee table in front of the couch. Ed and Marty are side by side on the worn gray couch. Ed holds Marty's right hand in his. Marty cradles one of Josey's sweatshirts and one of Cindy's sweaters in her other arm. Her thoughts are occupied by the visions of her two children happily playing in the kitchen or in the yard at home in Massachusetts.

Rob is sitting in an old recliner chair next to the fireplace. He is concentrating on what lays before him and his two friends once the dogs arrive. "Is Ed okay with me being here?" he wonders. He knows this is where he needs to be. Even the closed windows and doors cannot keep out the haze of the reflected dust and smoke in the beaming sunlight. The haze fits the mood of the room.

"Shouldn't they be here by now?" asks Marty. "How long can we wait?"

"They have left Clifford," says Rob. "It's not going to be easy to get in on that old road."

"No one can get in the other way," says Ed. "I can hear the fire trucks even this far away trying to get through." Marty clutches Josey's and Cindy's clothing closer.

"I can't wait much longer. I need to do something. I need to be out there looking."

Rob leans forward. "We have to wait. Without those dogs, we don't know where to look."

"We know where they camped," says Marty.

"Once the dogs pick up the scent, it will be much easier," says Rob. "We have to wait."

Marty sinks deeper into the couch and sighs. "I know. I know, but this is the hardest thing I have ever done in my life. I feel so helpless."

Ed puts his arm around Marty. He looks at Rob. Rob looks away.

"Will the smoke affect the dogs' ability to smell?" asks Marty.

"I don't think so," says Rob. "Not if they lock on the scent of the kids' clothing."

Ed looks around the room. Both Marty and Rob are silent. No one wants coffee or tea. They are beyond bodily comforts. Everything that can be said has been said. They want to take action, but they have to bear the waiting. The old wind-up clock in the kitchen marks the passage of each second. The ticks hang in the dusty air as if time itself is trying to hold back its inevitable passage.

"How much time have I wasted agonizing over the things that I have control over?" wonders Ed. "I've created a good life for us. If it's not quite what I want anymore, I can change it. There are alternatives that will work for both Marty and me. Now would be the time if I can only resolve what is happening out there—out in what I've always thought of as my refuge, a sanctuary, a place where I was in control. Instead, it has become threatening, menacing and horrifying. I feel like I am—we all are—on the downward run of an out of control roller coaster. Maybe the roller coaster is in control, but we certainly are not."

He looks at Marty, his wife of…how many years?…twelve? Rob is one of his best friends.

"We're all in this together. Can I hold Marty and Rob's mutual attraction against them? Does it matter now that she's made her choice to stay with me? Does how I make a living matter that much? Marty is here with me. She is not giving up. Rob is here. He could go off on some other call of duty, but he has stuck by us. He is here, here for all of us. It seems to have never occurred to him to leave. He cares as much about what is happening here as Marty and I do. I know Rob is thinking and analyzing the best strategy to find Cindy and Josey. Marty is thinking of the family and our two kids. She never wavers."

Ed knows he will do what he has to do. All that other stuff does not matter—not the life in Massachusetts, the affair, the exhaustion, the ineffective communication between Marty and him. They will find Cindy and Josey. The rest will take care of itself.

Ed looks up at Rob. "Thanks for being here," he says.

"I wouldn't have it any other way, Ed," says Rob.

Chapter 25

The light green Jeep Cherokee works its way slowly through the washed out rocky path that had once been a full-sized road. Long streams of sunlight appear among the dirty, smoky haze that permeates the forest. The Cherokee creeps along, climbing slowly, wheel by wheel, over the larger gullies and rock mounds. Harry clutches in and out without going out of first gear. It is necessary to come to a full halt just before most of the rocky mounds in order to avoid scraping the bottom of the Jeep as its front and back alternately jump up and down over the uneven roadbed.

Now and then, the road turns into a fairly even straightaway. Tire tracks from previous vehicles form ruts that clearly define the grassy mound that runs through the middle. These stretches allow Harry to shift into second gear and gain a little speed. The intervals are short, as the road suddenly reverts to washed out hardscrabble. In some cases, the road virtually disappears into the underbrush, only to reappear some yards later.

The SUV slowly works its way down a long hill. In such places, the track has been washed out by past spring run-offs and pounding thunderstorms. Large rocks have worked their way to the surface and the Jeep's tires spin trying to find a grip over the rounded edges, then bounce back down, only to repeat the process again. Harry and George ride silently. Harry has a white-knuckled grip on the steering wheel. George hangs on tightly to the handgrip at the top of the passenger's door. The vehicle continues its slow dance along the exposed road.

Harry watches the dogs in the back through the rear view mirror. Mutt and Jeff are his pride. He loves those dogs. In over twenty years of service, the veteran trooper has trained two generations of dogs from eager pups to the misfortunes of old age—senility and an inability to effectively lie down or stand back up. He is good with the dogs because he forms an attachment to them. Dogs know he is their friend. It is something they can sense, but it gets harder for him as each generation passes. How many times can you watch a once energetic old "friend" as it waddles unsteadily on stiff hind legs, in and out the door, only to stand and wonder why it is where it is? This dog has been your companion for years. You spend more time with the dog than with your own family.

One of his past shepherds, Molly, used to stand in the same place for hours looking bewildered. When she finally decided to move, she circled around again and again trying to find a comfortable way to bring herself to the ground. She would finally take the dive and fall painfully to the floor. Harry knows that Mutt and Jeff will be his last dogs. By the end of their ten-to-twelve-year life span, Harry will have retired. The first time you take on the responsibility of your dogs, you are young and you don't think much about the future. Now Harry knows. Given enough time, Mutt and Jeff will slowly meet their respective demises.

The life cycle of his dogs reminds him of his own vulnerability. He thinks about his parents, who are starting to slow down. Actually, so is he. The cure for the loss of a beloved dog is a new puppy. What could be the cure for the loss of his parents? What could be the cure for Ralph's and John's families?

Harry thinks about his wife and kids. His kids are in college now. Regina, his wife, even after twenty-three years as a cop's wife, worries about whether Harry will come home after his shift. He pictures John's and Ralph's wives as the cruiser pulls up to their homes. He envisions the funeral with marching regiments coming from all over the country. He sees the riderless horse with boots reversed in the stirrups.

"Maybe it is getting to be that time," he thinks. He has made sergeant and he knows that, even though he is competent, he will never go much further. Does he want to become a detective in order to become a lieutenant? Law enforcement is a fellowship. He has a bond with his fellow officers that he will never share with those in the civilian community. Cops tend to hang out with cops. Harry is easy going. He has done his job. He loves his dogs and gets them to perform well. The politics in Concord, brownnosing to be considered for the next promotion, the pushy news reporters, the gruesome car accidents and the domestic disputes are all starting to take their toll.

How hard could it be to catch this mountain lion? Dogs hunt them down all the time out West. When he gets home, he will look into retirement. The faces of John and Ralph haunt him. How could this happen? They were not only good friends; they were good cops. Competent. None of this should be happening. He knows Regina will be happy with his decision to become a civilian.

George smells the smoke and thinks about other cats he has tracked. Mountain lions are normally reclusive. They avoid human contact, but the number of attacks has been increasing in the past few years.

"Why?" he wonders. "If we leave them alone, they normally leave us alone. Maybe that is the problem. Maybe we're not leaving them alone. Our presence alone might be enough. We keep grabbing more and more space."

George has often wondered if humankind is not a sort of cancer, spreading across the planet. Don't we, indeed, live off the planet just as cancer lives off the body? Maybe the immune system is just kicking in.

"Oh, for Christ's sake!" George rebukes himself, almost aloud.

In any case, on the East Coast, mountain lions were completely killed off by the early 1900s. However, a small number are rumored to be returning east and lions are being spotted in areas that have not seen signs of such carnivores for generations. George has heard of attacks and sightings in Ontario, Minnesota, and even Connecticut. These are areas where mountain lions are "known" to be extinct. Christ, the chances of being hit by lightning are greater than that of being attacked by a mountain lion. Sure, there have been instances, but people are sometimes hit by lightning, too. As more and more people move into lion territory, you can expect more lion attacks. However, the human being has been much more harmful to the mountain lion than it has been to us. What was the figure? Over 16,000 lions killed in British Columbia alone from 1910-1955. In California, over 12,000. In 1931, an act of congress provided money to hunt and kill cougars. As late as the 1960s, bounties were still being offered.

Now, most mountain lions are protected from trophy hunting. George is all for preservation. Although he has seen the results of lion attacks on various ranches, and although he has helped track down a few rogue cats, his sympathies tend to be with the lions. He understands the frustration of losing livestock and sees merit in both sides of the issue, but he shies away from the extremes.

What is happening here in New Hampshire? All lions are territorial and mark out their respective territories by urinating on small piles of leaves and pine needles. The only time lions don't hunt alone is when they are mating. A male's range can be over one hundred miles. A female is likely to have a range of about sixty miles. How can one show up here? It is way out of range. What is this lion doing? It shouldn't take long to hunt one lone cat in this part of the country.

"Is it only one?" he wonders. The females will roam to new areas looking for a mate. Younger males are sometimes forced out of their habitats by older cougars. Suddenly, the car jerks to a stop. George hears the spinning tires.

Normally, you have to work to find the cat. This one—a catamount they call it in these parts—finds you.

"So much for this vacation," he thinks.

"Shit!" says Harry.

The ever-present smoke and the approach of dusk combine to create a haze around the Rollins' cabin. Rob stands outside by his truck and watches the smoke crawl eerily around the walls of the cabin. The light from the full moon streaks through the muggy air. He is going into a second night without sleep and has that not unfamiliar queasy feeling that accompanies a lack of sleep. He feels punchy but he knows he has to go back into the woods. They must find the kids. The fire and the cat are secondary. Marty and Ed have also not slept and they are getting edgy.

"Where are Harry and that guy from out West?" Rob holds the two-way mic. The front door opens and Ed comes outside. He can hear the radio crackling in the darkness.

"Any sign of them?" he asks.

"No," says Rob. "It's going to be a while."

Ed looks at Rob. "Why?"

Rob puts down the mic. "It appears that Harry managed to bury the Jeep in mud."

"Jesus Christ!" says Ed. "How'd he do that? There hasn't been enough rain to create any mud."

Rob leans wearily against the truck. "The river created a new path during spring run off, I guess."

Ed looks back toward the cabin. "Marty is getting antsy."

Rob picks up the mic. "I know. We all are. Let me see what else I can find out."

Ed looks back toward the house again. "We have to go back after them."

"I know," says Rob.

"Soon," insists Ed.

The smoke is black on the horizon above the fields behind the Roberts' farm. A red glow emanates from the tops of the trees and blends into the darkness above. The moon illuminates the tall grass, scattered groups of trees, and dilapidated fences that make up Ike Roberts' field. On the porch, Southard puts down the two-way radio.

"Man! Harry and that other vet just called in. They are stuck in a mud hole over on the tote road. They're in deep. We're going to have to send someone over to help. Do you have a winch, Ike?"

Ike gets up from his chair. "Yeah, I got one on that old Jeep out in the barn. Do you think we can get over that way?"

Wright looks at the map on the table. "I don't think the fire has gotten over there yet. Can we use your Jeep, Ike?"

Ike throws up his hands. "Why the hell not? You are using everything else of mine. If we don't stop this friggin' fire, I ain't goin to have nothin' left anyhow. Speakin' of which what are they doing about that?"

Southard looks out over the field. "They're doing what they can. The bulldozers are coming in to make some firebreaks. The planes have already started dumping and they are bringing in some jumpers."

"What about that friggin' cat? Do they know about that?" Ike asks.

"They know, Ike," Wright replies.

"Just wondering, that's all," says Ike. "Just wonderin' what it's up to, that's all."

"Well, let's stop wondering and go get those guys before it is too late," says Southard. Ike, Southard and Wright all pick up their hunting rifles and head outside.

"I'll get the Jeep," says Ike. "It might take a bit of coaxing to get her going."

Inside the barn, the starter motor turns over and over and then quits.

"Maybe we'll need to think of something else," says Southard. "Ike isn't always the best at maintenance."

"No I suspect he isn't," says Wright. Suddenly, the choo choo of the starter motor turns into the intermittent clicking of four valves as they attempt to run in sync. Finally, the faded green, battered, doorless Army jeep pulls out of the barn. A blast of black smoke explodes from the rusted-out muffler.

Chapter 26

The fire is slowly working its way around the bog. For the moment, Cindy and Josey are safe. They swim far enough out into the shallow but substantial expanse of water to escape the fire. The Clifford Bog consists of a series of small ponds that are linked by narrow canals. Each channel winds its way through thick patches of dense lily pads and reeds. In spite of the poor drainage, the water further out—unlike its stale, murky counterpart near the thick vegetation close to the shore—appears to be clean and clear except for the coating of grayish black flecks that fall like snow from the nearby inferno. The thick black muck and tangled weeds that populate the bottom of the bog make it difficult for Josey and Cindy to stay afloat. They are one hundred yards into the open expanse of bog water. They are far enough away from the fingers of flames that so recently tried to devour them, but an infernal heat radiates out across the small pool that protects Cindy and Josey from certain death. Salty sweat streams off their red faces. Black splotches of soot soil their cheeks and sting their eyes. Both children are treading water to stay afloat.

"I'm tired," pants Cindy. "This is really hard without my life jacket. The stuff in the water keeps pulling at my legs, and I can't see."

Josey goes under to clear his face.

"Go under. It's cooler," he says. Josey's eyes still sting.

He points to the left. "We have to get over there before the fire does."

Cindy looks and then goes under. Reappearing, Cindy struggles to avoid swallowing the soot-covered bog water.

"There's no place to get out. It's too far Josey. I just learned how to swim last summer."

Cindy goes under again. She comes back up. "I can't…"

Josey turns over on his back. "Try to float like Dad taught us."

Cindy paddles. "I can't Josey. I never could…"

Ike's old Jeep works its way along the narrow tote road. In the moonlit smoky haze, two deer jump out in front of the streaming headlights and flee off into the woods.

"The fire must be over there. The animals are coming from that direction," observes Wright.

"Deer ain't about to jump out at me like that durin' huntin' season, by Jesus!" says Roberts.

"Since when did you pay any attention to when it was hunting season?" asks Southard.

"You callin' me a poacher?"

"Call it what you like," says Southard. Ike Roberts leans forward from the back of the Jeep.

"You ain't goin' to catch me doin' nothin' illegal."

Southard turns toward Ike. "Catching and doing are two different things."

Driving slowly, Wright peers around the side of the Jeep. "I think the wind is shifting."

The smoke begins to move with purpose forming a ghost-like pattern of parallel streams of billowing gas.

"It's blowing this way," says Southard.

"I see something up ahead," says Wright. "This moon is about the only break we have gotten."

Marty is pacing in front of the fireplace. "I can't wait much longer. It's already dark."

Rob sits on the edge of the stone fireplace. "It doesn't make sense to go back in without the dogs. We'd just be wasting our time."

"I know. I know," says Marty, "but I need to do something."

Ed brings a cup of coffee from the kitchen. He hands it to Marty.

"It can't be long now," he says. "Once they find them, the tote road isn't that far from here."

Marty accepts the cup, then puts it down. "I know that, but...I can't drink this. My stomach...I feel like I am going to be sick."

"I know. I'm just trying to keep busy. Do you want anything, Rob?"

Rob holds his two-way radio. "No, thanks, Ed. I'm okay."

Ed sits down in the old gray easy chair. All three sit in silence. The backpacks and the rifles wait in the corner by the front door.

Marty clutches the two shirts that will give the dogs the scent they need to smell out the invisible trail left by her two lost children. She, too, waits. The chatter on the two-way is constant. Everyone is fighting the fire. No one is looking for the kids. She waits for the call to Rob.

"Will it ever come?"

"Up ahead...I think it is them," says Wright. "That's the front of the Cherokee. It's a good thing we're coming in from this side."

George and Harry are sitting inside the Cherokee. Ike's Jeep edges closer.

"It's them all right," says Ike. "Careful now! We don't want to get into that muck ourselves."

George and Harry get out of their vehicle, step out into the mud and approach the old Jeep. Wright stops and gets out.

"Christ, you are in deep!" he says.

Harry looks back. "Yeah, there is a bend off the river and the water is starting to take over this part of the road. It's all sand. We buried both axles and even in four-wheel drive we can't get out of here."

"This here winch will drag you out," says Ike. "It's gotten me out of more than one tight spot. Let's get my Jeep a little closer, but keep her on solid ground."

Wright gets back in and the Jeep creeps forward.

Ike puts up his hand. "That oughta do it." He takes the hook at the end of the old rusting cable and starts to pull.

"When's the last time you used that contraption?" asks Harry. "It looks kinda rusty."

"Just you wait and see," says Ike. "Start the motor."

The electric motor kicks in. The cable starts to unroll, making a loud squeaking noise as the metal wire cable separates from the strands below. Then it stops. The motor whirs loudly.

"Turn her off!" cries Ike. "She'll blow!"

Southard throws up his hands. "Christ! Now what?"

"This has happened before. Get me that can of oil in the Jeep. I'll fix her!"

Wright fetches the oil. Ike pours it over the rust-encrusted strands. He jerks hard and the strand comes loose.

"Try her again!" he yells. The cable springs off the winch and continues to unwind. When he has enough length, Ike connects the hook from the cable to the hook under the front bumper of the Cherokee.

"All right, set her back the other way!"

Wright flips the switch. Harry gets back into the Cherokee.

"Okay, let's give her a try!" The winch starts to pull. Harry slips the SUV into low gear and presses lightly on the gas pedal. The Cherokee inches forward. The cable from the old Jeep goes taut and vibrates hard under the strain. The four wheels on the Cherokee start to spin and then grab a little. The left front wheel crawls up onto solid ground. The cable groans and the right wheel creeps up, too. The vibration on the cable grows more intense and then, with a load crack, it snaps. The cable flies back and slaps into the windshield of the old Jeep, snaps over its top rim and spins around like an attacking rattlesnake, striking Wright in the back of the head. The Cherokee starts to slip back. Harry steps on the gas. The back wheels spin. The front wheels spit dirt but grab. The Cherokee lunges out of the mud and comes to a stop.

Harry leaps out of the SUV and runs to the jeep. The front windshield is completely smashed. Pieces of glass are strewn over the ground, the front of the Jeep and all over Wright's body. The shards closest to Wright are dark with the blood that flows from the large gash on the back of the trooper's head.

"Don't die!" cries Harry, as he leans over Wright's drooping head. The others hurry over to the Jeep. Harry checks Wright's pulse.

The cat smells the fresh blood. It is different from the blood that it licks off the bullet wound that is coagulating on its right front shoulder.

"He's alive!" says Harry.

Chapter 27

The radio crackles. Rob picks it up.

"This is unit 2. Over. Okay, I read you loud and clear. Over."

He listens to the radio and then looks over to Ed and Marty.

"Get the gear. The dogs are coming. We're going to meet Harry and Mason at the crossroads where the tote road comes in. They're not sure how to get here."

Rob puts the radio back up to his mouth.

"Okay I got you. We'll meet you there, over and out."

Ed and Marty are already at the door. Rob comes over.

"We should be able to meet them in about fifteen minutes. Harry got stuck in the mud. I'm not sure what happened but they said that they finally had everything under control. Ike and some troopers are there with Ike's Jeep and a winch."

All three throw their gear into the bed of the pickup and climb into the cab. Sitting between the two men, Marty still clutches the kids' clothing.

"I guess that's why it took them so long. Let's get going!" urges Ed.

They drive beyond the Rollins' cabin.

"That tote road is only about three miles long, isn't it?" asks Marty. "I never paid that much attention before."

"Maybe a little more," says Ed.

"How far are they from the crossroads?" she asks.

"Not far. In fact, they should be there by now," says Rob. He picks up the two-way radio. "That's funny. I can't seem to reach them. No one answers."

"They're probably just not near the radio," says Ed.

The road is beginning to become bumpier and the truck lurches back and forth as Rob works to avoid the largest rocks and the deepest ruts.

"The crossroads are right up here, up around the bend," says Rob. He tries the radio again. "For some reason I still can't reach them." As they move around the last turn, the headlights illuminate the four-cornered crossing ahead.

"They're not there!" gasps Marty. "Where are they? They should have been here before us."

"They'll be along soon," says Rob, trying to hide his concern. "Something must have held them up."

"What could have held them up? All we do is wait," says Ed, looking at his watch. "Christ! It's 10:30 already. Another night and we are no further along in finding Cindy and Josey than we were last night. How long can they hold on out there in the middle of a forest fire? I don't even want to think about that animal."

Marty clutches the kids' clothing even tighter. The sweater smells faintly like Cindy.

"I have a lot of faith in Josey," says Rob, "even if he is only ten years old. Both of your kids are smart."

Then Rob's radio comes to life.

Wright begins to move. He hears Harry say that he is alive. His head hurts. He doesn't know why. He puts his hand up to his head. It is wet and sticky. Slowly, his eyes focus. Harry?—yes, it is Harry—is leaning over him with a towel. He is wiping the liquid. What liquid?

"Harry, what are you doing?" The thought forms clearly in his mind, but his words are, at first, thick and incoherent.

He tries again, "Harry?"

Harry yells to Southard. "Get the first aid kit. He's coming to. Have you got a towel or something I can use to clean up this wound?"

"You don't need to talk, Roger," says Harry.

"What happened?" asks Roger. His thinking is growing clearer, but the clearer he gets the more the pain throbs in his head. Harry continues to clean the wound.

"The cable on the winch let go and snapped back and hit you in the head. I think the front windshield saved your life." Ben Southard comes over with a first-aid kit and the white undershirt he has taken off moments before.

"How you doing, Roger?" he asks. "I've taken the shirt off my back for you."

"I've been better." He smiles weakly.

"Let me take a look," says George. "I am a doctor of sorts you know." Harry moves aside. He goes back to the dogs. George inspects the wound and cleans the blood.

"Not really all that bad. I'd say you were pretty lucky, young fella. We should get you to a doctor. You'll probably need a few stitches. The Jeep deflected the brunt of it." Using the first-aid kit, he applies disinfectant and bandages the cut. He holds up three fingers.

"How many fingers am I holding up?"

"Three."

"How old are you?" asks Mason.

"Thirty-eight," answers Roger.

"Where do you live?" the vet asks.

"Sixty Back Lake Road in Lancaster."

"Who's president?"

"I didn't vote for him," answers Wright.

George smiles. "I think you'll be all right."

"My head just hurts like hell. I can see okay though."

The eyes watch and move closer.

Human noises.

Harry yells from the Cherokee, "I told Rob we would meet him and Ed and Marty Rollins down at the crossroads. George, if Roger is all right, we should probably get down there. It's just up the road a little ways."

Harry lets the two shepherds out of the back of the Cherokee. Both dogs start to growl.

"What the...? Stay!" he orders. Nervously, the dogs obey. Wright looks up at George and then he sees the light of the Cherokee's headlights reflected in the two yellow eyes.

"My God!" he shouts. "Behind you. There is something behind…"
George spins around. "What?"
He sees it. The dogs start barking. George hits the ground and crawls
as fast as he can under the jeep.

The cat springs. George feels the cat as it passes over his legs. He spins his head around to look. The eight or nine foot black apparition lands and lets out a blood-curdling scream. Ike freezes. Southard grabs the side of the Jeep. Wright struggles to make out what is going on through the windshield. Harry looks around the back of the Cherokee. He hesitates. The dogs are frantic. They spring forward. The cat turns and stares. It screeches, and then it flees. The dogs leap into pursuit. Harry whistles but Mutt and Jeff don't respond. Harry whistles again. Conflicted, the dogs stop, but immediately start to run again.

With all the authority, he can muster, Harry yells, "Stay!"

Reluctantly, the two dogs stop. They are still agitated and ready to run.

George breaks the silence. "Is it gone?" He peers out from his hiding place.

"I hope the Christ!" sputters Ike. "Fuckin' A, I was too scared to even get my gun."

The dogs have quieted down. "I think it's gone," George says.

He cautiously crawls out from under the Jeep. He stands up.

"Well, now we know what we are dealing with. That is bigger than any cat I have ever seen out West, and it did not look happy."

Harry calls the dogs back and gets them back into the Cherokee. He approaches the old Jeep.

"It doesn't seem to like dogs, though," observes Southard. "Who would have thought it? It seems like that thing could have a dog for breakfast."

"Yeah, they don't like dogs," says George. "Who knows why not?" He turns toward Roberts. "Ike can you still drive this thing?"

Ike comes over and clears the broken glass off the hood.

"The engine oughta work. Here, let me give her a try."

Harry and Ben open the passenger side door. "How are you doing, Rog? Can you move over here so Ike can get in?"

"No problem. It will probably be easier to get out and come around. I don't know if I can get around the stick shift." Ben goes over to the driver's side and helps Roger step out.

"How does it feel to walk?" The two men move slowly around the front of the hood.

"I feel okay," says Wright. "I'll be all right."

Ike brushes broken glass off the seat and then gets in. He turns the key and the engine springs to life.

"Just like a pussy cat," says Ike.

"Christ, Ike! Couldn't you come up with a better analogy than that?" asks Southard.

"Nope, I couldn't. I thought it was real appropriate."

Harry approaches the Jeep. He holds his radio in his right hand.

"Ike, can you and Ben take Roger back to your place? Have someone take a look at Roger when you get back." Harry returns to the Cherokee.

"George, you and I need to meet up with Rob and the Rollins. It's getting late. Judging from all this smoke, that fire isn't going away. Neither is that cat. We need to find those kids, and then we can concentrate on going after that thing."

"We got one big, angry animal on our hands," says George.

"If it is so dangerous, why didn't it attack?" asks Ben.

"Probably because of the dogs," says George. "They don't much like dogs, but that might not always stop this one. If you're all right Roger, I'm ready to go."

Ike backs the Jeep to the side of the road. George and Harry drive on. Ike backs the Jeep into the underbrush and then comes forward. After two tries, the Jeep is turned around. Ben climbs in the back and closes the tailgate.

The CL-215 water bomber is coming up on the fire. In the moonlight, the acres and acres of forested land spread to the horizon in all directions. The lights of the small village of Clifford are cut out of the wilderness at about 2 o'clock. The black, irregular form of Lake

Mackapaque that extends well into Canada is becoming larger and larger towards the north. A circle of fire and smoke, at 10 o'clock, appears to be blowing toward the big, dark body of water. There is still a substantial amount of forest between the lake and the fire line. The pilot will drop the fire jumpers into that area. The pilot looks at the map. The near end of the fire is working its way around what has to be Clifford Bog. The bog itself makes an excellent fire dam, but the prevailing winds are carrying the fierce flames around both the east and west banks of the stale water. From the plane, the fire looks like a perfectly shaped red horseshoe. The plane veers off toward the big lake to drop off the first jumpers.

Not far behind, the first full load of water is on its way. The second plane heads toward the bog and the billowing clouds of smoke. Once over the fire, a blanket of chemically treated water flushes out of the airplane and six tons of pink liquid spreads over the burning inferno. As the wall of water hit its target, treetops snap like twigs and full trees topple and crush the sizzling underbrush that, now smothered, smolders on the forest floor. The plane banks around. The smoke increases, but the fire and smoke continue to flow southward, undisturbed. The pilot flies low on the off chance that he might spot the two missing kids in the moonlight. It is unlikely, but he might even see the big cat that is causing such a fuss. He follows the faint white line of an old logging road that is just beyond the smoke. At first, he sees nothing. Then as he climbs to head back toward the big lake to refill, he sees the hazy headlights of two vehicles near what might be a crossroads below.

The smoke is light and wispy. The pickup truck's lights pierce through the haze. Ed, Marty and Rob stare out through the windshield. They hear the plane overhead.

"They're still not here," complains Marty. Suddenly, the headlights of the Cherokee break through the haze, and Harry and George pull up to Rob's pickup. Harry rolls down the window.

"Okay, let's get back to where the kids went into the woods."

"Just follow us," says Rob. The pickup turns around and heads back to the Rollins' cabin. As the two vehicles bump and heave along their way, planes and helicopters can be heard overhead, but the smoke seems to be getting thicker and thicker. The Cherokee and the pickup park in front of the Rollins' cabin. Marty opens the door of the truck and runs over to Harry. She hands him the two shirts. Harry releases the dogs out of the back of the SUV. He holds Josey's shirt under the nose of one of the shepherds. The other gets Cindy's. Rob, Ed, George and Marty all put on their packs. Ed and Rob sling their hunting rifles over their shoulders and start toward the back of the house. Harry grabs his gear.

"Let's go," says Rob.

The dogs are ready. They sniff wildly on the far side of the stream. Then they pull towards the woods. As expected, the dogs follow the trail to the spot where Josey and Cindy had camped. For the dogs, the next choice is easy. They pull hard down the river, toward the fire and toward the bog.

Chapter 28

The intensity of the flames dwarfs the increasing brightness of the morning. The water in the bog reflects the red and yellow conflagration. Josey and Cindy, in the water, appear to be engulfed by the fire. Both are holding on to edge of a substantial expanse of moss. The water is shallow and the muck from underneath pulls on their feet. The fire burns hot at the outer reaches of the area of level mossy growth.

"Josey?"

"What?"

"I can't anymore. I can't…"

Josey pushes his arms up onto the moss. "My arms are so tired," he says. "It's slippery but it might hold us."

"Why haven't Mom and Dad found us?" asks Cindy. "It has been so long. How are they going to find us here? They can't come through the fire. They'll never find us now. I know they won't. I just know it. And I just can't swim anymore."

"We can't give up, Cindy. Dad told us to never… We have to keep…" Josey looks up. A plane swoops down over the treetops right next to the bog. Cindy watches the plane as it comes rapidly closer.

"What is it doing?" she cries. The bottom of the plane opens up and the massive mattress of pink liquid plummets out of the sky.

"What's…?"

Josey grabs Cindy. "Go under! Go under! Now!"

The chemical water hits the trees on the side of the bog. Branches and colossal missiles of wood sail to the forest floor and into the water. The field of moss is left covered with smoldering debris and slippery masses of pink viscous goop.

Ed, Marty, Rob, George and Harry work their way around the smoldering rubble. Though the fire has burned through much of this side of the bog, it is possible to work their way around the edge of the bog next to the water. Picking up the scent on the untouched edge of the bog, Harry's dogs pull enthusiastically, drawing the group forward to a small peninsula. The sandy soil still reveals the presence of child size footprints, a conglomeration of dog prints and two large cat prints.

"They were here!" exclaims Marty.

Something is moving out on the bog.

"What's that out there on that small island?" asks Rob.

George points, "My God! I think it's a dog."

"He's alive!" Ed cheers. "That's not a dog. That's Virgil."

Virgil tries to stand up on the tenuous, mossy floor that barely holds his weight. His front paw is covered with drying blood. He yelps as he tries to put his weight on the wounded paw. The moss holds, but the other paw goes through.

"Come on, Virgil! You can do it!" yells Marty.

"Come on, boy!" cries Ed.

With determination, Virgil creeps into the water. Once in, his front paws propel him forward, as he responds to the frantic commands of his masters. Ed and Marty continue to urge the resolute dog on.

George watches and then scans the bog. "What's that over there?"

Rob looks. "It looks like a doll. Marty, is it...?"

"It's Stina!" she cries. "Ed, that's Stina! They were definitely here."

Harry's dogs are pulling toward the side of the bog.

Marty hesitates. "Oh no! Not in there. They can't be..."

"It doesn't look like the kid's went in here. The dogs want to go that way," says Harry. Ed continues to call to the struggling dog. Wiggling one paw in front of the other, he is working his way toward solid ground. Ed crouches on the edge of the mossy knoll. Virgil is almost there. The dog takes one more leap forward and Ed grabs him underneath his front paws and pulls him onto the ground. Virgil yelps with a combination of pain and joy. He whimpers with excitement. In spite of his wounded leg, Virgil runs around and around in convoluted circles. Then he races off in the direction of the fire.

"Virgil, come back!" cries Ed. "Virgil, stay!"

Virgil pauses, looks back and then he is gone. Harry's dogs try to follow.

"Heel!" commands Harry and the dogs obey, but look at their master in dismay. Marty is looking over the edge of the bog.

"We have to get Stina," she says. She searches around and finds a long blackened stick floating next to the edge of the bog. She picks it up and stretches out over the water, but she cannot quite reach the rag doll.

Ed grabs Marty around the waist. "Maybe, if I hold you, you can reach it."

Marty tries again. The stick misses once, then twice. Then, with a groan of effort, Marty is able to flip the doll over. Instead of moving closer to shore, however, the doll plops further out.

Tears appear in Marty's eyes. "I have to save Stina!"

Harry's dogs want to move. "The kids have to be that way," says Harry.

Rob looks toward the billowing smoke. "Can we go in there?" he asks.

"We have to try," says Harry. "We can't wait much longer."

Marty reaches out again for the doll.

"I know it is important but..." says Rob.

"It is important!" Marty snaps. "Can anybody find a longer stick?"

Ed lets go of Marty's waist and looks around. "Try this."

He pulls hard on a long, thin, badly bent birch tree. Rob grabs on and the two men pull together. The half-rotten tree, a victim of an ice storm, breaks off at its roots and jerks free. Ed returns to Marty and casts the narrow trunk and branches out over the water. The thick scraggly appendages at the tip of the birch paw at Stina. Ed pulls slowly back until the doll is an arm's length away. Marty reaches out and grabs the doll.

"I got her!" she cries. She picks up the soaked doll and hugs it tightly. Marty puts Stina to her nose.

She chokes. "It smells like Cindy, even in this smoke."

Ed comes over and hugs Marty and the little stuffed doll.

"She wouldn't leave Stina," says Marty.

"I know," agrees Ed.

Marty gasps, "Not if she had any choice."

"Come on, then," urges Rob. "Let's go get them. We'll find a way through this."

They all follow the dogs into the direction of the thick smoke and flames.

Cindy's and Josey's heads reappear, like bubbles on the water's surface. The fire that has been burning intensely along the edge of the bog now sputters in the pink gooey liquid. Large and small broken tree limbs are scattered throughout the smoldering mass and on top of the dirty bog water. Cindy spits out water.

"Josey, I can't do this anymore. I'm so tired. This water tastes awful."

Josey paws his way to a fallen limb. "Grab one of these, Cindy. It'll hold you up."

Cindy pushes her way through the flotsam and throws her arms over a large floating log. She looks like an old, dirty, wet towel that has been thrown over a back porch railing. Josey kicks his own buoyant tree limb toward his sister.

"Hold on, Cindy! I think we can crawl over there. The fire never got that part."

"I don't think I can, Josey." She starts to cry.

"Josey I'm so tired. We have been in the water so long. I'm shivering. I just can't...I want Mommy and Daddy. I want to go home. Please Josey, I want go home. I want to go home. It is not fair."

Josey maneuvers near the shaking, shivering girl.

"I can't..." she cries. "Let me sink." Cindy starts to slide off the bobbing limb.

"Cindy! No! Don't let go!" yells Josey. He lurches forward. Cindy's face goes under. Her arms go straight into the air. Josey grabs her nearest arm and jerks her back out of the water. Her head appears. She coughs up water and humps over the log. Josey continues to pull her closer. Cindy starts to slip back in. Josey pulls harder.

"Hold on!" he cries. "Please! I've got you! Please, just a little longer! We can get out over there."

Weakly, Cindy grabs onto Josey's log and holds her head above the lapping water.

"Just push over to that sand. We can do it. The log will keep us up. Over there, by those green bushes. This log is big enough for both of us. Just hold on so I can help you."

Josey sidestrokes feebly next to his sister. With both of them kicking, the log moves slowly but steadily forward. The small patch of sand draws nearer. The fire has not reached this part of the forest. The green bushes that stand on the edge of the small sandy outcrop rustle slightly. Neither Josey nor Cindy notices as the cat settles in to watch.

The two children make their way to the shallow water.

"I can touch bottom," gasps Cindy. "But it is all muck."

"Keep going," urges Josey. "We're almost there." Then the log hits bottom.

"That's it!" he cries. As he stands up, the muck sucks his feet into the quagmire. He is in ankle deep. He pulls Cindy straight up. The black ooze envelopes her ankles. Josey pulls his right foot up out of the muck. Black water fills the suctioning hole where his foot has been. He pulls Cindy forward and out comes her first foot and then the next. Once again buried ankle deep, the two struggle and squish their way out of the water. Reaching the sand, both Josey and Cindy fall to the ground. The brown sand sticks to the white, wrinkly, exposed skin of their faces, arms, and upper bodies. Neither child is aware of the swarming black flies or the black leeches that are working on the tired blood that still runs through their veins.

They lie there as the eyes in the bushes watch.

Ed's thoughts wander. He wonders how many times he has walked through these woods. Black flies and ticks are a major annoyance, and you have to be careful of bears, but he has never considered the north woods itself to be a dangerous place. For Ed, a walk down Tremont Street in Boston seems much more threatening. Driving on Route 128 scares the hell out of him. Up here, he has always felt safe. Now, these same trees and waters have turned malevolent. His kids are missing. Perhaps hurt. Perhaps dead.

"No!" He cannot let himself think like that. Not that!

What would life be without Josey and Cindy? How can his harmless stories about a catamount have become such a nightmarish reality? This must be a dream. But it is not. This is all too real. In a dream, the rules of cause and effect and logic are suspended. The odds of all this happening are almost nil, but this is no dream world. He had known John and Ralph. The effect on their families will be real. The whole place is burning up, and his wife has been sleeping with Rob. He hates his work, but what does that matter? Does that reality even exist? That seems like another world, another time, another place. Here he is, with no sleep, heading into an inferno looking for his kids. It is absurd, but it is happening. He wonders if he will ever be the same again.

"We have to find Josey and Cindy," he repeats to himself. "Forget the rest. Nothing else matters."

Ed, Marty, George and Harry follow the dogs. Marty stumbles on a root and falls to the ground.

"Christ!" she thinks. "I can't even walk. I'm so tired. Too tired." Months of pent-up anger has loosened itself from the hidden reaches of her mind. "I'm so angry. If we had not come up here, this wouldn't be happening. My children? They're my life. It's Ed's fault. No, I know it's not! It's nobody's fault, but why are we here? Why is this happening? What did I ever do? We just have to find Josey and Cindy. What did they ever do? They're only kids. But then, so are the kids in Africa dying of AIDS. It is not fair. Nothing is fair. Why can't it be fair?"

Marty continues to hold onto the ragged doll. "I just want my children. I want to go back home."

She watches Rob and Ed as they follow Harry's lead. Rob is quietly competent. Attractive even in the midst of all this.

"God, what am I thinking? What a mistake that would be, to leave Ed for him. Rob would never make it down there. I'd never make it here. How can I be thinking about these things when…? What kind of person am I? Cindy and Josey!"

Ed walks alongside of Rob. He also appears capable and confident. Marty wonders what Ed is thinking.

"Ed's a good man. Why can't I just love him? Christ, I do love him. Everything is good. Why can't he just be happy with what we have? What's wrong with what we have? We have a nice home. A good business. We have friends. We have two great kids. Oh God, please don't let me lose them. We have everything you are supposed to have. None of that matters. Please don't let me lose Cindy and Josey. Why can't Ed? If it weren't for Ed, we wouldn't be here. No, it's not his fault. It's not my fault. It's not Josey or Cindy's fault. Why did they go into the woods? Because they're kids, that's all. The damned stories about a catamount! That's really all. What a price to pay for just being kids. I want my kids. I want our lives back. We have everything that is supposed to make us happy. Why aren't we happy? Why aren't my kids safe at home? Why aren't we all safe? Why aren't we home? Why isn't Ed happy? Why are we here? When we are safe, why are we all so dissatisfied? I am so angry! So damned angry!"

Ed extends his hand to Marty. She takes it. Ed pulls his wife back on her feet.

"Damn it! Damn it! I am so frustrated!" cries Marty, as she allows her thoughts to surface. "I want to find those kids and go home! God! Please! I am not asking for anything more!"

"I know," says Ed. "I know. That's all I want, too."

The dogs continue to lead the group forward.

Rob scans for signs of the kids or the cat on the ground. "I've been here all my life. I've never seen anything like this. This fire is right up there with the fires of 1947. Whole towns wiped out. There are still traces of that fire down in Brownfield. There were fires all over Maine. Josey and Cindy…just playing kids' games. I don't know. Have they paid with their lives? Can kids that young survive all of this? They are all like family. I'll probably never have my own. Until…until I screwed up. All of the women in the world and I had to pick my best friend's wife. What a complete asshole! I don't know why, but Ed seems to have forgiven me. If we can find those kids, I can deal with all this. I am trained to work a fire. I can track down that cat. I can kill it. I just don't understand why it's…What's it doing? This doesn't happen around here. Christ! What's happening here doesn't happen anywhere."

Rob continues to walk on. He turns to George.

"What do you think is going on with this cat?" he asks.

"I don't know," says George. "Now and then, one will go on a rampage and kill more than they need. I guess it could be because the prey is there. I don't know."

"There isn't all that much livestock up here. Not that many people farm anymore."

"I don't know why it's attacking animals, or people for that matter," says George.

"I thought cats lived mainly on deer and small animals," says Rob. "We have plenty of those. It's not like Clifford is overrun like North Conway."

"Well, according to Doc," says George, "more and more people are putting up places. The snowmobiles are everywhere in the winter, the ATV's in the summer."

"As invasive as some of that can be, what would that have to do with this cat coming out of nowhere and doing all of this?"

"Probably nothing. I really don't know. We'll most likely never know. I just know the habitat is disappearing in many places where the mountain lions do exist. Maybe they are moving on."

"This far?"

George lets his breath out. "It doesn't seem too likely, does it?"

"Not really, but we do know it's here, and we do know it is wounded. That is not a good combination."

"It caused enough damage even before it was hurt. All I know is that this isn't your normal mountain lion. Not even close."

George thinks about his family. They are probably shopping in North Conway. They like to shop at Settler's Green. About the only places he likes to spend his money are North Country Angler, White Birch Books and the L.L. Bean outlet. He also likes IME and EMS. At least his family is safe. He is not so sure about himself, but knowing what is happening up here, he knows he would not want to be anywhere else.

They follow the dogs along the edge of the bog. They are coming closer and closer to where the fire has been. The smoldering remnants of what has once been a beautiful forest now stand as blackened silhouettes in the foggy mist of smoke and steaming firefighting water. The dogs lead them to a small sandy beach. There are small kids' footprints on the ground. They lead to the water. The soft wet sand has also captured the tracks of the big cat.

"They were here. It looks like the kids went into the bog," says Rob. "The prints go that way."

"The fire in all probability forced them in," says George. "It burned right up to here."

"The cat was here," cries Marty.

"There is no sign of anything happening," says Rob. "The tracks are on top of the kid's tracks. It was here after they were here."

"It went that way away from the fire," says Ed. "It's funny how nothing burned over there. The kids must have swum out there. Thank God, we taught them how to swim."

"It's almost like the fire left a path for the cat to escape. Mutt and Jeff point to the water, but they can't follow the kids there," says Harry. "We'll have to go around along the edge of the bog."

He points to the left. "They'd have to come out somewhere over there."

"Let's go, now!" cries Marty. "Let's find them! I want this nightmare to end. That's the same way the cat went."

Ed starts forward.

"Let the dogs go first," says Harry. "They may pick up the trail again wherever the kids came out of the water."

"Some places are almost burned out on the right," says Ed.

"Yeah, don't ask me how but there are some green areas that the fire hasn't hit over there to the left. It's way too far to swim over the other way. They must have gone this way."

Crouching, Rob and George look at the cat tracks. Rob stands up.

"You know, if this cat is so close, maybe George and I better go looking for the it," he suggests, "before it comes after us. Harry, can you stay with Ed and Marty? Leave your radio on. Let me know if you find the kids."

"Okay," says Harry. "Let us know if you get the cat."

"If we get into trouble, we'll fire three shots," says Rob.

Ed and Marty come over to Rob. Marty hugs him.

"Thank you, Rob," she says. "Thanks for your help."

Ed shakes Rob's hand. "Take care you guys," he says.

"You too," says Rob. "We won't go far. If we don't find anything, we'll meet back up with you." He and George pick up their gear and their rifles and head into the woods. Ed, Marty and Harry continue around the edge of the bog.

Chapter 29

The sand is hot. The air is sweltering. Diffused sunlight reflects in the smoky haze. Josey and Cindy begin to stir as the heat makes its presence felt on their worn-out bodies. Josey pushes up on his elbows. Through swarms of undulating black flies, he looks over to his sister and asks if she is okay. Cindy's swollen eyes open and quickly close again to avoid the penetration of the brutal sunlight and the swarming tiny insects.

"Josey, I hurt all over," she says.

Josey squints up at the sky. He waves his arms in front of his face.

"I think we have been sleeping," he says. "The sun is much brighter. I feel a little better."

Cindy starts to get up. "I am hungry, Josey."

"I know. I am, too. There's nothing here. Not even any berries."

Cindy stands up and leans over to scratch the flies off her legs. "Oh no! I am covered with leeches, again!" She looks at Josey. "So are you!"

"Okay, I'll do you first," says Josey. "It's going to hurt. Take off your shirt."

"I know. I used to hate bloodsuckers. Now, I don't care anymore. I guess they won't kill us."

Josey pulls a large, blood-swollen leech from Cindy's neck.

"Ouch!" she cries. "That does hurt!"

"They are really on there. This is going to take awhile."

Finally, Josey succeeds in pulling another of the leeches off.

"These bugs are so bad, I can hardly do anything. I wish we had some salt. We could kill those leeches." Josey throws the leech into the bushes. "But I guess it doesn't matter."

Something moves. Neither Cindy nor Josey stir.

"Did you hear that?"

The bushes rustle again and stop. Josey starts to remove another leech. The bushes remain quiet.

"Should we look?" asks Cindy. Another sucker comes loose.

"Let's get these off first. If it was a catamount, it would have gotten us by now," says Josey.

Something moves rapidly toward the two figures on the beach. It is running fast. Josey hears the pounding feet. He turns.

Cindy screams, "It's Virgil!"

The dog comes tearing out of the woods and circles around the two children. Panting, he comes to a full stop. Cindy throws her arms around the animal. Josey kneels down and pats the dog's torso vigorously.

"Good dog, Virgil!" he says.

Cindy squeezes harder. "Virgil, I love you so much!"

As suddenly as he has arrived, Virgil pulls away and starts to growl. The dog's nose is in the air.

"It's back!" cries Cindy. "I can feel it!"

"Where?" asks Josey.

The dog leaps into the bushes.

The cat rears back, screeches and disappears into the woods. Virgil stops and continues to bark. Josey and Cindy pull the bushes aside. Virgil stops barking and sniffs wildly all over the clearing in the sand where the cat has been. Some stains of absorbed blood darken the sand. Smaller but distinct droplets of murky red still maintain their round shape on top of the sand, at least until Virgil's tumultuous search causes the top soil to become a mixture of sand, blood and paw prints.

"It was here!" says Josey.

"How long?" asks Cindy. Virgil continues to sniff the ground madly.

"Looks like a while," says Josey. "Some of that blood is half dry."

Cindy swipes at the black flies and takes Josey's hand.

"Why didn't it eat us?" she asks. "It could have gotten us while we were asleep."

Josey puts his arm around his sister. "I don't know. It must be afraid of Virgil. I think it's gone."

Cindy starts to cry. "But Virgil wasn't…"

Hearing his name, Virgil stops. He points his nose straight in the air, and then he walks slowly over to Cindy. She throws her arms around the agitated dog.

"I'm glad you are here, now!" she coos.

Josey turns back toward to the sandy point. He pulls another leech off his arm.

"Let's get these leeches off and get out of here," he says. Cindy gets up and Virgil follows.

"At least the fire hasn't reached here yet," says Josey. "The smoke is getting thicker, though."

"What was that?" cries Rob.

George stops. "I don't know. It sounded like a dog barking."

Then a loud shriek echoes through the woods.

Rob stops. "What the hell was…?

"It's our cat!' says George. "I've heard that sound a couple of times before. I don't know what a banshee sounds like, but that has to be close. I definitely heard a dog, too."

"Wait a minute. Listen. There is something else, too," says Rob. He listens more carefully. "It sounds like…"

"It sounds like kids' voices," says George. "It's got to be them! It's coming from that direction."

Rob starts to move quickly. "Let's go!" he says. The faint voices stop as abruptly as they began. "It came from over there."

Rifles ready, the two men move back toward the bog. Soon they are walking around the charred remains of what has so recently been dry underbrush among the evergreen pitch pine. They approach the water. The smoke from the fire has worked its way well beyond the bog. They are able to move quickly now that they are away from the slippery edge of the bog.

"The fire is headed toward the big lake," says Rob. "That should make it easier to control. It'll have no place to burn."

"It'll also make our job easier," says George. "I'll wager the cat is being pushed that way, too."

"Probably most everything is," says Rob, "although some animals burrow into the ground during a fire. I wonder if a mountain lion would do that. Not this one, I bet. The kids would have to head that way or stay here. I'll radio Harry to let Ed and Marty know that we think we heard Josey and Cindy."

George looks across the pond-like expanse of bog water.

He points. "What's that over there?"

"I don't know exactly. It looks like it could be clothing."

"You got a pair of binoculars?"

Rob takes off his pack. "In here," he says as he pulls them out.

Through the binoculars, two small pieces of clothing come into view. He hands the binoculars to George.

"It looks like clothing. It certainly could be kids' clothing. What do you think?"

"I think we have to look," says Rob. "Christ! It looks like they must have swum from way back where we saw the prints to that point there!"

"If they did, they're two amazing kids."

Rob nods. "Actually, they are. It looks passable along that edge. We should be able to work our way over there now that the planes have dropped that stuff on most of that area."

"Should we call Harry and tell them?" suggests George.

Rob takes out the radio. "They're already going that way, but I can't see them. I think we are ahead of them."

"We *think* we heard voices," George says, carefully. "Well, if nothing else, when they get here, the dogs can check that clothing out. There's no scent where the dogs are now, if the kids swam over here. Marty and Ed will also know if that clothing belongs to the kids. You saw them. Do you remember what they were wearing?"

"Not really," says Rob. "I wasn't paying much attention to them when…when, you know, when they took off." Rob puts the radio to his mouth. "I'll tell them we're just ahead of them. You know what, George?"

"What?"

"I know I heard their voices. I am sure of it."

Ed, Marty and Harry all stop. The loud screech hangs in the air even though it had only lasted a short moment.

"My God! That awful sound again!" cries Marty. "Wait a minute! Listen. That's Virgil! I know it is." The dog continues barking.

"It is Virgil!" says Ed. "Listen, I can almost hear..." Suddenly, it is silent. "I thought I...never mind."

"Thought what?" asks Marty.

"I don't know. For a moment, I thought I heard Cindy and Josey talking, but I guess I was dreaming."

"No, you weren't! I heard them, too. I know I did!"

Harry picks up the radio. He listens.

"They heard them, too."

The black mountain lion slides through the underbrush away from the approaching smoke and flame. Even with her bleeding paw, she springs elegantly to the top of a small, rocky ledge. She lies down and is almost invisible as she uses the height of the ledge to look around a clearing below. Her yellow eyes penetrate whichever direction she chooses to survey. The smoke and flame continue to come from behind. The large area of water lies ahead. She licks her wounded leg. She moves her head to the rear. Human noises. The small ones. The ones with the barking animal. Then there are others. More of them. Her blank eyes stare back from where she has just come. They always bring danger. Absolutely still, she blends in with the top of the ledge. Not far below her, a herd of white tail deer moves cautiously away from the oncoming fire through the clearing into the woods. She remains silent, uninterested. A large flock of birds flies overhead.

Rob holds the radio to his mouth. "I think we heard them, too. We're headed in that direction. We're near the edge of bog. Can you see us?" Rob looks around and waves. "Okay, work your way over. I think we found some of the kids' clothing. Somehow we got ahead of you."

He pauses. "Wait! I think I hear something." He listens again. "It sounds like them. Get over here! I'm going to look." The radio crackles and Rob puts it to his mouth.

"Yeah, the fire has moved away from the bog toward the lake. You can make it. You're not far. Just keep coming around the edge like we did. I'm going to look. It's got to be the kids."

Rob cups his hands around his mouth. "Cindy! Josey! Can you here me?" he yells.

Josey and Cindy, covered with black fly bites, soot, muck and leech welts, sit on the small sand bar in their soaked underwear. Virgil lays resting, but alert. His eyes concentrate on Cindy and Josey. Exhausted, both kids stare vacantly at each other.

Josey looks up. "What was that?"

Cindy comes to. "What?"

This time the call is louder. "Cindy! Josey! Can you hear me?"

"It's them!" cries Cindy. "It's them! They found us! They found us!" Virgil jumps up.

"Over here!" cry out both kids, not quite in unison. "We're over here!"

Rob and George run through the woods. Rob runs ahead.

"Cindy! Josey! Where are you?"

"We're coming!" yell the kids. "We're right here!"

Rob comes upon a small clearing next to the bog. George crashes through the underbrush. In the distance, Ed, Marty, and Harry are catching up. Ed and Marty yell for the kids. Harry's dogs bark.

"It's Mom and Dad!" cry the kids. "They found us!" The early afternoon sun beats golden through the murky, lingering smoke. George sees her. Rob does not. Not until too late. He looks up.

There she is, ready to spring—and she does!

Rob dives to the left. He can still hear the kids calling, "Uncle Rob! Mom! Dad!"

Rob's rifle jams into the ground as the cat's teeth tear into his left arm and flip his body over like a rag doll. The rifle drops, but before George can react, the cat is gone and so is Rob. George takes aim, but there is nothing. Josey and Cindy are rushing toward the voices when they see it. The black figure slides into the trees dragging something with her mouth. Josey and Cindy freeze. George appears out of the woods.

"Who are you?" Josey asks, out of breath. "Where's Uncle Rob? I know I heard him."

The two kids stand motionlessly, arms around each other, looking at the stranger. George lowers the rifle to his side. Virgil takes off into the woods.

Chapter 30

Harry's dogs are pulling hard. The black smoke makes the forest feel like a dusky cave.

The sunlight creates repetitive slices of illumination in the haze. It is hard to see. Harry, Marty and Ed follow the dogs. Their eyes smart from the smoke. They come into a clearing near a rock ledge.

"They can't be far," says Harry. "The dogs have the scent in the air." Then the dogs start howling.

"Look over there!" gasps Marty. "There's something there."

Ed goes closer. "This looks like blood. A lot of it."

The sandy soil betrays evidence of something having being dragged back and forth.

"Over here," yells Ed. "There's something over here. It looks like a pile of brush, but…"

Ed gets closer. Two arms and two legs protrude out of the pile of sand.

"Oh God! It's a body!"

Marty runs up. Harry heels the dogs.

"It's not…" she whispers.

Harry removes the sand from the top of the pile. "It's an adult. At least, it was. Turn around! You don't need to see this!"

"Do you know who it is?" asks Ed. Harry takes a pair of latex gloves out of his pocket and wipes the sand away from the bloodied face.

"No, I don't." He continues to remove the sand off the pile. He feels for a wallet. It is there. He fishes it out of the bloody pants pocket.

"His name is Dave Johnson." Harry pauses.

"Christ! That is the missing fisherman. How did he get here?"

"Do you even have to ask?" says Marty. Her stomach turns as she looks at the body. She knows she should feel something like pity, but she does not—just revulsion and frustration. Only one thing matters—Cindy and Josey—and they are not far away. Finding them will make all this end.

"Let's just keep going. I don't hear the kids anymore. We can't do anything for this poor fellow."

"They can't be far," says Harry. "I know we heard them, and we know they're alive. You are right, there is nothing we can do for this man. Cover his face. When this is all over, I'll come back and get him."

Ed also feels surprisingly indifferent to the body in front of them. "What about the fire? If it is headed to the lake, it will burn through here."

"If it comes this way…there is nothing we can do," says Harry. This is one of many bodies Harry has seen in his career in law enforcement. You never actually get used to it, but he realizes they are too late to help. It is best to concentrate on what can be done.

"I suppose we could dig a hole. Can we take the time?"

Marty's response is immediate. "No!"

Ed looks at the body and at Marty. "Okay, come on," he says. "I guess we are living by different rules. Burying the body is just what naturally comes to mind. It makes no difference at all."

"Now!" yells Marty. "I want to find them now!" She starts to call their names as loudly as she can. She is growing hoarse. Ed joins in.

Even though it is in the middle of the day, headlights are needed to bore through the murky smoke.

"I'm still not quite sure what we expect find out here," complains Roberts.

"The kids might have worked their way back to the road," says Wright. Southard shifts gears.

"Well, we can't get too much closer to that fire," says Ike. "I can see the glow right in front of us. I cain't hardly breathe."

"I guess you're probably right. We'll turn up ahead." The forestry pick up creeps forward.

"What's that?" cries Ike. "There's something in the road."

Southard stops the truck. "It's an animal, I think."

"You get out and look," says Ike.

Wright gets out and leans over the dark mound in the road.

"It's a dog. Somebody's dog."

Josey and Cindy stand quietly. George leans the rifle against a fallen tree and sits down on the trunk.

"I'm Dr. Mason…uh, George. You must be Josey and Cindy. We've been looking all over for you."

Cindy breaks into tears. "You found us! You found us!" is all she can say. She runs up to George and hugs him tightly around his waist

"Your Mom and Dad will be right along," says George. Josey fights to hold back his tears.

"You guys did great!" says George. The sound of Harry's dogs barking grows nearer and nearer.

"Josey! Cindy!" The voices pierce through the forest.

"Mom? Dad?" cries Josey. Suddenly the dogs burst into the clearing and Ed and Marty follow.

"Josey! Cindy! You're okay! Oh, thank God!" cries Marty. Harry heels the still restless dogs. Harry pulls hard.

"What's the matter with you guys?" The dogs want to run.

"What the…?" cries Harry. "Look!"

All the humans turn.

They look straight at the beautiful, graceful, black apparition that watches. Its yellow eyes pierce through the haze. It turns and picks something up. Then, it disappears into the smoke and the trees.

The Rollins family stands together in a tight circle. They hold each other in a big hug, tears running down their faces.

"Let's stay together for ever and ever," says Marty. They all hug harder. Quiet now, the dogs lie on the ground, panting but alert. George and Harry sit on the fallen tree trunk.

"Now what?" says Harry. "Where's Rob?"

"Just before you got here, it…it took Rob," says George, shaken. "It happened so fast."

Cindy starts to cry. "Oh Mommy, it did. It took Uncle Rob. I want Uncle Rob back. I want everything to be okay again."

Marty holds her clinging daughter. "I do, too," she says. "I do, too. We'll find him. I know we will."

Ed, his arm still around Josey's shoulder, turns to the two men on the log. "Christ what do we do, now?"

Harry looks up. "The wind has picked up. I don't think we can stay here," he says. "I don't think we can go back either. The fire is bound to burn this way, too."

"Christ!" says Ed.

"What about Rob?" asks Marty, subdued.

"Why did you lie to us about the catamount?" whimpers Cindy. "It took Uncle Rob."

Ed looks down at Cindy. "What do you mean?" he asks.

"You said it didn't exist." Ed draws both his son and daughter close and holds them tight.

"I didn't think it did," he says. "I'm sorry, I didn't think it did."

Marty stands to the side and looks at Ed.

Harry picks up his radio. "I'll try to get some help. Maybe we can get a helicopter in here to get you guys out." The smoke is getting thicker and thicker. The sky is becoming redder.

"You can try," says George. "But I think we better get out of here, now. I can hear the fire burning." Harry holsters his radio. "It moves fast."

"Grab everything. Let's go. There's only one way."

Marty picks up Cindy.

"I lost Stina!" wails Cindy.

Marty starts to put her daughter down. "It's okay, pumpkin. I've got her."

Ed turns back. "Not now, Marty. We gotta move."

Marty's mind is racing in different directions. Cindy and Josey are with her. Rob is gone. He is most likely dead. This man has been her lover, her friend. She cannot hold the two ideas in her brain: the joy at having just found the two dearest people in her life and the abject grief of having lost Rob. Rob is not just a dead body in the woods, like that poor corpse they have just abandoned. Rob is a part of her life. He is a part of who she is. Will they abandon Rob, too? What else can they do, though? She has to be there for her kids. She has to deal with Rob later. What about Ed? What is he thinking? In spite of everything, Rob is his friend too.

Ed's intestines growl. He runs into the woods to release whatever is left in his, now, liquid, bowels. He bolts behind a copse of trees.

"I'll be right back," he yells.

The grief of losing his friend hasn't completely hit yet. His misery grows into rage. He is elated to be reunited with his children, but livid that this damned cat, this cursed, out-of-control horror, is destroying their lives. He cleans himself with leaves and emerges from behind the trees. He will protect his kids and his wife—at all costs. This thing, this catamount, is not the harmless fantasy a father created to entertain—and yes, even playfully scare—his kids. It will pay.

Chapter 31

The CL-215 water bomber banks back toward the big lake.

"The fire looks worse than when we started. It's heading that way toward the lake," says the pilot, Pete Reny.

Co-pilot Don Fredrick looks into the billowing smoke and angry flames. "It always amazes me. From up here, it almost looks like lava flowing through the smoke. You can actually watch the flames jump from one tree to another."

Another water bomber flies by at 1 o'clock, heading back from dumping its load.

"How we doing?" asks Pete.

"The fire is close, but behind us," says Don.

"I'm going to bring her down some. See if we can see Harry and that family. They're down there somewhere."

"What about the cat?"

"I don't know. They're still looking, I guess. They think it might have it gotten the fish and game guy, Rob Schurman."

Dan looked out the window. "Have they found him, yet? Christ once you are in the smoke, you can't see anything."

Pete banked the plane to the left. "I don't know. All I know is what the kids supposedly told Harry. They said the cat picked Schurman up in its mouth and dragged him into the woods. The guy from out West saw it too. Man, it's got to be hot down there."

"I wouldn't want to be them," says Dan. "It's funny how the fire jumps from here to there and then leaves some areas untouched. That whole road down there is untouched. It's headed toward the bog again."

"Yeah, that's how they got the bulldozers in. There are the breaks over there. The lake ought to help." Pete brings the plane back around.

Don looks to the left. "As long as the wind does not shift. If it does, it's going to burn right around the lake on the right."

"The damned fire is bad enough," says Pete. "On top of that they got a psycho mountain lion after them."

"They all gotta be heading the same direction. Even a maniac cat ain't going to head back there, into that. Not unless it's suicidal."

"I wonder what would cause a mountain lion to go nuts."

"I don't know. It's funny, I read an article somewhere. It said a bunch of house cats went nuts and attacked their owner. It had something to do with too much mercury in cat food. Or they ate canned tuna, something like that."

"Huh," says Pete. "It's as good a theory as any, I guess."

"I guess. They got those signs up everywhere telling you not to eat the fish you catch."

"I eat them anyway. There's nothing like fresh fish over an open fire for breakfast. I like to get up early, catch a few trout, have breakfast, and then have a morning nap."

"Yeah," Don says. "I like them fresh. Frozen just doesn't do it. I know a guy, a worm fisherman, who follows the stocking truck and fills his freezer."

"Each to his own, I guess," says Pete. "Not much sport in that. You know, we might as well get another load. I think we can do more good by doing that. Besides they're still trying to get the helicopters in here."

Pete shakes his head. "I sure wouldn't want to be any of those people down there."

She drags the limp body by the arm through the moonlight. Her eyes smart in the heavy smoke. She hears the rumble. Something big flies swiftly through the murky smoke. What is it? She drops her load.

Suddenly a voice echoes from the body.

"Rob, can you read me? Rob, answer please. Can you read me?" Again and again, the voice pleads and then stops.

"Human voice," she thinks. "Where?"

She notices the pain in her front paw. Her hind legs ache. She slowly crouches. Attentive.

Nothing.

She smells smoke. She smells the human in front of her. Nothing else.

She bends over the body. She pushes it around. Tentatively, she starts to play with it. One toss.

The voice again. "Rob, are you there?"

She looks around. Walks in a circle. Returns to the body. Sniffs. Bats it with her good paw. Paces around again. The smoke is getting stronger. She kicks a pile of pine needles over the still body, circles one more time, then slides into the woods and disappears into the smoke.

Harry puts the radio back in his holster. "I can't raise him."

"We can't leave him," says Marty. "We don't know if he's…"

Josey and Cindy stands next to the adults. Cindy grasps Stina.

Josey looks up at Ed expectantly. "What should we do, Dad?"

Ed looks at George. "Is it possible that he is still alive?"

"Probably not," George says. "But under these circumstances, who knows?"

"We do know they went that way," says Harry. "The dogs want to go."

"That's back toward the fire," says Ed.

"George and I could…" Harry starts to suggest.

Marty goes over to Josey and Cindy and puts her arms around the two children. "I don't want to split up again."

"I guess I agree," says George. "I think we're safer together. I think we all want to be with the dogs. Even the big cats don't like dogs."

"What about Virgil?" asks Cindy, quietly.

"We can only hope he is okay," says Marty. "He's done about as well as any of us up to now."

"He saved our lives," says Josey. "But where did he go?"

"He'll find us," Ed assures him. "Right now, I think we have to keep moving. That fire is getting closer."

*   *   *

— 175 —

The group of humans grows nearer.

"I think we should at least look," a human voice says.

Another voice says, "If we can't go that way, we can turn back to the lake."

A figure moves toward the canines. They are going wild—howling, barking, yipping. The human with the dogs is pulled to the side.

She will go for that.

Harry turns around. "What the…?"

She leaps. Harry throws his radio. As if in slow motion, it floats in the air. Harry goes for his service revolver. His hand drifts toward the holster. The cat rips at his throat. Harry's head jerks from left to right, right to left. The gun stays holstered as Harry's hand motion changes direction to grab his bleeding neck. The blood pumps like an uncapped oil well. He falls to the ground. The cat screeches. Ed spins and hauls the rifle off his shoulder, brings it around and fires. Another ungodly screech. Before he can fire again, the cat flies by him. The side impact knocks Ed to the ground. The rifle whirls out of his hand. It hits the ground. George hurries to pick it up—too late. The cat is gone. Marty, Josey and Cindy run to Ed.

"Daddy! Daddy!" cries Cindy.

Tentatively, Ed pushes himself up. Both Josey and Cindy watch in anxious silence as he starts to stand. Marty rushes over and takes his hand. When he is finally upright, his wife and children all wrap their arms around his waist in a tight hug. Ed returns the hug, holding on to each one as tightly as he can. Ed is more stunned than hurt. He feels the comfort of his loved ones, but a wave of frustration quickly overtakes that solace. He has failed. He had a chance to kill it. Then at least one part of this horror would be over and done with. He has failed Rob. He has failed his family and now…

Ed turns toward Harry. George is kneeling next to the bleeding body. The dogs are still howling. Ed starts toward George. He turns back to Josey and Cindy.

"Marty, take them over there. Stay near the dogs, just in case it…just in case."

Ed picks up Harry's radio. "Is he…?"

"Yes, he is," says George. "He is. I just met him today, but you know I really liked him. One minute he was here, and just like that…he's gone. Just like that. I just…I don't know. I mean, why?"

Ed feels almost dead himself. He looks away from Harry's blank staring eyes. He is ashamed. He should have done more. He should feel more. In a moment that passed faster than Ed could accurately squeeze a trigger, Harry has lost everything: his being, his family, his dogs, his hobbies, his hopes for the future, his remembrances of the past, his ability to experience pain and pleasure. Everything! However, Ed is still alive and, strangely, he feels nothing, just exhaustion and frustration at having failed. The words to that old Queen song spin inside his head. "Another One Bites the Dust, Another One Down…" His senses have become so numb that he does not care if he is next. Then he hears Cindy start to cry and he reawakens to the fact that this is not just about him.

"Odd, what goes through your head sometimes," he thinks. "That song. What a time?"

He looks at the radio in his hand.

"I'll try to get help." George looks at Ed and shakes his head. Cindy sobs louder. Marty holds the little girl close and, in spite of her attempts to be strong, breaks into choking sobs herself.

"The radio doesn't work," says Ed. "Nothing."

George gets up. "It hit the ground pretty hard."

Ed speaks in a low voice, "What now?"

"We have no choice," says George. "We can't go back. We have to head that way."

"Toward the lake?" says Ed. "That's where it went, too."

"We can't go back into the fire," says George.

"What about Rob?" asks Ed.

"What are the odds?"

"Christ!" says Ed. "I guess we have no choice but to figure out what we can do and what we can't. Do you think we can get it before it gets us? We have got the dogs, though the dogs didn't seem to scare it this time."

George looks over toward Marty and the kids. "I think it's wounded. That makes it a whole lot more dangerous. I want to, but we can't do anything for Harry or Rob. We have to go. Now."

"I can see the red sky," says Ed. "I don't know if I hit it or not."

"No idea," says George. "You want my opinion? We need to get it before it gets us. We need to do the hunting, all of us together."

"Even with the kids?" asks Marty.

"I don't know what else to do," replies George. "We don't have a whole lot of choices, do we?" He picks up Harry's revolver. He points it away and fires into the ground.

"This still works," he says.

The green pick up comes around the corner. Up ahead, in what had once been a large, remote logging yard, a group of jumpers are preparing to head into the woods. Ben Southard pulls the truck into the low growth underbrush that has started to reclaim the old yard.

Roger Wright, his head wrapped in a white bandage, peers into the rear seat of the pickup. "How's the dog doing?"

Roberts continues to rub behind Virgil's ears. "Ole Virgil ain't doin' badly at all. I'll bet he'd like to be reunited with the Rollins. I bet we get him some water and something to eat; he'll be as good as new. He seems mighty anxious to get going."

Wright tries his radio. "I still can't reach Harry. I hope nothing has happened to him."

Southard gets out of the truck. When he opens the back, Virgil jumps up, pushes his rear paws against Roberts' leg and bounds out of the truck.

"I'd say he's feeling some better," observes Roberts, rubbing his leg. "Christ, that hurt!"

"I bet he could lead us to those kids," says Southard. "The kids are in good hands, but we can help get this mountain lion. My water bottle is just about empty. Let me get some water from these guys. Maybe something to eat."

"Virgil can have half my roast beef sandwich," says Roberts. "Bet he won't mind that none."

"Christ, Ike! You didn't tell us you still had some food left. My stomach has been growling for hours," says Ben.

"You didn't ask!" says Roberts. "Besides it's more important to feed the dog."

"What about that other half? What did you do with that?" asks Southard.

"Ate it, of course. A man's gotta keep his strength up. I need to get out of the truck and stretch my Christly legs." Roberts gets out. "If you want the damn sandwich, it's yours."

"Let's see what these guys have got," says Southard. After a few minutes, he returns to the truck carrying an old bucket. "We have to be careful with drinking water. Old Virgil here probably doesn't mind drinking from this bucket of rainwater. I found it upright on the ground. It still has water from that storm."

"Have they got enough water for us, Ben?" asks Wright. "If we keep going, we're going to need to stay hydrated."

"I ain't drinkin' no rain water," says Roberts.

Southard puts the bucket down and calls the dog. "I brought this for you fella," he says. Virgil walks over with a slight limp and starts drinking.

"I'll bet Virgil's willing to share," says Ben.

"I'll bet he just might," says Ike. "But what have they got over there?"

"They'll take care of you," says Ben. "It'll feel good to get some food and water. I think I can keep going, now. Some of those guys heard a shot a while ago. They don't know anything more. They can't reach Rob, or Harry either."

"Can we get in there?" asks Roger.

"Maybe. The fire is headed toward the lake. It hasn't hit the far side of the bog yet. It most likely won't unless the wind shifts. We can probably get around that way."

Roberts comes back toward the truck eating a Cliff Bar. "I feel better now. Here I brought one for you, Rog." He hands Wright an apple and a granola bar. "They want us to move the truck further over there so they can get the equipment in. This road's the only way in. This is 'bout as far as we can go with this here truck anyhow."

Virgil is lying down, but looks at the three men expectantly.

"What do you think?" asks Southard.

"It looks like Virgil's ready to go. It's our job," says Wright. "Let's go do it."

"What about you, Ike?" asks Southard.

"Course, I'm comin'. I didn't bring that big gun for nothin'. 'Sides, I've known them kids since they was born."

Southard heads toward the group of firefighters. "I'll get some provisions. I bet those kids haven't eaten anything. I don't know if they even have water."

"Okay," says Wright, "I'll get our gear together." Virgil jumps up, anxiously.

"What'd ya think?" asks Roberts. "What are their chances?"

"If they kept ahead of the fire, they could be…"

"What about that cat thing?" asks Roberts.

"I don't want to think about it. Let's get to work." Wright takes out a topographical map and compass. "It's going to be tough going," he says.

"Yup," says Ike. "I guess probably."

The bright red fire truck works its way slowly up the long hill. Two firefighters ride on the back step platform of the truck; two more ride in the cab.

"Can't we get this thing going any faster?" the man in shotgun asks.

"I'm doing the best I can," replies the driver. "Oh Christ! What's that up ahead?" He engages the loud siren. Parked directly in the middle of the road is a big, brand new, shiny Lincoln SUV.

"Some asshole left his car right in the middle of the goddamned road," says the driver.

"I don't believe this."

The four firemen get off the truck.

"Do you see anybody?"

"Not a soul."

"What now?"

"I'd say we push this thing right out of the way," says the driver.

The owner of the Navigator does not care. He is under a pile of pine needles in a ditch down at the bottom of the steep incline that reaches up to the road. His broken Winston Fly Rod lies next to the pile. The smoke slithers freely through the trees.

"Are we going to get out to that farm in time?" asks one of the firefighters.

Chapter 32

George attempts to heel the excited dogs. Cindy and Josey are protected between Ed and Marty. Ed keeps his rifle ready. He is not going to miss if he gets another shot at the catamount. He wears Harry's service revolver at his side. George carries Harry's 30.6 over his shoulder.

"The dogs are certainly onto something," he says.

"If I hit it, there's got to be some blood," says Ed. "They'd pick up on that."

George rubs his red eyes. "I haven't seen anything that looks like blood. Have you?"

Cindy stumbles on an exposed root. "Mommy, I am too tired. Can't we stop and rest?"

"Cindy, we have to…"

"You know," says George. "It might make sense to rest for a short time. If it wants to turn on us, it can do it whether we're moving or not."

Ed agrees. "Let's stop over there. The smoke isn't too bad for the time being. Hard to tell, but I don't think the fire is right behind us at the moment. Maybe we should take advantage of it. The kids can lie down next to that log. We can sit right next to them. We need to be ready to move, though."

The kids both lie on the ground. Ed and Marty face the forest in front of the log. George faces the other way. Both men are ready with their hunting rifles.

Ed hands Harry's gun belt to Marty. "Just in case."

She takes it gingerly. Ed looks down. Both kids are asleep.

"They look so peaceful," says Marty. "I wish I could sleep like that."

"You will, but not now," says George.

"I don't think I could now, even if I wanted to," says Marty.

"It's funny," says Ed. "I don't think I've ever been this scared, but I don't know that I've ever felt this alive. It's like I have gotten a second wind."

"I know what you mean," says George. "I should feel a lot more tired than I do. I even feel like, if we are careful, we might be able to get this situation under control."

"Yeah," says Ed. "Maybe."

Marty sighs. "I feel more than tired! I just want to get our kids home, and I don't mean the cabin. I mean home! Safe! That's where I'm in control. We aren't in control of anything here. That thing could come out at anytime."

"At least we know it is there," says Ed. "We know we have no choice but to try and get it. Do you think those people going to work on 9/11 knew what was there? They thought they were safe. We might actually have a chance, if we could get the time to shoot."

"Actually we do," agrees George. "I think we can find the cat and kill it. In a way, I hate to, though. I became a vet in order to save animals' lives, not to take them. I wish I had my tranquilizing gun. They were supposed to get it to me, but that's not going to happen. No one knows where we are."

"I don't know, George. That thing is definitely out of control. I think we have to kill it. It's done so much damage. It was already a legend before it ever became reality. Can you imagine a catamount in a cage? What would you do with it even if it were tranquilized? We have to get it. If we don't, we'll have a bunch of crazies trying to hunt it down—probably already do. On top of that, I owe it to Rob."

"I just want to get out of here," says Marty. "I want Cindy and Josey out of here. You don't owe anything to Rob. You owe us."

"Nobody knows where we are," says Ed. "We don't have a choice."

"Yes, we do," says Marty. "We can head for the lake. They have to be looking for us there. There's nowhere else we could come out. Ed,

I really don't care about the catamount. It can stay here forever, as far as I am concerned. I am never coming back, ever."

"We have to get it," whispers Ed.

"And if we don't and someone is there to rescue us, will you come with your family or stay here?"

"I don't know," says Ed. In the smoky miasma, the sun is a diffuse yellow ball coming in from the side, just at the top of the trees. George holds his peace.

"We shouldn't stay here too long," he thinks. "The days are longer this time of year and it is a full moon, but it would be good to find the lake before dark."

Fred Jordan, the crew chief, is looking over the topographical map.

"We have a few things in our favor, if the wind doesn't change."

Josh Redman looks at the map and orients his compass.

"If it does shift, this could be worse than the Bitterroot fire. There's a lot of dry fuel out there. Right now, though, it's headed toward the lake."

"Yeah, that was a bad one," says Fred. "That blew into thousands of acres within a few hours."

Josh turns around and looks up. "The smoke went so high that the planes flying overhead couldn't see anything. It's pretty bad here, too."

"That's right, I've heard the smoke was over 30,000 feet high at Bitterroot," says Fred. "Let's hope we can keep this contained. The lake is over here." He points to a spot on the map.

"We got ground crews over here to the right. They are cutting and creating a substantial break." Josh points at the map. "It's burned from this point to here. That crew is keeping it from going back the other way. That whole area here is gone."

"Where's the Roberts' farm?"

Josh shows Fred on the map. "Back that way. So far, nothing over that way has been threatened."

"It could come back around this way, though."

"Yeah, it could. Let's evacuate this group over here near that part of the lake. It's getting real hot there. If we put them here, we can try to create a fire road there and protect this part. How are the Heli-baskets doing?"

"They're still getting around."

"Okay, send a copter over to get those guys and put them back there," says Fred.

"How are we doing over here?"

Fred looks at the map again. "The bog seems to be keeping it from heading east."

"There is one area over here that isn't water," observes Josh.

"We just put a crew over there. That's near where those kids are missing. Have we heard from any of the searchers, the trooper with the dogs? Still nothing about what happened to Rob Schurman?"

"Nothing," says Josh. "But they have to be in here somewhere. Along with quite a few animals, I would imagine."

"That cat, you mean?"

"Well yes, I would think the space is getting tighter and tighter. Where else are they going to go?"

"It's funny, the big animals just kind of walk away from the fire. The small ones burrow underground and the birds fly away, almost like they have been trained to do it."

Josh winces. "We kill more of them with our bulldozing and chemicals than the fires do."

"Yeah, that's true, but we have to do what we have to do. Humans come first."

"I suppose we do," says Josh. "The loss of radio contact worries me. That cat has a better chance of surviving than those kids do in there."

Fred studies the map. "At least we know the adults found them. The trooper got through before his radio went dead. Can we spare one of those Heli-baskets over by the lake here? Just in case. They have to come out here somewhere, if they are still..."

"Still alive?" asks Josh.

"Yeah, still alive. Let's hope."

*   *   *

The smoke creeps like fog through Clifford. Main Street carves an oxbow through town and then branches off north straight to Canada, ten miles away. The town itself has a general store with gas pumps, one small family-style restaurant, a bar, and an eight-room K-12 school. There are a dozen or so large Victorian houses, all of which support L-shaped, cluttered front verandahs—the storage shed of choice in Clifford. A block that once housed a series of storefronts now stands empty and in disrepair. The nearest IGA is thirty miles away in Cold Brook. About two miles north of the town, the Ace in the Hole Bar and Grill sits next to Morrison's, a modern general store featuring everything from an agency liquor store to a fresh meat butcher department and a magazine rack featuring *Field and Stream, Better Homes and Gardens,* and an array of cellophane-wrapped special interest titles such as *Nugget, Cherie* and *Leg Show.*

The large parking lot is uncharacteristically full of official and unofficial vehicles. A number of state police cruisers are congregated near the storefront. The Ace in the Hole is also doing a brisk business, profiting from all the activity. An area large enough to accommodate a landing helicopter is cordoned off toward the back of the parking lot and a number of rescue vehicles stand waiting. TV news vehicles are parked to the side. Newscasters prepare to broadcast the latest developments in what has become "The Wildfire and Wildcat Crisis in the North Country." High-resolution broadcast cameras are placed so that the flaming red sky looms ominously behind an attractive newscaster as the latest worrisome intelligence is disseminated to the inquiring minds to the south.

The videographer is set up on the far edge of the parking lot. He hopes to capture some dramatic close-up digital images for what appears to be an eager market. He studies the map on his front seat. Can he get inside somehow? He has tried to drive, but all the roads are blocked. No one is allowed to go in or out. He is determined to find a way. He goes back to his Jeep. One of these roads must lead into the area. If he can get a shot of the cat or some actual footage of the fire, he will be way ahead of the reporters. It could mean real money, big money. He looks at the map. Some of these old roads might be passable. He goes over to his equipment, unscrews the lock nut on his tripod, stows away his camera and collapses the legs on his tripod. He will give it a try. He brushes off the black soot falling on his equipment.

"I have to be more careful to keep this away from the camera," he thinks.

Suddenly, he hears the whoop, whoop of helicopter blades. A helicopter with a large Heli-basket approaches the makeshift landing area. A group of about fifteen exhausted, soot-covered firefighters climbs out of the basket. Fresh replacements wait as the helicopter raises the basket and completes its landing maneuvers. The videographer watches as a big Mercedes flies into the parking lot and screams to a stop. Peter Schmidt jumps out and runs toward the helicopter pad. A trooper blocks his access.

"You can't go in there," he says.

"I'm Peter Schmidt. Mary, my wife, she is at our farm in there. I need to get in. Money is no object."

"Sir, it has nothing to do with money," says the officer. "It's too dangerous."

"My house isn't far from that fire. Who's in charge here?"

"I am," says a tall trooper with captain's bars.

"Can't I drive in?" pleads Peter.

"We can evacuate your wife," says the man in charge.

"I want to save the house," cries Peter. "Don't I have the right?"

"I think we already have a fire engine out there to soak the house," says the trooper. "Or at least it's on the way."

"I want to be there myself," says Peter.

"I can understand that, but…"

"Please," says Peter. The captain turns around and goes to talk to the helicopter pilot.

"Peter! Mr. Schmidt!" cries the videographer. "Peter, can I come with you? Remember me? I did the videos of your place."

*　　*　　*

The catamount comes into the clearing.

The heat radiates through the trees. Smoke permeates the air.

She is in pain, but she will bring this one with her. She creeps slowly over to the pile. She brushes the pine needles away with her bloody paw.

It is gone. The human is gone.

Chapter 33

On the move again, George allows himself to be pulled along by the dogs. They seem to have a purpose. He does not really know what they are following. According to the compass, they are still going north towards the lake. The narrow swath through the underbrush provides just enough room for one person to move through, so the group follows. The once again intensifying smoke creeps through the trees like a prowling animal.

"Much like a cat," thinks Ed. "A lot like us. I wonder who is hunting whom."

Rifle held ready across his chest, Ed keeps his thoughts to himself. Josey and Cindy move slowly between their parents. Marty keeps her hand on Harry's pistol, hanging loosely on her hip. Periodically, she pulls it up to keep the gun belt from sliding down her legs.

The catamount moves slowly, almost invisibly across the narrow path. Off to the side, she waits.

The narrow pathway disappears back into the smoke. She hears the barking of the canines. The overhanging branches up the trail begin to move. The canines burst through. They are approaching, closer and closer. The barking increases.

She is ready. They are almost here.

Mary Schmidt carries a box of photographs out on to the front driveway. Jake follows behind carrying framed family portraits. The flames leap from pine tree to pine tree like a track runner jumping over hurdles. The large piles of heirlooms are thrown helter-skelter into the driveway. Sweating, Jake puts down his box.

"We should get away from here. When the fire reaches those trees right behind the house, the house is going to go."

"I know. I know. I just want to get my mother's china. Can you get the generator going? You can use the hose to water down the side of the building."

"I can try," says Jake. He heads toward the barn. "I knew we should have cut down those pitch pine trees," he mutters to himself. Mary hurries back into the house. In the dining room, she goes over to the antique hutch and starts to take down the carefully sorted dishes. The generator comes to life in the barn. The lights flicker back on in the house and the radio comes alive.

"The fire in Clifford is not yet under control," says the announcer's voice. "Anyone in the woods should evacuate immediately."

Mary turns the radio off. "Tell me about it," she thinks.

She hears the whap of the streaming water from the hose hitting the backside of the house. She looks at the pile of antique china.

"I'll need some more boxes," she thinks and heads into the kitchen and down the cellar stairs. Jake watches anxiously as the leaping flames careen toward the house—one clump of trees and then the next. Suddenly, the trees above Jake burst into a brilliant fire. Clumps of scalding flames rain from above. Jake drops the hose and runs toward the house. Moments later, the roof bursts into flame. Clumps of burning pine rubble cover the roof and the ground surrounding the structure. The water that Jake has just sprayed evaporates instantaneously. Fire starts up the now-dry gray clapboard wall. Jake runs around to the front of the house.

"Mary!" he cries. "Where are you?" He hurries into the house. He sees the china on the floor. The house is already full of smoke. He looks around. Suddenly, the back wall explodes into a slab of fire. Jake hits the floor.

"Mary!" he calls. "Where are you?" He does not know which way to go. Should he go to the kitchen or the back bedrooms?

Mary hears the blast. She runs upstairs. The kitchen is full of smoke. The back wall of the kitchen is covered with angry red flames that reach out for the combustible material above. She hears a muffled whoosh. The ceiling and the walls all around her are suddenly on fire. The front door stands open.

"Can I make it?"

The entire room is now engulfed. Jake breathes in the raw air down low to the floor, takes a deep breath and bursts through into the kitchen. He spots Mary in the cellar doorway. He notices the open kitchen door. The flames form a precise replica of the outside outline of the door's molding. The outside appears invitingly through the hollow opening. Jake sees Mary start to move.

"Mary, no!" he cries. "Go back down." Mary hesitates just as the front door collapses and the opening to the outdoors fills with flames. Jake dives for the open cellar doorway, slams into Mary, pulls her around and heads down the stairs.

"Out the back cellar door!" he explains as he leads Mary into the cellar. The ceiling overhead burns brightly, as Jake pushes open the heavy metal doors that cover the concrete back cellar entryway.

Unexpectedly, the black apparition appears in front of the dogs. The dogs go wild. George loses control of them and lets go. The two shepherds instinctively start to circle. Momentarily, the cat cowers. Her back arches upward. Her bloody paw comes off the ground and with one powerful swoop she connects with the first approaching dog. Mutt flies back toward George and Ed. He hits the ground, yelps, but is up again. Both dogs continue to stalk.

Ed cries, "Mutt! Jeff! Out of the way! I can't get a clear shot!"

Jeff leaps forward. Mutt follows. Both dogs attempt to lunge for the cat's neck. The cat moves back and, with one powerful swoop, she connects with both dogs. They fly back onto the ground. Cowering, bloody and defeated, the two dogs hold back but then cautiously move toward where the cat has been. It is gone.

"I couldn't get a shot," says Ed. Josey and Cindy are rigid. Marty holds them close. George goes to retrieve the dogs. The brush behind Marty begins to move.

"What's that?" gasps Marty. The brush moves again. Marty spins around and pulls out the pistol. Ed aims his rifle. His finger is on the trigger. Marty is ready to shoot. The scrub oak moves again. It appears. Marty freezes and then dives as Ed fires. The shot rings through smoky wilderness. Marty and Ed are both on the ground.

"What the...?" asks Ed, angrily.

Panting, Marty says, "It's Rob."

Ed looks up. Rob lies face down on the ground, his feet still hidden in the bushes.

Ed sits up and stares. "How...?"

The firefighters and Peter Schmidt all stand in the basket.

"Where's your place?" one of the firefighters asks.

Worried, Peter points in the direction of the bright red sky. "That way," he says.

The videographer tries to hold his camcorder steady. The brilliant sky is dramatic stuff, but the bucket bounces from one side to the other.

"Has the fire gotten to your place?" asks another firefighter.

"I don't know," replies Peter. "The ground phones are out and the cell phones don't work out here. I know they sent a truck out to water the buildings. They weren't sure if it could get through all the traffic on the roads."

"Yeah, I heard that old farm house became quite a zoo," says the first fireman.

"That's closer to town," says Peter. "It belongs to Ike Roberts."

"Is your wife out at your place by herself?"

"I hope Jake is still there. He takes care of the place. I don't think he would leave. On top of all of this, my cattle apparently got attacked by a mountain lion or something."

"Yeah, we heard about that, too."

Peter looks toward the horizon. "That's the least of my worries now. We should be able to see the house soon. It has to be up over that hill. It's hard to tell from up here and with all this smoke."

The helicopter banks to right and up over the rise. The red sky bursts open in front of it.

"Holy shit!" cries one of the firemen.

Below the house and the barn appear to be constructed of flames. The clearly defined outer walls and roofs of the buildings are completely engulfed in fire. A moment later, they collapse in on themselves in a great whoosh of sparks and billowing smoke. The videographer continues to shoot.

"No!" is all Peter can say. "My wife!"

One of the firefighters in the basket picks up his two-way and contacts the pilot of the helicopter.

"We're going to need a crew here," he says. "We also need to look for this guy's wife. How about over that way in the field? That hasn't burned yet, but the fire is headed that way. What's that on the ground?"

The helicopter veers toward the field. The videographer swears as the bucket tilts wildly. To the left, a fire truck lumbers up the driveway.

"Good timing," observes a fireman.

The man with the radio pauses. "Okay," he says. "We might be able to hold the fire back here. Can you come down a bit? Maybe we can get the truck over by the field where it might do some good."

As an answer, the helicopter descends toward the ground. The truck heads toward the field.

"Christ! Those are dead cows!" says a firefighter. "Look at them all."

"Do you see my wife?" cries Peter.

"Not yet."

The man with the radio asks, "Can you put us down?"

The helicopter responds by moving to a clear flat section of the cow pasture. It hovers. The bucket lowers to the ground. Ten firefighters, Peter and the videographer walk out onto the ground. The smell of decay permeates the air.

"God!" gags one of the firemen. "This is awful."

The videographer sets up his tripod away from the men. Peter runs toward the burning house.

"Mary! Mary! Can you hear me?" he yells, over and over again. "Jake! Can you hear me?" There is no response. The videographer pans his camera from the house to the field. He zooms in and then he yells.

"There's something moving over there!"

"Where?" asks a fireman.

"Over there!" the videographer points.

Southard, Wright and Roberts follow Virgil.

"Christ! That dog is impatient!" complains Roberts, wiping his brow.

"It's a good thing, Ike," says Southard. "I can almost feel the fire jumping those bull pines, coming after us."

"Yeah, I don't think the fire could give a shit about us," says Wright. "It going to go where it's going to go."

"Well, I guess, since we got a choice, we better stay away from it," says Southard. "Come on, let's keep going."

The three men move quickly around the bend. Virgil stops abruptly. Roberts follows suit.

"Holy shit!" he says.

In front of them stands a large black bear. It rears up on its hind legs and whirls around as if caught with its pants down. The bear's eyes express what the bear itself cannot say. It, too, would be using some type of expletive, if the bear was able to speak English. Confused, it starts to move toward the three men and the dog. Then it twirls around, goes down on all fours, and hightails it along the only path available, its rear end high in the air.

"Oh, Jeeze!" says Ike. "It went where we're going."

Wright looks down the path. "That bear is the least of our worries. If we leave it alone, it'll leave us alone."

Roberts swings his rifle around. "Yeah, that's what you said about the goddamned cat."

"Come on," says Southard. "I'd rather deal with that bear than what's coming up behind us."

Virgil still looks uncertain, but starts cautiously down the path. In the rear, the fire roars like the crashing surf on the rocks at the ocean. In front of them, something howls like a banshee. On either side, branches from the thick underbrush reach out to grab them. The smoke burns their lungs as they push the overgrown branches aside. Roberts holds a branch, so as not to snap it back into Wright's face, and Wright performs the same favor for Southard. Virgil moves the easiest, panting low to the ground.

Another shriek sounds ahead, this one much closer than the last.

"What the hell was that?" asks Southard.

"It's that goddamned cat," says Ike. "Ain't nothin' else sounds like that."

All three men unsling their rifles from their shoulders awkwardly.

"There's nothing like trying to thrash your way through scrub oak," says Wright. "Be careful!"

"Christ almighty!" says Ike. "We got a goddamned fire behind us and a man-eating wild cat in front of us—not to mention the Christly bear!"

Ike pushes a branch aside and steps into a small, narrow clearing in the path. He starts to hold a branch aside. He lets go. The branch snaps back and slaps Wright in the face.

"Ike, what the hell?"

Roberts readies his rifle and points it to the left and to the right. Wright pushes his way into the clearing. Southard follows. Virgil whimpers and looks back at the men as if expecting an answer. Then, as if possessed, he starts sniffing back and forth in all directions.

"It don't look like we have to worry about the bear none," remarks Ike. The three men move slowly, weapons ready, toward the large carcass that is still weakly spurting blood from its neck.

"Have you ever seen anything like that?" asks Southard.

"My God!" says Wright. "A cat that would attack and kill a bear?"

"Jesus Christ!" says Ike.

"It's two people!" yells the videographer.

Everyone turns toward the far corner of the field. The two figures are running. Peter hurries toward the approaching man and woman.

"Mary!" he calls.

"Peter!" she responds.

Peter meets Mary and they throw their arms around each other in the middle of the field. Jake catches up, out of breath. Both Mary and Jake are covered with dirt, soot and dripping sweat. Mary breathes heavily.

"It's all gone, Peter. It's all gone. The horses…everything."

The once beautifully renovated home and barn are a heap of flames on the ground. The fire has worked its way from the barn into the field. The dry tall grass ignites and the inferno is spreading like lava. Peter continues to hug his wife. Mary sobs. Tears trickle down Peter's cheeks.

"The only thing that matters is that you are okay."

"Thanks to Jake," says Mary. "He saved my life."

Peter looks at Jake. He takes his hand and then gives him a quick hug.

"I don't know what you did, but thank you. Thank you. Anything you ever need."

"I think we saved each other," says Jake. "I'm just glad you're here."

The videographer watches the three figures in his viewfinder. One of the firefighters rushes up quickly. The camera pans around toward the fire. The videographer shrinks back. In the viewfinder, the fire is right in front of the camera. He stops taping, collapses his tripod and runs toward the woods.

Mary, Peter, Jake and the fireman hurry toward the helicopter. The fire is wild. It spreads through the field like brilliant spilled water.

"We have to get the helicopter out of here," says one of the firefighters.

"When the fire gets going in the woods over there, we've got trouble. That could reach Clifford."

A fireman takes Mary by the arm. "Come on! We need to get you guys out of here!"

Peter, Mary and Jake climb into the basket.

"Where's the guy with the camera?" shouts the fireman standing next to the basket. The fire progresses ever closer.

"He went over there to the woods," says another fireman.

The first fireman closes the gate and gives a thumbs-up to the pilot.

"I guess that guy is on his own. You guys are out of here."

The helicopter takes off and heads back over smoky woods toward Clifford. The two firefighters run toward the edge of the field where others are already attempting to create a workable firebreak.

"When you called in, did they say whether they're going to evacuate the town?" asks one.

"I suspect, it's a good possibility," the other replies. "Come on! We've got work to do!"

The videographer sets up his tripod at the edge of the woods. He pans with the helicopter as it flies away.

Chapter 34

"Uncle Rob!" screams Josey.

"You shot Uncle Rob!" cries Cindy.

Ed stands transfixed, with his rifle pointing toward the ground. Marty runs over to Rob's body, still lying on the ground.

Matted with blood and sweat, Mutt and Jeff whimper but then start sniffing back and forth across the path, first one way and then the other. Each dog limps, favoring a wounded limb. They both sniff their way over to Rob.

George kneels down to feel for Rob's pulse. Ed stares for a moment longer and then drops his rifle. Marty kneels down and puts her hands around Rob's head. Mutt licks Rob's wet, dirty neck.

Josey and Cindy approach cautiously.

"Is Uncle Rob dead?" asks Cindy, shaking.

George removes his hand from Rob's wrist. "He's definitely alive," he says.

He pushes Mutt and Jeff away. "Come on! Get off!" he orders.

Mutt pulls back. Confused, Jeff steps on Rob's back. Suddenly, Rob arches his back and cries out in pain. He rolls over and starts thrashing.

"Get off me!" he screams. "Get away! Get away from me!"

George tries to grab Rob's wrists, but the bloody body on the ground responds instinctively in self-defense. Rob's knees spring back and then kick out with such a force that George bounces onto his back. George lies on the ground gasping for air.

Rob leaps to his feet, adrenaline flowing, ready for combat or flight. He looks around quickly from side to side.

"Rob! Rob!" cries Marty. "It's us."

George struggles up and puts his head down between his legs, trying to regain his breath. Ed starts toward Rob but hesitates. Rob appears ready to lash out.

"It's okay. It's okay. Rob, it's us," says Ed, quietly.

"It's us," cries Josey. "Uncle Rob, it's us."

Cindy runs up to him. "Uncle Rob!" she screams and bursts into tears.

Rob starts to lunge. Then he cowers back. His eyes dart back and forth. Fear changes to confusion, and then he collapses to his knees and starts to shake. As he comes to his senses, Rob's battered body pulsates with pain.

"Oh, my God!" he moans. "Oh, my God!"

Marty tentatively approaches Rob. "It's okay. It's us."

Rob peers up. His arms fall to his side. Marty kneels down and gently puts her arms around his beat-up torso. Rob melts into her grasp. His arms hold on tightly as the rest of his body goes limp. Ed kneels next to his wife and Rob. He wants to put his arms on his wife's shoulders but holds back. Josey and Cindy inch forward.

"Uncle Rob?" asks Cindy. "Uncle Rob?"

Slowly, Marty pulls her arms back.

"Are you all right?" asks Josey.

Rob looks toward him. His face, in spite of the dried matted blood and dirt, manages a smile, as the crust on his cheeks and lips pulls tightly against his skin.

"I think so," he says, softly. "I think so."

The smoke continues to grow thicker and thicker.

"Am I alive?"

The Old Abenaki.

It is not a big island, but it was Molly's favorite place. This rock was their place. The Indian feels Molly's presence as he closes his ancient eyes. He buried her here on this island years ago. How he wishes she could be there in body when he opens his eyes again! How he wishes to be in the past, sitting with his Molly! What would their lives been like, had it not been for the whites?

Molly was a name given to her by the white men. Unlike him, she had known no other. What would she have been called, had their lives not been so altered by the arrival of those from across the great water? They understood so little about the land. He had helped them to survive, they that had to control and conquer everything in their path.

When he opens his eyes, he can barely make out the expanse of the great lake. His old eyes are failing. This will be his last visit to Molly's island. He will no longer be able to come here by himself. Soon the blindness will come and he will have to rely on the kindness of the white men. He will go back to the white man's village and wait to join his beloved Molly. His time will come. He has lived his life. Has it been a compromise? Soon it will not matter.

The old canoe approaches the shore. The old Abenaki expertly brings the canoe to the edge of the sand. He stumbles as he climbs out. He secures the canoe and then walks slowly away.

With his fading vision, he does not notice the big black animal that watches unhidden at the edge of the forest.

He stops as if he senses something, but then moves along.

The State of New Hampshire Parks and Recreation party boat moves steadily across the middle of Lake Mackapaque. The large, shallow lake is safe to cross full speed in the middle, but close to shore, the ubiquitous New Hampshire granite rocks lurk right below the surface of the water, ready to prey on any unsuspecting boater. In the best-case scenario, the boat may slide to a sudden stop sitting on top of the invisible stone formation causing only a few dents and scratches. The occupants would be obliged to climb into the water and work, by pushing and shoving, their craft off the rocks and back into a safe depth. In the worst-case scenario, the bottom of the vessel may be permanently damaged or torn open.

The driver of the state boat speeds on confidently through the fog-like smoke that hangs close to the surface of the lake, much like morning mist. The driver knows most of these waters. Much of his time is spent transporting campers to remote sites around the lake. The flat party boats can easily carry two or three canoes or kayaks plus all the provisions necessary to keep a group supplied for several days and nights. Each site requires a special set of skills and knowledge in order to maneuver the boat close enough so that the temporary tenants can unload or load their prodigious piles of gear. The days of living simply, for many, are no longer a part of the isolated backwoods experience.

Viewed from behind, the flat canopied boat is a silhouette against the bright red burning sky that blazes on the horizon. It appears to be sucked into oblivion as the boat disappears into the smoke and haze. The boat has just passed the well-known small island called Molly's Rock.

Mike, the twenty-one-year-old bearded driver, wheezes.

"Did we get all of the campers out of here?" he asks.

Brenda, his thirty-something companion wipes her stinging eyes.

"Yeah, they're all gone except for that group from the brewery." She coughs. "They can still see pretty well but there is a light haze emanating from the fire up ahead. It takes two boats to get all their stuff."

"They usually just leave the kegs in the water anyway," says Mike.

"It's good beer, but it's a pain getting those big kegs out of there. Everyone is taken care of other than those guys. Do you think the fire could burn around the lake?"

"It'll go wherever it wants to. It's so dry—depends on the wind."

"How close do you think we can get?"

Mike holds his hand over his eye. "If they are going to come out, it's got to be somewhere over there. I'd want to hit that sandy area."

Brenda takes out a pair of binoculars. She squints toward the approaching shore.

"It's getting close, but I don't see any people. There are a couple of row boats locked to a tree"

"I think we better hold back here," says Mike." I'm not sure about the rocks over there. The fire has a ways to go, but it can move incredibly fast. It's down to the water over on that point."

Brenda looks over to the left. "It looks like the Fourth of July." She hands the binoculars to Mike. "Can you see anything?"

Mike looks hard. "Actually, I can see pretty well. The smoke is mostly above the fire. I don't see any people. If they are there, they should be able to see us in this boat.

"Whoa! What's that?"

A large black apparition flicks ghostlike in the smoky mist. Through the binoculars, the large yellow eyes appear to be staring directly at Mike.

"Holy shit!" he says. "Look at this!"

"It looks like there really is a mountain lion, and it's coming into the water," says Brenda. "Did you know they could swim?"

The videographer pushes aside a pile of pine brush that reveals the remains of an expensive, decomposing Scottish cow. He endures the smell long enough to grab a few short spurts of footage. Then, he moves back into the field. The fire has spread rapidly across the dry grass. He can smell the burning bovine flesh that was scattered here and there. Each one that the fire has reached creates its own chimney of smoke, so the effect is like a series of Native American smoke signals. He sets up his video camera on the edge of the woods and pans over the field. He watches the viewfinder as waves of flame flow over the brown grass. He zooms in and records the flames as they leap into the bull pines at the far end of the field. He has heard that these trees actually germinate in a forest fire. A forest fire every twenty to thirty years helps keep the forest healthy.

"Well, it had been that," he thinks. "The fire still hasn't gotten over here. Maybe I can get up in one of those trees and get some better footage."

He looks over at the firefighters working to build a break. He can see them digging with their shovels and pick axes. He needs to get closer. This is good stuff. He is in the thick of it. None of the TV stations are getting this. This might be his break.

"Lord knows, I need one."

He works his way closer to the firefighters. One runs over toward him. The videographer tapes him as he approaches. In the viewfinder, the man looks distorted, almost an ethereal part of the smoky atmosphere.

"None of this is real," thinks the cameraman. "It's only tape."

"Are you crazy?" the man yells. "If you're numb enough to stay here, we could use your help."

The videographer waves the man off. "I'm fine," he cries.

The firefighter yells, "There's another helicopter coming. You need to be on it."

"I'm fine," repeats the man with the camera. "Let me get a little more footage and I'll come and help."

The firefighter throws up his arms. "It's your life buddy."

The videographer waves the man off again. "I'm fine. I'll be over soon." He picks up his camera and heads for the woods.

The firefighter warns him. "Don't go in there. The fire has jumped into the trees and is circling back around."

The figure with the camera waves as he slips into the woods. He cannot hear the man's voice above the crackling and the roar of the fire and the resonance of the wind.

He opens the tripod and positions the legs. He lights a Marlboro and inhales tobacco and wood smoke in what seem like equal quantities.

"If you you're going to smoke, you may as well go all the way," he thinks.

He coughs and looks around. If he can get some height, the effect of his pan will be even more dramatic. If he does a hand-held shot with the camera, he can make it up a good climbing tree. He can see the bright red sky to his right. He throws down his cigarette. Out of habit, he crushes it out.

"Why'd I do that?" He exhales. "What am I going to do, start a forest fire?"

He walks along the edge of the woods until he spots a good tree, one with some low branches.

"I only need a few seconds, then I'm out of here." He takes the camera off the tripod.

"Thank God for small digital cameras," he thinks. He throws the strap over his shoulder and moves toward the tree.

"Boy, when I woke up today, I didn't think I would be doing this."

He does a chin-up to the first large extended limb. Breathing heavily, he works his way up two more. A layer of sweat coats his skin. His hands are so wet, it is hard to grip. The coarse bark scrapes against his sweat-soaked tee shirt and blue jeans. Finally, he squirms into position. He inches forward. The branch creaks under his weight but holds. A little more and he will have a clear shot. There it is. He can pan everything from the burning remains of the house on the left, to the ocean of fire in the middle, to the helicopter hovering over the retreating firefighters on his right.

"What a shot!"

His greasy hands reach for the camera. He brings it to his eye. He presses the record button. The whoosh and the roar are deafening.

"What was that?" he wonders, momentarily distracted. A loud crash, a sucking noise and a sharp concussion. Was that an explosion? He looks up. A large mass of flame and sparks fade to white. The camera slides off the videographer's shoulder and falls to the ground.

The catamount is out of the woods. She moves back and forth along the abbreviated shore. The heat radiates from the forest behind her. She stops. She stares across the lake.

The large flat object comes closer and then stops. More humans.

She moves easily into the water and slides into an elegant swim. It is cool. She swims back and forth enjoying the coolness of the soot-covered water.

The flat object is still. The loud noise it made when it was moving is now a soft, purring sound. Then it stops.

The mountain lion treads water, watching the woods, the brightness in the distant trees, and the smoke. She waits. In the water, the pain is not so bad.

Ed kneels down next to Rob.

"Thanks to Marty, you're alive," says Ed. "I almost shot you. Are you all right? How did you…?"

Rob gingerly tries to sit up. He pushes on his left arm.

He grimaces. "That hurts."

Marty grabs Rob's other shoulder and helps him pull himself onto a blown-down log. Rob puts his hand on his bloody left shoulder.

"Get the first aid kit out of Harry's pack," yells Marty.

George opens the pack.

"I'm not sure what happened. I found myself under a pile of pine needles and leaves and the cat was gone."

George brings the first aid kit. "You are one lucky guy. Mountain lions usually break the neck of their prey. We're always told not to play dead."

"I wasn't playing dead," says Rob. "I was out cold."

"That's a nasty cut!" George says as he gingerly pulls Rob's shirt off his wound.

"It just grabbed me and threw me. I remember flying though the air. That's it. Then I was under this pile. I crawled to here. I wasn't that far away."

"Well, excuse my French, but you are one lucky son of a bitch." He finishes wrapping Rob's shoulder and fashions a makeshift sling from the remnants of Rob's shirt. "Can you stand up?"

Rob starts to push on his right arm. "I think so," he grunts. "I think so."

George gives a pull and Rob is up. He limps around in a wide circle.

"I think I might live," he says," "but I hurt all over."

"Hold still," George says, as he inspects Rob's bruised body. "I don't see any other serious problems, but you are going to feel it for awhile."

"I guess so. Thanks," says Rob. "I think I'll still sit over here for a few minutes."

Marty is the first to notice as Rob wobbles and looks like he might black out. She rushes over and helps George hold Rob up.

Rob stiffens. "Let me try it myself," he says. He limps over to the blow down and carefully sits down. He reaches for his radio.

"Christ! I lost it! Does anybody know where we are?"

"Harry's radio broke," explains Ed.

"Where is he?" asks Rob.

"He wasn't so lucky," says George.

"Christ! I've known Harry for years. Man!"

Josey and Cindy come over and sit on either side of Rob.

"We love you," they both say in unison.

"I love you, too," he says. His head is bowed. His right arm wraps around Cindy. His left shoulder hangs limp. He struggles with his left hand but manages to get it to Josey's knee.

"Do we know where we are?" he asks Ed.

"Yeah, I think so," says Ed. "In any case, we're near the lake."

Rob looks up at him. "Ed, I'm…"

"It's okay. It's okay. Let's worry about getting out of here. Like I said, we're not far from the lake."

For a passing moment, Ed feels like justifying himself but decides that this is not the time.

"Whatever I say won't help anything, now," he thinks. "Anytime I say what I think, I only end up in conflict. I wonder how many people just grin and hide what they really think." He smiles a little.

"Come on, let's go," he urges, cheerfully. Rob manages to smile back—not much of one, though, since his whole body hurts.

He thinks about Harry: "Why would…?" Then he realizes there is no satisfactory answer to his question.

Chapter 35

The helicopter hovers over the nearly deserted parking lot in front of Morrison's General Store. Peter helps Mary out of the basket. Jake follows. Another fifteen firefighters scramble into the basket and the helicopter rises, then banks off and disappears into the approaching fire. Even the news vans and satellite dishes have moved out. A few, forlorn, forgotten old automobiles keep the Schmidt's new Mercedes Benz company.

Most of the firefighting equipment has either been assigned to areas in the woods where the fire is actually burning or has been placed in strategic areas in the village, in case the fire threatens the buildings. Fire departments throughout the North Country have been deployed to the Clifford area. Professional fire fighters have been flown in from around the country. Yet the resources are still spread thin. The best hope is that the winds will carry the fire away from the populated area toward the lake. Fortunately, a large logging conglomerate owns most of the land to the north and the land has been spared the kind of dense development that has taken place on the water in the southern part of the state. In spite of the lack of development, land usage has increased dramatically in recent decades.

One lone tanker is hosing down Morrison's and The Ace in the Hole.

"Do you think it's worth saving that old dive?" asks one fireman.

"This is my second home," the other replies.

"More like your first." Peter, Mary and Jake run toward the Mercedes.

"What's old Jake doing with them city folk?"

"Works for them."

"I wouldn't want to do that."

"Yeah, and what are you doing with your life? Standing here with your thumb up your ass trying to stop the biggest fire in the history of the state?"

"I'm volunteering, that's what. What's your excuse? Just down right ignorance, more'n likely."

"Well, I ain't so ignorant as to want to stay here much longer. That fire ain't all that far away." The bright red sky dominates the horizon. "For what it's worth, let's give her one last soaking. It's hard to tell which way the wind might blow that fire."

Peter drives the Mercedes. Mary is next to him with her hand on his thigh. Jake sits in the back. No one speaks. Even though the late afternoon sun is bright, it is diffused by the gray, curling smoke. The headlights of the Mercedes burn two swaths of light through the thick mass. The air conditioner filters the air coming into the car. Through the closed window on her side, Mary watches the misty images of Clifford's abandoned homes and businesses flash by and then disappear.

"Will I ever see these places whole again? Will we ever come back?" she thinks. "What now?" she asks no one in particular. "Our home is completely gone."

Driving with his left hand, Peter put his right one on hers. "You're alive," he says softly. "That's all that matters. That's all that matters."

Mary looks at Peter and then back out of the window. They are in the woods heading south. "Will this all be gone, too, when we come back?"

"Either way, we'll be back," says Peter.

"It was your dream!"

"It's only money. We'll be back."

Mary turns to Jake. "What about you, Jake?"

"It's the only place I know," he says. "I ain't got any insurance, but I'll come back. Can I go to Cold Brook with you? I got friends there."

"Absolutely," says Peter.

"Could we swing by my trailer? I'd like to get my Dad's old fishing rods. The rest I can't do much about, I guess."

"Jake, whatever you need," says Peter. "We owe you."

"You don't owe me anything. Mary and I helped each other."

"That's not what Mary told me."

"We want to help you out," says Mary.

"I'll take my job again, if you come back. That's all."

"That goes without saying," says Peter. "You've got a job for life as far as I'm concerned. And it's not if—it's when."

"What about the cows and horses I let get destroyed? That's a lot of money."

"Jake, that wasn't your fault," says Mary.

"Besides," says Peter. "I think I can safely say that catamount, or whatever you want to call that cat, is probably the least of our worries now."

"I wonder where it is," says Jake. "It's somebody's worry."

"I doubt if it is in Cold Brook," says Peter. "Where's your place? Let's get your fishing poles and whatever else we can fit in the car. It isn't like we have a lot of luggage with us."

"Much obliged," says Jake. "I am much obliged."

Froggy stumbles out of his tattered, tarpaper shack. He throws another bottle on top of the large pile of empty half-gallon whiskey bottles and tin cans. Smoke creeps out of the blackened corncob pipe that hangs from his mouth.

"It's kind of smoky," he thinks. He inhales and sways back into the shack. He returns with a bag of fish, which he throws onto an existing pile of half-eaten fish carcasses. The sharp, pungent odor, for a moment, almost awakens his alcohol-deadened senses.

"I guess I better get some more wood chips," he says to himself. "It's getting kind of rank. Right now I could use a drink."

Froggy weaves his way back to the one room structure and its adjoining outhouse. He disappears inside and reappears with a full bottle of Old Boston and a small single-use Kodak camera. He sits down on a dirty old Adirondack chair that he built himself in his more sober days when he had quite a reputation as a talented woodcrafter. This chair is propped in front of the large, ancient stone chimney that he discovered many years earlier. He especially likes the built-in smoking chamber that he sometimes uses to cure the fish he catches. Building around an existing chimney saved Froggy quite a bit of labor and allowed him more drinking time.

"I'll show them," he thinks. "I'll take a picture of that cat. Then they'll believe me."

He takes a few more swigs and slumps into a deep sleep in his classic chair. He does not appear to be at all affected by the smoke that drifts by his cabin and on down the long path that leads to the lake. His old spin fishing gear is propped next to the chair. A rusty, old Shakespeare lure dangles in the wind. It makes a low, clicking sound, but Froggy does not hear it.

"How far are we from the lake?" asks Southard.

Roberts stops and wipes his brow. "I ain't never come this way by land before, but it can't be far. I've only seen this end from my outboard. It's pretty good bass fishin' up this end."

"I went trout fishin' up on the Mahuco River that comes into the lake. There's an old logging bridge up there," says Wright.

"You ain't one of them Christly fly fishermen that can cast into the wind but never catch anything are you?" asks Ike.

"I should have figured you'd be a wormer," says Wright.

"At least I catch fish," says Ike. "Sometimes worms is the best, but I was fly fishing before you were born."

"I've caught plenty of fish. It's a hell of a lot more fun on a fly. And much more elegant."

"More what? Christ, now we gotta be elegant when we go fishin'." Ike looks up to the sky. "Pardon me, Lord, for not always being elegant."

Virgil stops and looks back.

"Don't look at me," Southard says to the dog. "I'm not taking sides on this one."

Virgil continues. Southard follows.

"I'd say we better see if we can catch us a cat using any method we can."

The three men push their way through the overhanging branches.

"This trail, iffin you want to call it that, don't get used much," observes Ike.

"It's better than bushwhacking through what's on either side of us," says Wright. "How far are we in, anyway?"

"I'd say about twenty miles," says Ike.

"We should hit that logging road before long," says Wright. "If we can get to that bridge, we can walk along the inlet and hit the lake."

"Then what?" asks Ike.

"I'm not sure," replies Southard. "I am counting on old Virgil here to take us where we need to go."

"How in hell does he know?" asks Ike.

"He does seem to know where he wants to go," says Wright.

Southard takes out his radio. "There's still no response from Rob or Harry...I'm picking up the firefighters. Wait a minute...I've got the park rangers."

Southard listens. "They see that cat. It's in the water by the rocky point at the end of the lake. Do you know where that is, Ike?"

"The cat in the water?" he asks. "What's it doing there?"

"How should I know? Do you know where the rocky point is?"

"Not exactly."

"I'd say we get down to the lake and try to work our way from there," suggests Wright.

"At least, we know where that thing is. If it's there, it ain't after us."

Suddenly, Virgil disappears.

"Where's...? Look! There's a road!" cries Wright.

"Let's go!"

"Which way?" asks Wright.

Southard hauls a DeLorme map out of his pack. "Now that we have a road this should do us some good. It must be page 28."

He shows the map to Wright and Roberts. "It's got to be this road."

Wright looks over his shoulder. "Then we need to go that way."

Virgil reappears.

"I don't know how many times I've ended up in East Bejesus using these maps," Ike remarks.

"If we go back the other way, we're heading toward the fire," observes Southard. "The lake can't be that far. This will take us to the bridge."

Virgil starts walking down the road away from the fire.

"I guess that settles it," says Wright.

The cool, black, silky-covered water is soothing.
The flat object bobs up and down out in the water.

She turns.

The brightness above the trees is a constant palpitating glow.

Her eyes sting and her breathing is deep and heavy, almost painful. In the distance, her ears sense them coming—the sharp bark and howl. Through the heavy pungent mist, she scans the forest.

The bushes are swaying.

She moves, almost invisible, through the soot-laden water. Black on black. She swims a short distance, turns and slips out of the water into the underbrush and then is gone.

In the boat, Brenda hands Mike the binoculars.

"I can't see it anymore. In this smoke and with all the soot on the water, it blends in."

Mike takes the field glasses. He scans the water and the smoky shoreline.

"I don't think it's there." He hands the glasses back to Brenda. "Take another look. I'll call the search party and tell him we lost it. They must be getting close."

"Should we get any closer? How well do you know this part of the lake?"

Mike reattaches the radio to his belt. "They're not far away. They're headed for the inlet up by Bridge 15. I guess we should try to get closer, in case they need help. They're going to try meet up with the kids and then go after the catamount."

"It's kind of a shame. It looked like a pretty animal. In any case, they'll have to work their way around the inlet," says Brenda. "I've fished up there. It's not easy going. I always use a walking stick."

"One of the troopers said that he had fished up there, too. He knows where he's going now. It's amazing."

"What is?"

"When you think about it, everyone wants to see a catamount. Here we got one. It's big and beautiful, but everything is all screwed up. Why would it go after people? Cows I can understand, but that many?"

Brenda puts her hand over her brow and squints through the smoky mist. "I don't know. Why is anything messed up? I'm up here pretending I didn't go to college and running away from a lousy marriage. You're pretending you're not gay. Neither one of us likes having many people around. It seems a shame, though."

"What, that poor cat or us?" asks Mike.

"Maybe both."

"Well, I don't think I'm about ready to get violent. That cat, the catamount or whatever you want to call it, is pissed off at something."

Brenda continues to spy across the surface of the dark water. "Well, yeah, I can understand that. I'm kind of pissed off at things myself. I also have to wonder who is supposed to be here—her or us."

Mike leans against the front of the boat. "I'd say at this point in time, he, she or whatever it is, will probably lose. The moment our ancestors showed up, it was all over."

"So, maybe she's practicing a little animal terrorism."

"How do you know she is a she?" asks Mike.

"Just feels like it," smiles Brenda.

"Shit, and here I thought it was a guy!"

"Nah, she's a female. I'd bet on it."

"Whatever you say," says Mike, smiling, "but I guess we better see if we can help. It's a straight shot that way. The troopers should be coming from the right, over there, shouldn't they?"

Mike turns on the engine. He pushes the drive lever forward and heads toward the shore. He moves steadily, but slowly, across the surface of the water.

"I'm just not so sure whose side I am on," says Brenda.

"I am," Mike says, smiling again, "but I guess we better go help anyway."

Brenda looks to the side. Then the boat comes up short and stops as if it was snapped from behind. The engine pops out of the water, the propeller spinning. Brenda grabs the rail. She almost flies over the side. Mike pulls the emergency cord on the engine.

The boat sits, stranded.

Brenda looks into the water. "Didn't you know about these rocks?"

Mike does not answer.

Chapter 36

The two dogs pull Ed and George through the brush into the rocky clearing that opens up into the large expanse of Lake Mackapaque. Josey and Cindy pop out behind, followed by Rob and Marty. Rob limps and supports himself with a makeshift walking stick in his right hand. She watches from aloft on a large limb as the figures move toward the water. She is so close that she can see everything below her through the smoky haze. The heavy, darker smoke billows overhead from the fiery tress that are still a good ways behind her. The dogs pull hard. They sniff wildly among the rocks.

"I bet it's been here," says George. "Those dogs smell something."

Josey and Cindy sit down on a pile of larger rocks.

"I don't see anything now," says Ed. He looks around. "There's one of those party boats out there. I wonder who that is."

George takes out a pair of binoculars. He focuses in. "It's a state park boat. I wonder what it's doing there."

"Hopefully here to help us,'" says Marty. "Maybe they can get us out of here." She starts to wave her hands.

"I can't see too well in this smoke," says George. "Something is wrong. They are out of the boat." Marty continues to wave. George refocuses. "It looks like they're grounded. How deep is it here?"

"Not very," says Ed. "This lake is not all that deep, but they should be able to push themselves free. All of this was created by the dam on the other end." Ed turns to Marty. He takes off his shirt. "Here, wave this at them. If we can see them, they can see us."

Marty waves the shirt. Ed looks around. The dogs continue to sniff nervously. Rob looks back in the direction from which they have just come. The smoke filters through the trees like the smoke escaping from the butt ends of just-puffed cigarettes. The smoke and the dense forest blend into low contrast obscurity that hides the detail in the tree, the underbrush and the foliage.

"If you stay low, you can still see pretty well. Why don't we tie the dogs to that old boat mooring over there? All we can do is wait," says Ed. He puts down his rifle and leads the dogs toward the old, weather-beaten, padlocked rowboat. His eyes sting as the sweat on his face drips into his them.

Marty continues to wave, hoping to raise the attention of the would-be rescuers out in the lake. Her fruitless beckoning wanes and then stops. She sits suddenly, or rather flops, to the sandy beach. She unbuckles the heavy gun belt she has been carrying around her waist and sets it beside her. Aware that Josey and Cindy, who huddle together on a projected blow-down, are watching her, she attempts to stifle her sobs of frustration. She scratches the leech welts and bulging black fly bites that cover her exposed neck, arms and face. Her neck feels like she has the mumps. At least, thanks to the fire, the torturous insects that plagued them earlier have vanished for the time being. She stares off across the lake, oblivious to its smoky beauty.

If a photographer were there, he would find the late afternoon light coming off the horizon, mixed with the fog-like smoke curling out of the trees, quite photogenic. Its beauty belies the all-too-real dangers. It may be an once-in-a-lifetime shot, the kind of thing National Geographic would pay big money for. The nearest photographer, however, is not there to capture the moment on film, disk or tape as his charred remains still lie on the forest floor waiting to be found some day in the future.

Cindy and Josey, also covered in dried muck and covered with welts and insect bites, still sit side by side on the rocks. Cindy pushes herself up and goes to sit beside her mom. Josey follows. They both put their small arms around Marty's back. Marty pulls her two children close and hugs as tightly as she can. It helps. After securing the dogs, Ed moves slowly over to his family. He kneels down behind and puts his arms around his entire family. He will never take them for granted again.

George watches the forest, rifle ready. He glances back. He looks at the Rollins family and thinks of his own. When will he see them again? He sighs. One way or another all of this will end. As his grandmother had always said, "This too, shall pass." For thirty years, he and Mary have been together. He remembers Mary coming into his fraternity house for the first time back in 1967. She had worn a mini that showed off her wonderful legs. He sported a droopy mustache and yellow checkered pants. Supper consisted of peanut butter and jelly in the fraternity kitchen along with uncounted numbers of beers. Mary had gotten sick. George had looked over at her lying on an old tattered couch. "Someday, we'll look back at this and laugh," he had thought at the time. That day had come.

He knows Mary and their three daughters are in their vacation condo waiting, waiting for him to come home. He cannot complain about his life. "In many ways it has been a charmed existence," he thinks. Through it all, he and his family stick together. There has been one daughter who battled anorexia and another who had to come to terms with alcoholism. He and Mary lost all their parents within a two-year period. Their love and support for each other has not waned even when facing these challenges. The family grows closer during the hard times, and there are many good times too. He needs to get back and he will.

Then he thinks about the pile of bills in his car, waiting to be paid. George checks his rifle.

"What a strange time to be thinking about that."

Rob limps toward the tied up dogs and sits on the edge of the dilapidated rowboat. He glances back toward Marty, Ed and the kids. He watches the waves of smoke drift across the water.

He struggles to bear up against the throbbing pain on the entire left side of his body as he takes in the scene of Marty and her family sitting together.

"What now?" he thinks. He has never felt so alone.

Chapter 37

In silence, Ed waits with his family and finds his thoughts wandering. What now? If we get out of this, I cannot go back to all that. Even in the midst of all this, he flashes back to the customer standing before the counter and complaining. Why do the hassles remain in your brain in perfect clarity while all the successes merge into an indistinct haze?

"You ruined our Christmas!" the man yells. "You said the right ski pants would be here by then. My wife got nothing for Christmas. It's your fault!"

The guy is ready to jump over the counter and punch the sales person out. Ed steps in with a smile on his face, ready to do whatever he must to keep this bully from hurting someone. Meanwhile, the line of customers holding yellow Rollins' Sport Shop bags grows longer. None of it is his fault. Ed aches to get up and leave, to be anywhere else but in that store. He will lose hundreds of dollars on the day after Christmas because "the customer is always right." In at least half of the cases, the customer is dead wrong—some of them even lie. The frustrating part is that Ed and his staff are not guilty of "ruining" everyone's Christmas, although, of course, they will not be receiving any sympathy.

Ed actually prides himself on his ability to deal with the various snafus that are inevitable in any business, to expedite, substitute, improvise or otherwise work out some ingenious solution, but some things are beyond his control. He is tired of having to apologize for being human when the issue is indeed his fault. If you hire the help you need, you cannot make enough money to live on. If you try to go it alone, you burn out on the endless hours of the same thing over and over again. Ed had started the sporting goods business because of his love of the outdoors. Instead of freeing him to spend more time there, it had trapped him behind a counter or chained him to his desk. He feels like a wild animal caught in a trapper's snare.

He has two choices: learn to rekindle his desire to continue what he is doing or find something new. If running the business makes him feel this bad, the second choice has to be the right one. He knows he cannot go back. After going through this, he knows he can no longer live that life. He will sell or liquidate. Hell, if Marty wants to run the place she can have it. It is all so trivial compared to what they are going through now.

He pictures Marty pulling Rob into the cabin, the two of them tearing at each other's clothes. That is the image in his mind—out of control desire. He and Marty are way beyond that after all their years together, but none of that matters. Marty is as frustrated in her own way as he is in his. Jealousy is also a trivial and destructive response to something that has less to do with him than it has to do with the chemistry between Rob and Marty. That part of Ed and Marty's life is good. He is a part of that. If anything threatens their marriage, it is not that Rob and Marty have been together. He has gotten beyond that, and he suspects that, by now, so have both Rob and Marty.

He pictures the catamount creeping up on his unsuspecting and vulnerable children. He imagines Josey struggling to keep Cindy afloat in the bog. He is so proud of how they kept going. Thank God, his precious son and daughter are alive, but they are sitting so still, abnormally so, for kids this age.

"What will the long-term effects be on them?" he wonders. "Will all this make them stronger or will they have mental scars for the rest of their lives? What about Marty and Rob?" He pictures Marty's orgasm—she would have one, she always does—Rob's face distorted.

He feels a stirring in his groin. What's that all about?

Maybe, he should…The woman in the store next door—long black hair, tanned face, and long legs, much like Marty's features.

Revenge? No.

Maybe we shouldn't be so conflicted about…

About what? About things that are natural? About things you cannot change?

You make choices. You choose.

I choose Marty. I choose my kids. I will also choose to deal with this situation that I don't like. I am not trapped there anymore than this fire or this mountain lion traps us. We are going to deal with it. I don't know exactly how, and I don't know what's going to happen when this is over, but know I have choices and I am going to make them. I cannot imagine not being with Marty. We have shared so much together.

Ed presses harder against Marty.
She shudders. She feels Ed pull close to her back.
She experiences a momentary revulsion. At the outset, she wanted to blame this all on Ed. His "dreams"... What about mine?
She looks over at Rob.
So alone, yet so damned sexy. Ed is in his own way, too. Her desire for Rob has nothing to do with Ed. It is just there. She pictures Cindy and Josey sitting safely at home. Josey is playing. Cindy is dressing her dolls. Peaceful. Ed is there. I am preparing supper. It's so serene. There must be a way. If we can survive this, we can find a means to do more than survive that. We are two different people, but two people who still want to share life together—not just for the kids, but also for us. I cannot imagine life without Ed. We have been through too much together. So much of what I have been unhappy about has been so insignificant compared to all of this. I need to decide what I truly want. So does Ed.

Marty pulls Cindy and Josey closer, inside her lap. She snuggles ever so slightly tighter to Ed.
"I wonder where Virgil is," she says.
"I don't know," says Ed.
No one asks about the catamount.

For the moment, the ghostly black figure lies on the obscured limb and also waits and watches.

Then they all hear a muted crash. A large, flame-covered tree thunders to the ground. Its tip falls into the water. It is close enough that a spray of sparks and white steam are clearly visible.

The catamount turns her head, too.

*   *   *

Mike looks over the side of the grounded boat. He can see the rock underneath. The water is very shallow.

"I can get out and swing the boat off these rocks. I'll pull the motor out of the water. You stay in the boat in case I get separated."

Mike goes to the back of the boat, releases the motor lock and pulls the engine prop out of the water. Then he jumps over the side.

"These rocks almost look like they were put here," he says. "There's a pile and then it goes off deeper again."

Mike stands on the narrow piling and starts pushing the boat back and forth. It does not move. He tries again. The bottom of the boat scrapes but hardly moves. He goes to the front of the boat and tries pulling on the mooring rope, but to no avail.

"Brenda, you're going to have to get out and help."

Brenda leaves the front seat and climbs over the side. The boat rests solidly on the pile of rocks and will not budge.

"Maybe if I push on the front and you on the back, we can swivel it off," she says.

"How the hell did this pile get here?"

"Probably stone walls from before they dammed the river. They served a purpose when they were put there by some long-dead farmer."

"That's right, this was all farmland—Indian land before that. I wonder how they felt about the dam."

"Probably not too happy. As soon as the boat is free, we're going to be in deeper water," says Mike. "We don't want to lose the boat."

Brenda moves toward the bow. "Come on, we can do this." She pushes and the boat edges grudgingly to the side. The back inches back toward Mike. Then he, in turn, shoves and the stern creaks forward. The bow slides slightly back toward Brenda.

"It's getting there!" she says. "I can see the paint on the rocks." She pushes hard again. The bow pops off the rocks. The middle of the boat turns. The stern jumps back toward Mike. His feet roll on the loose rocks and he falls backwards into the water.

"Shit!" he cries. He goes under back first and then resurfaces. His feet touch bottom. He stands chest deep in water. Brenda works her way along the edge of the boat. She holds out her hand. Mike takes it and she pulls Mike back up onto the pile.

"We're going to have to get wet anyway," she laughs.

Mike spits out lake water and begins to push. "Just push," he says.

They both push hard on the stern and the boat suddenly slips off a pile of loose rocks and then slides into clear water and immediately floats forward, easily propelled by the wind. Continuing to push, Mike and Brenda stumble on the loose rocks beneath their feet and splash forward into the water.

Brenda surfaces quickly in the deeper water. She is now over her head. The boat is moving away. Brenda spins around. Mike is floating face down, thrashing the water. She swims to him. A small slick of blood oozes from Mike's head and then dissipates into the water. Brenda maneuvers her feet up onto the slippery pile of rocks that had captured their boat. She grabs for Mike, misses, and then throws her arms around his waist and flips him over. Stunned, Mike tries to grab Brenda around the neck. He pulls her forward and drags both of them underwater holding Brenda in a tight headlock. Trained in lifesaving, Brenda grabs Mike's arm, spins him around and locks his right arm around his back.

"Take it easy," she says. "You're going to be all right."

Mike stops resisting and goes limp as Brenda puts her hands on each side of his face. She pulls up to the pile of rocks and lifts Mike up into a sitting position. Mike spits water and blood from his mouth. The blood is flowing freely from a cut in his forehead and it mixes with the water dripping down his face. Brenda kneels and looks at the cut. She pulls off her tee shirt and wipes the area around Mike's cut.

"It doesn't look too bad," she says. "I'm going to use my shirt to wrap around your head." She quickly tears the shirt down the middle. She rips off a small piece. "Hold this on your cut. Press hard."

Mike takes the piece of cloth and holds it against the cut. Brenda takes the two pieces of ripped shirt, ties them together, rolls them into thirds and then ties the elongated, makeshift bandanna tightly around Mike's head. A patch of red appears on the white cloth over the wound but the blood ceases to flow down Mike's face.

"That'll do for now," says Brenda. "You must have hit your head on those rocks."

Mike cups some water in his hands and washes his face clean. He looks at Brenda.

"Too bad you are not with someone who could fully appreciate those boobs. I stumbled on these loose rocks when the boat let go." He takes off his shirt. "Here, take this. I don't know how those people might react to a topless rescuer." He manages a smile.

Mike turns around and sees the boat floating away quickly.

"Christ! We've lost the boat! We should have thrown the anchor out."

George surveys the lake with his field glasses.

"They are definitely both out of the boat." He tries to focus in more clearly. "I can't tell what they're doing."

Ed comes over. "Why would they get out of the boat?"

"I don't know. Maybe they ran aground. How deep is it out there?"

Ed takes the binoculars. "This lake is pretty shallow in parts, but I wouldn't have thought there would be a problem out there. It seems to go off quickly here."

George holds his hand over his forehead and squints into the smoky haze. "I would feel better if we could get everyone on that boat and out of here before the fire gets any closer."

Ed looks back. Where the fire has reached the edge of the lake, the flames try in vain to find more fuel to feed their hunger. Billowing smoke and steam roll across the water as fiery underbrush blows out like fireworks from the red inferno and then lands and sizzles on the dark water's surface.

"We haven't got much time," says Ed. He hands George the binoculars "Maybe I can row that fishing boat out."

George looks again through the glasses. "The boat is getting away from them. The wind is blowing it back toward the middle of the lake."

Ed runs back to the old fishing boat. Rob sits motionless. Now and then, he squirms in pain. Marty, Cindy and Josey walk over to Ed. The dogs pull hard on their tethers as Ed approaches the old boat.

"Can we go home?" Cindy asks. "I want to go home."

"Me, too," says Josey. "I'm so tired. I want to get on that boat. I want Virgil to come back."

"Me, too," says Cindy. "I don't want to see a catamount ever again."

Ed examines the boat. It is old. It lies upside down. The spotted, faded-green, varnished canvas that covers the folded plywood surface of the bottom of the boat has started to separate, but there are no holes visible in the hull.

"We're going to try to get us all out of here," he tells them. He unties the dogs' leashes and hands them to Josey. "Hold them over there," he says.

Josey pulls the panting, whimpering dogs back toward Rob. He tries to calm them down, but they are acutely aware of a danger in the air that their human companions do not seem to comprehend. Ed picks up a large rock and bangs it against the old rusty paddle lock. After a couple of tries, he breaks the lock into two pieces.

"Marty, give me a hand," he says.

Marty comes over. They both pick up one side of the boat and flip it over. The wooden thwarts have started to pop out of the fastening that holds the gunnels to the boat. The oarlocks tip inward inside the softened block of wood that holds them in place. Two old oars lay on the ground where the boat was covering them. Ed picks up one. The varnish is spotty, but the oar is intact.

George helps Ed push the boat into the water. A number of tiny spouts allow water to begin seeping into the bottom of the boat. A small bubbling puddle begins to form. They all look at the boat.

"What do you think?" asks Ed.

"I think the leaks are slow enough that one of us could get out there and get that boat. It might work," says George.

"What other choice have we got?" asks Ed.

Chapter 38

Virgil works his way quickly through the underbrush, reaches a stretch of pebbled beach out on a point and starts to run. Wright, Southard and Roberts splash loudly through the water, trying to keep up. On the point, Virgil stops and looks back. He waits until the three men work their way sloppily to the patch of clear, dry land. The smoke curves around the corner of the point and stings their panting lungs. As soon as Virgil is sure that the three men are behind him, he bolts again in the direction of the smoke. Roberts stops and bends over with his hands on his knees.

"Christ! I ain't breathed this hard in years!" he says between spasms. "I'm regrettin' all them Camels when I was young." Both Wright and Southard are in better shape, but still sweating from the exertion of working their way against the wind through the knee-deep, choppy water that covers the rocky-bottomed edge of the lake.

"It's not so easy walking on those rocks," says Wright.

"I couldn't find a decent walking stick anywhere," says Southard. "That last fall kind of hurt."

Roberts straightens up again. "That mutt don't give up." Virgil stands further down on the side of the lake.

"We're coming!" yells Southard. "We're coming fella!"

Wright looks hard across the smoky water. "Have you got those binoculars?" he asks Southard. "I think I see something."

Southard takes off his backpack. He opens it, takes out the binoculars and hands them to the other trooper.

Wright holds them to his eyes and looks to his right. "I can see them," he says.

"Who?" asks Roberts.

Wright focuses again. "Who do you think? I'm sure it's the kids and that man and wife. I don't see Rob. There's some other guy."

Southard looks. "It's probably that vet from out West," he says. "What are they doing?"

"I can't tell. It looks like they are doing something with a rowboat. Can you reach the rangers out on the flatboat?"

Southard tries the radio. "There's no answer."

Wright pivots the binoculars out toward the lake. "The flat boat is moving toward the middle of the lake. I don't think the motor is running. It just seems to be moving with the wind. Wait! It looks like the rangers are out of the boat!"

Southard comes over. "Can I take a look?" He focuses. "That's what it looks like. I wonder what that's all about."

Roberts tries to peer through the smoke toward the small spec out in the water.

"Well, we ain't gonna do them any good out there, but we might be of some help to them people yonder. I 'spect we ought to get crackin'."

Southard turns the binoculars back toward the side of the lake. "For once, Ike, I think you're right."

Virgil waits restlessly up ahead for the three men. He starts to bolt and then stops, turns back, and waits, not yet ready to leave his followers behind. Southard scans the edge of the coast one last time. He stops.

"Christ! Look at that! That cat is right up there on that ridge watching everything they do."

Ike comes over and takes the binoculars. "Where?" he asks.

Southard points. "A little more to the right."

Roberts adjusts the binoculars. "Holy shit! Look at the size of that thing! So that's the devil that attacked my sheep."

Wright takes the field glasses. "Man, what a beautiful animal! It's watching everything they are doing. They don't even know it."

Southard picks up his pack and his rifle. "We better get over there," he says, "before it decides to stop watching. Should I fire a shot to warn them?"

"I wouldn't," says Wright. "It might spook the cat."

The three men start toward the figures in the distance, back into the water and towards the smoke and the bright flaming sky. Noticing that the three men have finally moved, Virgil breaks into a run.

The agitated water slaps the old rowboat against the shore.

"It's floating," says Ed.

George brings the paddles over. "It just might make it. I think it's best if you stay here with your family. If I can get the boat, I can get the rangers and then get everybody out of here." George puts the oars in the boat. "I think there's enough shore here to protect you from the fire."

Ed looks back. "If it gets too close, we'll get in the water." Neither man mentions the catamount.

The two men look over to the rifles leaning against the blow down where Marty and the kids sit waiting.

"We'll be all right," says Ed. "You be careful."

George gets into the boat. He pauses. "I left the pistol over there, too. I won't need it out there. If I end up in the water, I don't want that pulling me down."

Ed gives the stern of the boat a good hard push. George starts to row. The boat repeatedly bobs up and over the swells. The water splashes onto the bow of the old boat and the water level inside rises as the liquid seeps through the tiny pores in the boat's ancient hull. More water slaps over the gunnels and flows inside and it is soon up over George's boots. His soaked socks slosh uncomfortably inside his hiking boots.

George rows harder. The extra weight from the water adds to the boat's resistance as it plows through the lake's surface. George turns back toward the bow. The ranger's boat is still floating on its own as it rolls with the turbulent currents out into the open expanse of the lake. The two figures in the water are now further behind and, from George's perspective, appear to be motionless. The rowing becomes more and more difficult as the water continues to fill the boat.

George turns toward the bow again. The flat boat is closer. It is moving faster in his direction than he is able to move toward it. Now, the two figures seem to be waving.

"Had they seen him? If I could only get to their boat," he thinks, "or if it can get to me."

His boat is sinking. The water is now halfway up his shins. Soon he will be sitting in the water. Rowing now is not only arduous but rapidly becoming useless, as the weight of the water inside the boat creates so much resistance that George's forward motion is overcome by the wind's backward thrust. George finally gives up. The boat sits motionless in the water—a dead weight. The water works its way up toward his waist.

"Sometimes the laws of nature suck!" he thinks as he unties his boots. "Maybe I can swim to that boat."

Virgil looks back impatiently. Finally, the three men work their way through the heavy underbrush and blow-downs and come up on a large rock. Virgil looks, panting toward the discernible motion on the sandy beach ahead. The figures on the pebbly beach are now almost recognizable. Wright takes out his binoculars and pans from left to right. He looks for the mountain lion. It is gone. The figures on the beach still seem to be oblivious to its possible presence.

Wright then looks out toward the free-floating ranger's boat. It is closer now. The old dingy wallows half submerged in the water. The figure inside stands up, jumps into the water and starts to swim. Wright continues to scan the water back and forth from the sunken boat to the flat boat to the shore. Then he stops.

"Come here!" he says as he passes Southard the binoculars.

"Holy shit! Look at this!"

The sleek black form is working its way toward the stranded rowboat.

Mike and Brenda stand on the elevated mound of rocks. The water is only shin deep but it splashes vigorously against their legs. They watch their boat drift further and further away. They can also see the wallowing rowboat not far from it. They can make out the rise and fall of the swimmer's head and shoulders as he works his way toward their boat. Mike puts his hand to the torn shirt wrapped around his head.

"It's frustrating not being able to do anything," he says.

"He'll get there before we could," says Brenda. "I just hope he makes it. At least the boat is going in his direction."

"A lot of help we've been," says Mike.

"Yeah! Well, we tried," says Brenda. "You can only do what you can do. It sure seems like not much is going right."

Mike holds his hand over his forehead. "What the hell is he doing? Why is he splashing and trying to swim so fast?"

"Beats me! He's swimming like something is right on his tail."

"What could be coming after him?"

"The mountain lion?"

"What?"

When George turns to look back toward the shore, he sees the slick black form swimming easily and steadily through the choppy water. He has never seen one do it, but he knows mountain lions are at home in the water. He recognizes it immediately. The boat is only fifty yards away and is moving toward him. He switches from a breaststroke to a crawl. He has to get to the boat. George is a runner and is in good shape, but it has been years since he, as a camp counselor and lifeguard, has used his crawl stroke for any extended period. His lungs ache. His arms feel like cotton batten. His shoulders cramp, but he keeps on. He is closer to the boat.

"Should he look back? How far away is it? Is it coming after him? What else could it be after?"

He keeps on. Can he sustain this pace? His whole body aches. He has to stop. Treading water for a brief moment, he looks back. It is still there, moving through the water with an ease he cannot help but envy.

He can still make it. He thinks about his family waiting in North Conway. How could his life have led to this moment? It cannot end like this. He has a family. He has a life. He is well known. People look up to him. It cannot end like this...

He knows none of that has anything to do with what may happen now. It is just him, the water, the boat and a killing machine that he cannot see or hear but that he knows is drawing ever closer. It has nothing at all to do with who he is. It is only that he is here, in this moment of time. The fire, the lost kids and an out-of-control beast that lives at the top of the food chain—is there a reason for all of this? He is lower on that food chain and no match, in any way, for the carnivorous strength that animal possesses.

"Christ, the hubris! With my big gun, I thought I could handle anything. Well, I don't have my gun now. Why would it go into the water just to get me? Why would it kill all those animals and all those other people? It has nothing to do with me. I'm just here. Those other guys were just there, too."

George keeps swimming hard.

"I'm about to die."

His body feels like it is saddled with lead weights. His mind is racing. Everything he has ever done passes almost instantaneously into his consciousness and then is gone.

"Just keep swimming, for Christ's sake! I am almost there. Just a few more strokes."

He has never hurt so much. His lungs feel like they have been ripped open. Finally, he lunges forward. He is there!

His right hand grabs for the large pontoon on the side of the boat. His hand fails to grip the smooth surface and slides off, but he is able to lean against the slippery cylinders and slowly move along the side of the boat working his way toward the back.

He does not want to move forward. He turns quickly to look back in the direction he came from. He does not see the black shape, but he knows it is there. It has to be! How far is it behind him? He peers around the side of the boat and...

There it is, coming around the other side!

George slides along the pontoons to the front of the boat. He leaps up to grab the edge of the flat platform. One last pull, a lunging pull-up, and he will be out of the water. Does he still have the strength? He has to have it! He heaves himself up just as the cat swoops around the corner of the boat. George's feet feel the smooth, wet fur as the cat swims underneath.

George lies flat on the boat. His lungs heave. The cat circles back around. He pulls himself up to a sitting position. Could the cat make it into the boat?

The black shape comes slowly around again to the front of the boat. George crawls over to the cockpit in the stern of the boat. He uses the driver's chair to pull himself up. Finally, he is in an upright position. He can hear scratching at the front of the boat. He puts his hand down to start the engine.

"Oh Christ!" he cries aloud. "Where are the keys?"

Using George's binoculars, Ed focuses in on the boat. It is difficult to see, but he can make out the indistinct outline of the flat craft. He stands next to Marty. Josey and Cindy lie next to the blown-down log, half-asleep. Rob is propped against the log. Now and then, Josey or Cindy will open an eye to see if anything has happened. When it is clear that the adults appear to be in control, the two children slip back into a fitful doze.

"Did he make it to the boat?" asks Rob.

"It looks like it," says Ed. "I'm not quite sure what he is doing. It is hard to tell."

"Is the cat still out there?" asks Marty.

Ed pans again. "I can't see it. I don't know where it went." He hands the glasses to Marty.

"It's got to be there somewhere," she says. "I saw it going after him. He's definitely on the boat. He should be safe there, shouldn't he?"

"I don't suppose there is a gun on that boat?" asks Ed.

"I wouldn't think so," Rob replies. "Why doesn't he just get out of there? That boat should be fast enough."

Marty looks again and then passes the glasses back to Ed. She sits down next to Cindy, who looks up for a moment. Marty puts her arm around her daughter. Cindy snuggles into Marty's armpit.

"When can we go home?" she asks.

Ed sits on the fallen log just above her and puts his hand on her shoulder.

"Soon," he says. "George is on the boat. When he comes back, you can go home and we can take care of the catamount. It's right out there."

Marty shifts slightly forward. "You know, Ed, I really don't care about that cat, the catamount or whatever it is. I just want to take Josey and Cindy home. I'll even settle for the cabin, if it is still there."

Ed starts to speak. Marty interrupts him. "It's okay, Ed. I know it is something you have to do. My job is to get the kids out of here."

"I know," he says.

George sees the huge, black paw come up over the front of the boat.

"It can't get in here!" he thinks.

The second paw, a bloodied appendage, appears.

"Christ!" He leaps forward toward the bow of the boat. He grabs a paddle, lifts it behind his back and slams it down on the wounded paw.

The two paws disappear. A short deep growl turns into a light splash. George stands ready. The paddle is high above his head. Breathing deeply, the acrid smoke flowing over the lake burns his lungs. He coughs. It is the only sound outside of the dull roar and crackling of the fire behind his back and the ever-present wind stirring up the water.

Where is it?

Does he dare look over the side? He inches forward. He peers over the right side—nothing but chop and smoke.

He moves toward the front. He comes up to the front gate. He pushes it open. He slips onto the front platform and looks over.

Nothing.

He sees a small pool of blood on the platform. Now he is sure that the cat is wounded. He knows what that means.

"Where is it?" he wonders.

"Where the hell is it?" he says aloud. He steps back. He moves to the left and looks over.

Nothing.

He lowers the paddle down to his side. He walks quickly back toward the stern of the boat. The boat bobs up and down in the rough water. George lurches forward and smashes his shin against a turned-over lawn chair.

"Shit!" he says and falls forward onto his knees.

The boat tips to his right. The chair hits the side rail and makes a low, tinny slap as aluminum hits steel. The black paw comes up over the pontoon and appears over the lower edge of the boat. For a moment, George watches the paw attempt to gain a grip on the smooth surface of the deck. It slips back and is able to hold its footing on the pontoon.

Then George hears something rolling in front of him. He sees a small tubular object rolling toward the edge of the boat. Momentarily, the boat rocks back. The object hangs still, but continues on its journey off the side of the boat when the craft lunges again back to the right. George suddenly recognizes the yellow float with the boat's keys. He lunges forward just as the black head and yellow eyes appear above the pontoons.

The unlatched side door flies open.

Chapter 39

"He's on the boat," says Mike. "What the hell is he doing?"

"It looks like he's waving the paddle," says Brenda. "What's he doing that for?"

Suddenly the boat springs forward. It gains speed, cuts into a wide circle and heads back toward the two park rangers. Abruptly, the boat veers off toward the middle of the lake…then back again…then away from them toward the shore at the end of the lake.

Brenda repositions her feet on the wobbly rocks. "What's he doing?"

Mike waves his hands over his head. Without warning, the boat turns back around, creating a large wake. It spins around so fast that it almost tilts on its side. Once again, it heads straight toward Brenda and Mike.

Mike continues to wave his arms. "I think he sees us!"

Brenda waves her arms. The boat continues its full-speed, straight course.

"He's coming on awful fast!" Mike says with alarm. "He's got to slow down! He'll hit these rocks!"

"Slow down!" yells Brenda.

The boat keeps coming closer and closer. Mike turns around. His left arm grabs Brenda by the waist.

"He's not stopping!" he cries and he pulls her out of the way of the oncoming boat as he dives into a belly flop onto the water. The speeding boat zooms onto the bulge of rocks just below the surface of the water. It lurches forward and then snaps backwards as if pulled from the rear. The large engine races wildly and slams up and down against the protruding rocks. The propeller whirls in the air. Brenda and Mike dog paddle in the deeper water next to the pile of rocks and the stranded boat.

"Jesus Christ!" says Brenda.

Using a breaststroke, Mike moves cautiously toward the boat. Brenda follows closely behind.

"I don't think there is anybody on there," he says. "We've got to stop that engine."

Brenda grabs the side pontoon. "What did he do? Fall out?" She starts to pull herself up further.

"Oh shit!"

"What?"

Brenda pulls her hand back. The inside of her palm is covered in a layer of red.

"What does that look like to you?"

Mike pulls himself up over the side of the rocking boat.

"What the hell?"

Blood is splattered all over the deck. His knees slip in a puddle of slippery red liquid. He turns around, still kneeling and pulls Brenda out of the water. She slides onto the deck. She stands up. Her knees and hands are dripping with scarlet goo. She runs to the helm and jerks the safety cord. The racing engine abruptly stops. Suddenly, it seems very quiet, in spite of the wind, the incessant slapping of the waves against the bottom of the boat, and Mike and Brenda's heavy breathing. The smoky air burns their lungs and the boat feels like death.

The speeding object roars away.

The cat moves steadily in the opposite direction.

The figures ahead on the land come closer and closer.

The sharp pain in its paws does not prevent its forward motion. A sliver of red trails behind the black specter.

Ed's binoculars spy the black apparition, but the creature's blood is invisible in the water's chop. Ed passes the binoculars to Marty.

"Do you see that?" he asks.

Marty points the glasses in the direction that Ed has been looking. Ed stands behind Marty and puts both his hands on her shoulders. He tries to maneuver Marty's search. He pushes her to the right.

"A little more that way," he says.

She shakes him off. "Let me find it," she says.

Ed withdraws his hands. Marty scans the water.

"I see it," she says. "It's heading off to the left. Out there, it doesn't look like the creature from hell that it surely is."

Cindy comes over to Marty. "Is the catamount coming, Mommy?"

"No, pumpkin! It is going the other way," Marty lies.

"Do you see George?" asks Ed.

Marty pans from left to right. "No, I don't. That boat seems to be back where it was stuck before. It looks like the rangers are out there. It's hard to see with all the smoke....There still seems to be something wrong."

"Where's the catamount now?" asks Josey.

Marty pans again. "I can't see it."

"I want to go home," whispers Cindy. "That's all I want and I am really hungry."

"There are some energy bars in that back pack," says Ed. "Do you want one?"

"Yes."

"I'll get them," says Josey.

Rob inches toward one of the backpacks and opens the top. He pulls out two bars and hands them to Josey.

"How are you doing, Uncle Rob?" asks Josey.

Rob manages a weak smile. "I've been better, but you aren't rid of me yet." Josey takes the bars.

"Is the boat coming?" asks Rob. Josey looks back toward the lake.

"It's out there," he says, "but there is something wrong. Mom and Dad saw the catamount out in the lake."

Rob starts to stand up. "It's out in the lake?" His legs start to give out and Rob pushes on the large blowdown with his left hand.

"Josey, give me a hand," he groans. Josey grabs Rob's right arm. Rob grimaces in pain and slumps back down.

"Here, take my left hand." Josey takes Rob's hand and pulls. Rob slowly stands up. He puts his arm on Josey's shoulder and the man and the boy move slowly toward the lake and the others. Ed turns as Rob and his son approach. Marty comes over and takes Josey's place, putting her arm around Rob's left shoulder. Rob looks back. The black smoke and jets of sparking fire fill the sky.

He says to Josey, "Take your sister over there by those reeds, near the water and eat these bars."

The two children move away from the adults. Rob turns to Ed and Marty.

"Ed, Marty, we have to get out of here. That fire will be like a bomb when it comes out of the trees back there. We won't be far enough away from it. And it is coming."

"What about the catamount?" asks Marty.

"Right now," he says, "we need to worry about the fire. Stay close to the water. We may have to jump in. What's with the boat?"

Ed hands Rob the binoculars.

"It ought to be coming," says Ed, "but it isn't."

Rob tries to hold the binoculars in his left hand. Marty is still next to him.

"Here, let me help you focus."

All of a sudden, the fire blasts through the trees on the next point over, only fifty-some-odd yards away. Missiles of burning pine limbs and disintegrating, blazing pine needles rain down on the entire nearby shoreline. Josey and Cindy rush to the waters edge and stand in the water. Ed, Marty and Rob follow suit. They can hear the burning debris sizzling on the water's surface not far away. The point of land that has provided their safe haven will be next. It is not easy to maintain their balance on the lake's rocky bottom, but there is no other way to avoid the inevitable, oncoming conflagration.

"Goddamn it!" complains Ike, as he trips over yet another hidden branch of a blowdown that projects out into the water. "There's more crap along this lake than you can shake a goddamn stick at."

"It's pretty rough going," agrees Wright. "It's incredible how thick the scrub oak grows in here."

Southard wipes his brow and inhales another breath full of dense smoke. He points further along the shore.

"I think we might be able to walk in the water over there. I fished in here once. It doesn't go off deep as fast over there."

"It's still all loose rocks. If that cat don't get us, slipping on these Christly rocks will!"

"Where's Virgil?" asks Wright.

Southard points up ahead. "He's having almost as much trouble as we are, but he's still way ahead of us." Southard takes out the binoculars. He pans from the shore out into the lake.

"Everyone seems to just be waiting over there." He points toward the shore. "The rowboat is gone. The ranger boat isn't moving. I can't tell what's going on. This damned smoke doesn't help much."

"What about the cat?" asks Wright.

"I don't see it out there." Southard pans back toward the shore. "Wait! Hold on! I do see it! It's heading right for them!"

Wright puts his hand to his brow. "Do they see it? Where can they go?"

"Nowhere. The fire is almost there. It has nearly reached them. What the hell is wrong with that boat?"

"Christ!" says Ike. "I don't think we can get over there in time."

Southard follows the black form.

"Can I take a look?" asks Ike.

Southard passes him the binoculars and points. "It's right there."

Ike focuses and pans. "It looks like a seal in the ocean," he says. "If it weren't so black, I don't know if I'd be able to see it. But there it is."

Wright takes the rifle off his shoulder. Ike continues to look.

"They don't see it coming."

Southard stumbles forward on the rocks. "They don't, but Virgil does."

Virgil jumps into the water and swims hard toward his people and the approaching cat. Wright fires his rifle off to the left in the air.

"Maybe that'll warn them." He fires two more times.

Mike turns around. "What was that?"

"Three shots," says Brenda. "Someone's in trouble." Mike climbs off the boat onto the rocks.

"Let's get this thing going."

Brenda follows. Both rangers push on the side of the boat. The pontoons screech as the boat slips off the rocks. The rocks roll out from underneath Brenda and Mike's feet, but they hold on. The boat breaks free.

Mike pulls himself up into the boat. He starts to crawl aboard, but slips on the slimy, blood-covered deck. Brenda stops his slide and boosts him from behind. Mike inches forward and grabs the stable partition that separates the helm from the flat back of the boat. Brenda stumbles forward. Mike hoists himself up and turns around. He grabs Brenda's hand. He pulls her on to the boat. The two rangers sit for a moment on the blood-soaked deck, breathing hard.

"Let's go!" says Brenda. "Let's get those people and get out of here."

Brenda lowers the motor into the water. Mike slides to the front of the boat, grabs the partition and hauls himself up into the driver's seat. He starts the boat, moves out toward the middle of the lake, makes a wide turn, spraying water like the crown of a rooster, and heads toward the shore and the stranded survivors waiting there.

In the water just beyond the reach of the searing fragments spitting out from the edge of the flaming forest, Marty looks around.

"The shots came from over there," says Ed. "I wonder who..."

"Look!" cries Marty, "The boat is coming! We're going to get out of here!" She starts waving her hands. The boat continues toward them. Both Cindy and Josey stand next to their Mom, waving.

"We're going home! We're going home!" cries Cindy. "We are going home!"

Rob sits quietly on the rocks near the shore. He motions to Ed. Ed leaves his family and joins Rob.

"It's near! I can't see it, but I can feel it," says Rob. "We need to get ready."

"That's not all we have to worry about," says Ed. "If that fire comes any closer to us, we won't be able to stand the heat. We" have to be in the water."

"Let's get ready. I know that catamount's here, someplace."

"The boat is coming," says Ed. Ed helps Rob up. He hands him his rifle.

"Oh no!" cries Marty. "The boat is going in the wrong direction again."

Brenda grabs Mike by the arm.

"Over there!" she cries. "Look over there! It looks like someone swimming."

Mike slows the boat.

"It must be that guy. He's still alive!"

Mike swings the boat around toward the waving hands.

George takes a deep breath and treads water. He can see the boat heading his way. He waves his fatigued arms once more. The boat has changed direction. They've seen him! It is almost there. Then the boat slows down and drifts toward George. Mike gives the boat a spurt of gas in reverse and eases the boat sideways right next to George. Brenda leans over the side, grabs the exhausted man's hand and, with a quick jerk, hauls him onto the boat. He sits on the bloody deck, breathing hard. He lowers his head between his legs.

"Thank God!" he says. "I was heading for the shore, but I don't think I could of made it. I wasn't sure if it would follow me or not."

"The cat?" asks Mike.

"It came right after me!"

"We wondered if that was what it was. They really can swim!"

"It was on the boat. I hit its bloody paw with the paddle. I got the keys into the ignition, but it kept coming. I got the boat going, but I had to dive over the side."

"Where did it go?" asks Brenda.

"What's all the blood?" asks Mike.

George is still struggling to get his breath back.

"You don't look like you're bleeding," Mike observes.

"It's the cat's blood," says George. "It's badly wounded. I think it may have been shot, but I can't be sure."

"Christ!" Mike says. "That would make it all the more dangerous!"

"That is absolutely right," says George. "A mountain lion in that condition is totally unpredictable and more than likely ready to kill. After I dove in, I was sure it would come after me again. Every time, I looked around, I thought that it would be there but it wasn't. At some point, though, it must have gotten off the boat."

"I wonder where it went," says Brenda.

"I think we better get Rob and that family," says George, "then we can worry about the cat. I hope that it isn't already too late! It has already killed humans. It will again. I'm sure of it!"

Mike pushes the throttle forward and slowly points the boat back toward the middle of the lake.

"I don't want to get stuck on any rocks again."

The cat moves slowly toward the figures on the edge of the shore.

The bright darkness emanates from the top of the trees.

She looks back at the figures.

They are all standing quietly. Josey and Cindy are knee-deep in the water.

Ed goes toward the blowdown. "We have to get everything over here. We'll have to get in the water. The fire is getting too close."

"I can hardly breathe," pants Josey.

"The boat is coming. We'll make it," Marty reassures him.

Rob sits on one of the wobbly rocks near the water's edge. He holds his rifle. Ed and Marty bring one of the packs to the lake's edge. The two pistols lie next to the pack.

Ed puts his rifle down. "Watch the gun," he says to Marty. "But be careful, it's loaded. Josey, come with me to get the other packs."

The cat creeps forward.

"It's close," shudders Rob. "I can feel it. I think I can smell the damned thing."

Over by the blowdown, Ed picks up a pack. Marty bends down to pick up one of the pistols.

Josey yells, "What's that? There's something over there!"

Ed looks. The yellow eyes look back. The black figure is ready to spring.

"It's too late," he thinks, instinctively grabbing his son and starting to run. As if in slow motion, Ed, holding Josey, leaps toward the shore. The rocks underneath his feet give way and he stumbles to the ground. Josey slips out of his arms and tumbles forward. He turns over.

"Look! It's Virgil!" he cries.

Virgil bolts out of the water. Just as the cat springs, Virgil leaps at the cat's throat. The cat screeches. Virgil holds on. Ed stumbles back to his feet and runs to the shore. Josey follows. Ed picks up his rifle. He aims. Virgil holds on as dog and cat whirl about in a wild tumble. Marty aims the pistol, but hesitates.

Ed aims the rifle again, but he does not want to hit Virgil. He decides he'll have to risk it.

"Dad, no!" cries Cindy. "Don't shoot Virgil!"

The young girl pulls on her father's shirt. Marty drops the pistol, pulls Cindy away and then moves toward Ed. Then the cat rolls onto its feet and flings the yelping dog away. Instinctively, Marty starts toward the dog.

"No!" she cries. The cat springs into the air. Ed fires. The cat seems to hang in the air. Marty stumbles. She looks up at the large, ominous, black body floating down on her, in what seems like slow motion. She sees the large, open mouth and the fierce, yellow fangs. She tries to scream, but the breath is knocked out of her lungs. She is crushed by the weight of the immense body and then, as quickly as the cat has fallen on her, it springs away. It vanishes into the woods, into the smoke.

Cindy stands immobile in the water. "Mommy!" she cries.

Still carrying his rifle, Ed rushes over to Marty. She heaves, trying to breathe. She is covered in wet, sticky blood. Josey and Cindy run over to Marty.

"Are you all right?" asks Ed. Rob is ready with his rifle. Slowly, Marty starts to breathe normally. Ed helps his wife up.

"Are you all right?" he asks again. It feels like a stupid question, but what else is there to ask? Ed puts his arm around his wife and helps her to her feet.

"Doesn't that thing die? I know I hit it! I know I did!"

"You did!" says Rob. "You saved Marty's life! I'm sure of it."

Ed hugs Marty harder. Still stunned, she hugs back.

"Where's Virgil?" whimpers Cindy.

Ed walks over to the lump on the rocks. He picks Virgil up.

"He's still breathing," says Ed. "I think he'll be okay."

As Ed carries the dog over to the others, the sound of an engine grows nearer and nearer. He unties Mutt and Jeff. In spite of their injuries, they race around frantically following the scent of the cat. Undaunted by his last run-in with the catamount, Virgil joins in with the other two dogs, sniffing wildly in every direction.

Rob turns around. "Come on! Let's get in the water. The boat is coming."

Ed walks Marty to the edge of the lake. The two kids follow. Rob steps in the water, rifle ready, waiting. The two kids start to swim. Marty starts to wade toward them and then jumps forward into the deeper water. Suddenly, flames burst out from the trees behind.

Ed throws down his rifle. "We'll have to leave the stuff."

The only sound is the steady hum of the approaching boat and the roaring crackle of the fire.

"Get out into the water!" cries Ed. "The fire is too hot!"

Suddenly, the black apparition appears out of the flames. It springs over Rob knocking him face down in the water. His rifle fires. Instantaneously, the stray bullet strikes Ed, sending him reeling onto his back. The cat is in the water. It moves steadily and surely towards Cindy and Josey. All three dogs bark. They pace back and forth on the edge of the water.

"No!" yells Marty as the cat glides toward Cindy. Marty turns back to the shore. She grabs a rock and flings it at the cat. It hits the cat squarely in its hind legs. The catamount lets out a screech. and reverses direction, swimming back to shore.

Marty runs to where Rob is trying to pull himself back up. She grabs his rifle and prepares to shoot. She feels like she is moving in slow motion as the cat appears instantly back on shore. The mountain lion turns toward Marty, ready to attack. The catamount's yellow eyes stare directly at her and its cold, wild look bores into her. Momentarily, Marty freezes.

Once again, the cat springs, just before the dogs race to attack.

A shot rings out. It is all Marty hears as, once again, the big, black body lands on her with a thud. Both the cat and Marty splash into the water.

Nothing moves. Even the dogs hold back, not sure what to do next.

Then Wright, Southard and Roberts appear out of the smoke.

"By Christ, I think you got it!" says Roberts.

Cindy starts to cry. The three men move into the water toward the motionless animal. Wright holds his rifle ready to shoot.

Ike kneels down next to the cat. "It's deader than a doornail."

Rob slowly gets up.

"Mommy's under there!" screeches Cindy. "She's under the water."

Roberts, Wright and Southard all heave the heavy cat to the side. Belly up, it bobs on the surface. The yellow eyes stare straight up to the sky. Marty's head appears out of the water. Then she opens her eyes. She looks dazed and bewildered.

Josey splashes through the water to the three men.

"Dad...Dad has been shot!"

Ed is on the edge of the sandy beach. His face is mottled from the heat of the fire. He is leaning on his left shoulder, trying to push himself up. A large, red wound bleeds profusely on his right shoulder. Slowly, Marty struggles up. She sees Ed. In a trance, she staggers over to her husband and puts her arm around his good shoulder. Her face is also bright red from the heat.

"We have to get in the water," she says. "It's all over."

She and Wright help Ed to his feet. Josey hugs Ed's leg and Cindy clings to Marty's hand. They wade into the water and, for a moment, they all look at the dead catamount. Marty has picked up Ed's rifle. Before anyone can react, she fires once more, sending a bullet into the head of the dead animal. Then she throws the rifle at the carcass and turns away. She hears the motor of the flat boat as it gingerly works its way toward the shore. Roberts leans over the animal for a closer look.

"Christ! It has one of them radio tags on it. What should we do?"

Ed looks back. "Let it be," he says.

They all move as best they can toward the boat.

"That fire is hot! Let's get out of this cursed place!" says Wright as he dives into the cool water.

"I'm ready!" says Ed.

Roberts turns back for one last look.

"Who's that?"

To his dying day, Ike Roberts will swear that he has seen an old man and woman standing in the smoke in front of the burning inferno.

"I don't see anything," says Wright impatiently. "Let's get on the boat. If you did see anyone, they would be dead by now. They could not survive that heat." He calls to Virgil and the other dogs and they follow into the water.

Washington D. C., one month later...

Ten scientists sit around the large conference table. The meeting has been called to order.

"I think we can contain this," says the leader. "The president is with us on this one. The media we control is prepared to discredit any reports from the survivors that they actually saw the mountain lion. The bigger story was the fire."

"What about that videotape that was found?" asks one of the scientists.

"We've got it," says the leader. "There was only one copy. The guy who took it died in the fire."

"You couldn't see much anyway," says another. "Only if you knew what you were looking for. The animal carcasses looked like mounds of just about anything."

A third man leans forward and puts his elbows on the table. "What about the people who killed it, and what about the ones it killed? What about the livestock? What about the TV coverage?"

"We have a scenario for each one. We have already sent out the official press release. We've discredited a couple of reporters. The whole mountain lion tragedy is being portrayed as an over-reaction by the media."

"What about that family, the cops and the others?"

"They'll be easy to discredit. They were under a lot of stress because of the fire. It'll just be one more alien abduction type of scenario."

"We've done it before," says the leader.

"Did anyone ever find the carcass?" asks the first scientist.

"No sign of it."

"What about the GPS tracking device?"

"That stopped working a long time ago."

"I thought it was infallible."

"It was," says the leader. "Nothing we can do now."

"What if the carcass shows up?"

"We'll deal with it, if it does. Are we all in accord on this?"

Everyone at the table nods, including the group's lawyer, Peter Schmidt.

"So this should be the end of the catamount legend," he says.

Epilogue

Ed turns the running of the store over to Marty. Ed becomes a mildly successful writer. He earns enough money to spend his time writing stories on hunting and fishing that he sells to various magazines. His only book, *CATAMOUNT, A NORTH COUNTRY THRILLER*, almost reaches the bestseller list. It is not in the public eye for very long. The urban critics cannot identity with the story, and many copies of the book disappear mysteriously from bookstore shelves.

In spite of marriage counseling, Marty and Ed go their separate ways amicably one year after the fire. Marty marries a man who owns the store next to Rollins' Outfitters, which she continues to operate while bringing up Cindy and Josey. They live in a nice suburban home and vacation in Cancun. Ed and Virgil move to the cabin in Clifford. The Rollins' cabin lay outside the path of fire and was never in any real danger. Virgil enjoys running free in the North Country.

Cindy becomes a New York lawyer and marries a stockbroker. She has no desire ever to return to the old family cabin in Clifford.

Josey becomes a Conservation Officer in northern Maine. He marries a North Country woman, lives off the grid and has three kids.

Rob retires from Fish and Game and buys a hunting and fishing lodge with Ike. That is a story for another book.

Roberts lives on his farm until he goes into business with Rob. He is locally renowned for his unbelievable stories about catamounts and ghostly Native Americans. After fifty years of marriage, Marion moves to live with her sister in Portland, Maine. When she leaves, she quotes Dolly Copp, pointing out that fifty years with one man is more than enough for any woman. If Roberts does not agree with her, he does not say so. Ike takes up fly-fishing again, but that, too, is part of another story.

Peter and Mary Schmidt rebuild their farm. Jake lives in the barn chamber full time.

George makes it back to North Conway. He and his family return to Montana. He tries to convince his colleagues that the catamount story is true. He writes a number of articles, but the mainstream press refuses to print them. Government scientists quickly repudiate those that surface.

Brenda goes back to school and becomes a wildlife biologist in Vermont.

Mike "comes out of the closet" and moves to Provincetown, Massachusetts where he runs a bookstore and lives in an isolated house near the dunes. He carries CATAMOUNT, A NORTH COUNTRY THRILLER until he can no longer find copies in print.

After taking some vacation time, Wright and Southard report back to duty and, as they are trained to do, keep their mouths shut. Southard keeps Mutt and Jeff as personal pets until they die of old age.

The catamount's body is never found.

Froggy survives the fire. Somehow, the fire split around his shack, leaving his place untouched. Local residents are sometimes heard to comment that God must look out for drunks. Froggy still reports seeing catamounts on a regular basis, but as in the past, no one takes him seriously.

Fortunately for the town of Clifford, shifting winds propitiously propel the fire toward Lake Mackapaque and away from the town. Outside of a snow-like layer of black ash that settles on just about every square inch of the village and surrounding areas, the town is spared.

The Old Abenaki's grave is in a small graveyard in northern New Hampshire, not far from Clifford. He is thought to have lived to be over a hundred and twenty years old. At the time of his death, he was blind, a pauper and a ward of the town. No one knows the exact location of Molly's resting place, but an island still bears her name.

This book is, of course, a unique combination of fact and fiction and the author hopes that no one will take offense at his liberal interpretation of local legends. The author has always been fascinated by the legend of Metallak and his relationship with his wife, Molly Oozalluc. The curse is fictional, and there is no historical evidence, as far as the author knows, that Metallak would have attempted to cast such a spell as the one that may or may not have caused such havoc as described in this novel.

The Legend of Metallak

There is conflicting information on Metallak's life. The following is the stuff of legend, and therefore may not be historically accurate.

He was a chief and the son of a chief of the Coo-ash-auke tribe.

It is said that he lived to be 120 years old. Most of his tribe had disappeared by the time of his death, perhaps from disease.

As a youth, Metallak may have fought against the coming of the white man, but later, after a vision from the Great Spirit, lived in peace with the invading Europeans and even proved to be a great help in aiding them in adapting to their new world.

Metallak was known as a highly skilled hunter and warrior.

Metallak's territory was the northern parts of New Hampshire and northwestern Maine.

Metallak and his first wife Keoka, who was very beautiful, lost their first child to wolves. Metallak took revenge on every wolf he saw. Keoka died at a young age.

Metallak's second wife, Molly Oozalluc, was not beautiful. Perhaps, he chose her so others wouldn't desire her.

It is believed that Metallak may have served in the U.S. Army in the War of 1812. His sons served the British during the same war, but they may have had no choice. In spite of this, Metallak found it difficult to forgive them for fighting with the British.

Metallak may have helped the white man, but he preserved his sense of his own native heritage and supported himself in traditional ways until he was too old to do so. He did not like farming and preferred to live from hunting and trapping. He was highly regarded by both his own people and the white men.

He was heart broken when he lost Molly Oozalluc and preserved her body by smoking it. Some stories say he buried his wife on the Narrows of Richardson Lake in Maine. Others say on Moll's Rock on Lake Umbagog. That lake is on the New Hampshire / Maine border.

Two books by Alice Daley Noyes are good historical resources on Metallak's life: *PRINCE OF DARKNESS*, (A. D. Noyes, 1992) and *METALLAK, HIS LEGACY*, (Colebrook, NH: Liebl Printing Company, 1992).

About the author

Rick Davidson is a public school teacher, award-winning professional photographer and sometime guitar player. For many years, Rick wrote a popular newspaper column about photo tips and operated Davidson Photography and Video along with his wife, Jane. He holds a B. A. in philosophy, with a minor in English Literature. Rick and his wife have traveled extensively throughout Europe and lived near Stuttgart, Germany for over seven years. They now enjoy their rural home in Freedom, New Hampshire. Rick is presently working on a mystery novel that cannot truthfully be described as a sequel to CATAMOUNT, A NORTH COUNTRY THRILLER, but that does feature some of the same characters.

photo by Jane Davidson